# Praise for *Called to Protect*

"Eason's page-turner is energetic and tense until the end."

*Publishers Weekly*

# Praise for *Oath of Honor*

"Explosions, gun battles, and a terrifying, cop-killing criminal pepper the rocket-powered plot. Author Lynette Eason's formidable female characters stand out, as do the male leads who trust the women's judgment without question."

*Bookpage*

"This nonstop, white-knuckled thrill ride will please devotees of police procedurals."

*Library Journal*

"Although concerned and delicate with both grief and romance, Eason's well-rounded story doesn't spend too much time bogged down in either as the harrowing plot unfolds. Eason's fans will enjoy this first installment of a promising new series."

*Publishers Weekly*

"Lynette Eason once again pens a gripping thriller with her latest book, *Oath of Honor*. I can't wait for her next installment of the Blue Justice series!"

Carrie Stuart Parks, award-winning author
of *A Cry from the Dust*

"Lynette Eason's *Oath of Honor* promises to be the beginning of another roller-coaster ride series. Readers are going to love Isabelle and Ryan's story while getting to know the entire St. John family. This engrossing novel will have them hooked from page one."

Lisa Harris, bestselling and Christy Award–winning author
of *The Nikki Boyd Files*

# CODE OF VALOR

# Books by Lynette Eason

### Women of Justice

*Too Close to Home*
*Don't Look Back*
*A Killer Among Us*

### Deadly Reunions

*When the Smoke Clears*
*When a Heart Stops*
*When a Secret Kills*

### Hidden Identity

*No One to Trust*
*Nowhere to Turn*
*Nothing to Lose*

### Elite Guardians

*Always Watching*
*Without Warning*
*Moving Target*
*Chasing Secrets*

### Blue Justice

*Oath of Honor*
*Called to Protect*
*Code of Valor*

# CODE
# OF
# VALOR

## LYNETTE EASON

Revell

a division of Baker Publishing Group
Grand Rapids, Michigan

© 2019 by Lynette Eason

Published by Revell
a division of Baker Publishing Group
PO Box 6287, Grand Rapids, MI 49516-6287
www.revellbooks.com

Printed in the United States of America

Library of Congress Cataloging-in-Publication Data
Names: Eason, Lynette, author.
Title: Code of valor / Lynette Eason.
Description: Grand Rapids, MI : Revell, a division of Baker Publishing Group,
    [2019] | Series: Blue justice series ; 3
Identifiers: LCCN 2018020853 | ISBN 9780800727048 (pbk. : alk. paper)
Subjects: LCSH: Murder—Investigation—Fiction. | BISAC: FICTION / Christian /
    Suspense. | GSAFD: Christian fiction. | Mystery fiction.
Classification: LCC PS3605.A79 C64 2019 | DDC 813/.6—dc23
LC record available at https://lccn.loc.gov/2018020853

ISBN 978-0-8007-3558-6 (casebound)

Scripture quotations are from the King James Version of the Bible.

19  20  21  22  23  24  25      7  6  5  4  3  2  1

Dedicated to those who go above and beyond:
To every law enforcement agency who fights for justice,
to the firefighters and medical personnel
who put their lives on the line
for those they don't even know.
We thank you, we appreciate you, and we pray for you.

## LAW ENFORCEMENT
### *Oath of Honor*

★ ★ ★ ★ ★ ★ ★ ★ ★ ★ ★ ★ ★ ★ ★ ★ ★ ★ ★ ★ ★ ★ ★ ★ ★ ★

On my honor,
I will never betray my badge, my integrity,
my character, or the public trust.
I will always have the courage
to hold myself and others
accountable for our actions.
I will always uphold the constitution,
my community, and the agency I serve.

★ ★ ★ ★ ★ ★ ★ ★ ★ ★ ★ ★ ★ ★ ★ ★ ★ ★ ★ ★ ★ ★ ★ ★ ★ ★

For the LORD seeth not as man seeth; for man looketh on the outward appearance, but the LORD looketh on the heart.

1 Samuel 16:7

# FRIDAY,
# OCTOBER 18

# 1

The broker rose from his chair and glared at the imbecile standing on the other side of the desk. "We paid you well to steal that boat. Where is it?"

Jeremy Hightower smirked. "Well now, that's the question of the night, isn't it? I went to a lot of trouble to get that boat for you. It took planning and cunning. Finding a marina worker uniform that fit and a couple of guys to help. Unfortunately, the measly twenty-five grand you forked over isn't going very far. I need more." He looked around. "And it's obvious you have plenty."

Rage pounded through him. He should have known better than to trust this worthless piece of an excuse for a human.

The broker rounded the desk and jabbed a finger at the greedy man. "Planning? Cunning? I planned it down to the last detail and simply told you what to do! Now tell me where that boat is and I might let you live!"

"Not until you wire another one million dollars to this account number." He tossed a piece of paper onto the desk. "I had to hire some help to get it done and they demanded payment up front. When I have confirmation the money's there, I'll tell you where the boat is."

"Do you know what happens to people like you? People who

betray me? They die. Just ask Reuben Kingman. Oh wait." He laughed. "You can't ask him. Because he's dead!" He slammed a fist on the desk and leaned forward. "And I'll kill you just like I killed Reuben."

"Then you'll never get the location of the boat."

The fact that his outburst and threats didn't seem to faze Hightower didn't sit well. His blood churned faster. He needed those pictures in the boat's safe. Pictures that showed him wielding the knife and killing yet another who'd betrayed him. "You had help. I'll find them and get it from them."

"Good luck with that. They're dead." This time it was a picture he flung onto the desk.

The broker studied it. Two very dead men stared at him with sightless eyes. He returned to his chair behind the desk, pausing a moment to draw in a breath and consider his options. The picture told him a lot. "You planned this from the beginning," he said.

Hightower shrugged. "It was hard not to."

"I've killed men for less."

"So have I." Hightower's stare remained solid. Unwavering.

And the broker knew this latest traitor wouldn't back down. "So. It's come to this, has it?"

"I've been your go-to boy for a long time now," Hightower said. "It's time for me to branch out."

"Pay him."

The two men turned at the voice that came from the corner of the room. The broker scowled. "Stay out of this. It doesn't concern you."

"Of course it does. If it concerns you, it concerns me. Now, wire Jeremy the money."

He reluctantly considered his friend's advice, then opened his laptop with one hand. With the other, he pulled his weapon from the holder he kept attached to the underbelly of the desk. He raised the gun and aimed it at the man who would dare try to blackmail him. At the brief flash of fear in Hightower's eyes, satisfaction flowed. "Are you sure you don't want to tell me now?"

"If you pull that trigger, you'll never find it."

"Oh, I'll find it."

"Put the gun down." His friend rose to his feet. "Think about this."

"I have."

Hightower laughed. "You shoot me and you'll all go to prison."

"What are you talking about?" the broker asked.

"I was followed. She had a tracker on my car that I found later."

"And?"

"She took pictures of me on the boat. She'll report it and the location, the cops will go get it and return it to its rightful owner, who'll then have access to the contents of the safe—and the pictures—and you'll be done."

For a moment, he thought his blood pressure might actually do him in. His eyes closed for a moment. "I'll find it," he muttered.

"No, you won't. I disabled the GPS, as you've probably already discovered."

The broker turned to his friend, who sat still, hands clasped loosely between his knees. "What do you think?"

His friend's jaw tightened, the only indication that he was affected by the scene playing out before him. "Pay him. And he and I will work together to get rid of anyone who knows anything." His eyes studied Hightower. "Don't make me regret this."

"No regrets. I get my money, you get your boat." Jeremy nodded at the man. "But we'd both better make sure that nosey reporter dies. She's the one who can bring everything down for all of us."

"We'll take care of her," the broker's friend said.

"I have a guy who can get it done and he doesn't ask questions."

With a scowl, the broker picked up the paper with the account number on it and turned back to Hightower. "Seems like you need her dead as much as we do. When it's done, let me know and I'll transfer the money." He jabbed a finger at Hightower. "And so help me, if you betray me again, I'll take my chances and just kill you. Am I clear?"

"Clear."

"Get out of here."

Hightower smiled as he exited and closed the door behind him.

"I want him dead," the broker said. "No one crosses me like this and lives. Have him killed." He paused. "No, don't."

"Don't?"

The broker snapped his fingers. "New plan. Keep Jeremy away from that reporter until you can get the location of the boat from her, then let him get rid of her. Once she's dead and we have the boat, I want you to bring Hightower to me so I can take care of him myself."

# WEDNESDAY, OCTOBER 23

# 2

Heather Gilstrap glanced over her shoulder as she pulled her keys from her pocket. With a click, she unlocked her car and heard the chirp—and something else.

She stopped to listen.

Yes, that was a footstep behind her. Not for the first time that day. For the past week, she'd felt watched. When she'd asked Emily, her best friend, if she felt the same, Emily had simply shaken her head.

Heather turned and saw no one. But someone was definitely behind her. Following. Stalking. But who? She'd been so careful to cover her tracks.

Not careful enough.

Rapid puffs of air escaped her lips as she resumed her rush to the vehicle.

Her heels clicked on the parking garage concrete floor, echoing in the quiet. Covering the sound of the person following her. Why had she stayed so late? Why hadn't she asked security to walk her to her car? She pulled her phone from the other pocket of her blazer just as she reached the silver Toyota Camry.

Heather opened the driver's door and slid into the seat. Slamming the door with one hand, she hit the locks with the other and lunged toward the glove compartment. The door fell open and

19

she grabbed for her Smith & Wesson 642. Only to find it gone. "What?" she whispered. But how? It didn't matter right now. She jabbed the key at the ignition, her shaking fingers betraying her as she dropped the set.

She leaned down to grab them, praying she had enough gas to get out of the garage. Why oh why hadn't she stopped to fill up the tank?

When she straightened, a figure was approaching from her left, walking slowly, clearly not in any hurry. Yet the threat emanated from him. She jammed the keys into the ignition and twisted.

Nothing happened.

"No," she whispered. "No, no, no." Terror centered itself in her midsection. With another glance at the person dressed in black, she grabbed her phone and dialed 911. And still he continued his slow stroll toward her. He was stalking her, toying with her. She put the phone on speaker, then switched the screen to her text messages.

"911. Where is your emergency?"

"I'm in the Cannon Street Garage, third floor. My name's Heather Gilstrap. There's a guy following me and I think he's going to kill me." She had to get out of the car, but she couldn't go out the driver's door. He'd catch up to her in seconds. She lunged across the seat and pulled the handle.

Nothing happened. What?

"The door won't open!" Heather yelled, cutting off the dispatcher's words. She pounded the door and tried again with a low grunt.

Again, nothing.

"I can't get out! No, no, no."

She tossed the phone onto the back seat and climbed over, tried both doors. Same result. No wonder he wasn't in a hurry. Somehow he'd jammed the doors. She was trapped. And he was enjoying his game.

She rolled on her back and kicked the window. Once, twice. It didn't even move. And there was nothing she could use that would smash through the glass. "I can't get out!"

With shaking fingers, she grabbed her phone and heard the operator above the rush of blood in her ears. "Heather? I've got officers en route."

"My car won't start and my doors are jammed. He did something to my doors!" Pictures. She had to send them. She punched the text string of the one person she could trust, and quickly tapped a message, added a photo from her gallery, then hit send.

Adrenaline surged, muffling her other senses. Another picture, the next text went. Then the next. Emily needed the pictures for evidence. If she simply texted the words and tried to explain, it wouldn't hold up in court. But the photos would.

"Heather? Heather! What's happening?" The operator's voice cut through her panic.

A frantic glance showed the man coming closer. She whimpered. "He's almost here. He has a gun. With a suppressor." *Please, Jesus. I love you, but I don't want to die today.*

"Do you know who he is?"

Another text went. If God didn't intervene and she was going to die, she was going to take down the people who killed her. Unfortunately, her texts might not be enough—but it was all she had.

"No. He has a ski mask on." Tears streamed down her cheeks. She sniffed. "Please, God, don't let me die in vain," she whispered as her fingers worked the phone. "Please, he's going to kill me—"

"I have someone on the way right now. You have to find a way out of the car and run."

"I can't!"

Maybe he would just take her. Demand to know what she knew. Force her to hand over the evidence she'd gathered. But he might not. Her breathing came now in harsh gasps while her heartbeat thundered in her ears.

She hit send on the final text, then started erasing them from her phone even as the dispatcher's voice asked her another question she missed.

"What?" No. She needed one more text. The location.

The lake where we

"Can you break the window?" the woman demanded.

"I tried," she whispered. "Tell Em I tried. Emily Chastain, tell her! Warn her she's in danger!"

The back window shattered. Glass rained over her and she screamed. The phone fell into her lap. Frantic, she grabbed for it. The last text shot off to Emily only half finished. She looked up into dark eyes that held nothing. Just empty black pools. He placed the gun against her head and she froze.

"Please, don't," she whispered.

He reached in and disconnected the call. Then took her phone and stepped back. He kept an eye on her, the gun in his left hand never wavering as he tapped the screen and scrolled. "Emily Chastain? What did you tell her? What did you send her?"

"Leave her alone. She doesn't know anything."

"Unfortunately, while that might have been the case three minutes ago, it might not be now."

Wait, what? Was he going to—

The gun lifted.

Heather screamed again.

The muzzle flashed.

Sharp pain hit her, then darkness.

# THURSDAY, OCTOBER 24

# 3

Brady St. John sat on the porch of the cabin he'd rented for the next two weeks and let his mind drift behind closed eyes. Unfortunately, the current took it to places he'd rather not revisit, so he lifted his lids and let his gaze settle on the lake.

Peaceful. Gentle. A great place to solo dive or fish for largemouth bass and catfish. He'd had the catfish for dinner tonight. Remnants of the meal that consisted of two ears of corn, a side of baked beans, and an apple pie now lay pushed to the side. Chloe had made the pie and insisted he take it with him.

On his vacation.

Because he'd needed a break before he snapped like a toothpick. Only now the October evening air had gone from brisk to downright freezing, sending goose bumps to pebble his skin under the long-sleeved sweatshirt. But he wasn't ready to go inside just yet.

He finished cleaning the Glock and wiped it down. Setting it on the table next to his empty plate, he shook his head as his sister's voice echoed in his mind.

"Go somewhere peaceful, someplace quiet," Chloe had said. "Where you can go diving or just sit. And be. Like the Drummonds' little cabin on Lake Henley. They rent it out on a regular basis, I think."

"Yeah, during the summer. Lake Henley's closed up for the winter."

"So sweet-talk them into letting you stay there. They probably wouldn't mind making a little extra money on it."

"Maybe."

"You need to, Brady, you've been through a lot. Don't think, just go. And just . . . be. And take your Bible with you."

He'd realized she was right. He probably did need a break. Especially after the latest case where a mother had driven her two children, ages four and six months, into the river, drowning all three of them. On purpose. Not to mention the fact that Krystal had managed to make a complete fool out of him. What had he seen in her anyway? She'd been smart. He'd liked that. And beautiful. That hadn't hurt either. And mercenary.

But he wasn't going to think about that. He was going to sit.

And be.

So here he sat.

Just . . . being.

And he was bored out of his skull. He sighed and leaned back to stare at the porch ceiling. No, not bored. There just weren't any distractions, which meant too much time to think about things he'd rather not think about. *That* was the real problem. He should have asked one of his brothers to come with him.

With a groan, he rose and raked a hand through his hair. Fine. He'd go inside and start a fire, warm up—and pack. So he could go home and do what he did best.

Which was to throw himself into work until he was so exhausted he fell into bed and slept without nightmares.

A scream ripped through the air and he froze for a split second before reaching for his weapon.

With the sun setting in the next several minutes, light was quickly diminishing.

Another scream.

Brady shot off the porch and into the yard, trying to discern the direction of the cry.

There. On the water.

A speedboat motored out to the middle of the inlet, aimed toward the open water, and the silhouettes of two people came into view. One sitting behind the wheel. The other sat on the bow, hands tied to the rail that ran along the side of the boat. She struggled, yanking and twisting against her bonds.

"Hey! Let her go!"

The driver jerked his head in Brady's direction. Then lifted his weapon and fired. Brady dove to the ground and rolled. The bullet missed but was a little closer than he was comfortable with. He lifted his head to see the man taking aim at his captive. She stilled, head ducked, shoulders heaving with her sobs. Brady fired while running toward the water. The man jerked and swung his weapon back in Brady's direction.

And then the woman was loose. She launched herself over the side and into the water. The man's curses reached Brady even as he settled back into the driver's seat and spun the wheel. The boat sped away.

Brady caught sight of the woman's head just above the surface, but her arms flailed, slapping the water.

She went under.

Brady ran to the edge of the dock, stopped long enough to shuck his sweatshirt and loafers, and dove in. The icy water wanted to steal the breath he held, but it wasn't the first time he'd swum in freezing water. He reached her in ten long strokes.

Just as she was going back down, he got behind her and slid his forearms beneath her armpits, lifting her head up once again. Her back pressed against his chest. She gasped and coughed. Started to struggle. "Hey, hey, it's okay, relax. I'm here to help you. Rest your head back on my shoulder and just breathe, okay?"

She gave one last hacking cough, then went limp. Hoping she

hadn't passed out, he kicked toward the shore. The dock would get them out of the water faster, but if the guy decided to circle back and start shooting again, he could pick them off.

"Are you conscious?" he asked. Then kicked, wishing he'd had the time to get rid of the heavy jeans, but he ignored the weight and aimed them for land.

"Yes."

"What's your name?"

"Emily," she gasped. "Chastain."

"I'm Brady. Are you hurt?"

"I d-don't th-think so."

But she was cold. "Can you swim?"

"No. I mean yes, but . . . no strength."

"All right. Just be still and don't fight me and I'll have us on shore in a couple of minutes."

She trembled against him. A combination of fear and cold. Finally, his feet found the sandy bottom of the lake and he hefted her into his arms.

She gasped, coughed, then wiggled. "I can walk. I'm too heavy to c-carry. P-put me down."

He wanted to laugh. "Be still. I bench press more than you weigh. A lot more."

She stilled and he set her next to the dock, out of sight of the lake, protected by the wood. "Stay here for just a second."

Shuddering, she nodded. At least he thought it was a nod. Keeping low, hunched against the wind that sent shudders whipping through him, he made it to the end of the dock, all the while feeling like he had a target on his back.

But no one fired. He shoved his feet into his shoes and grabbed the sweatshirt. He hurried back to find Emily curled into a ball, back against the dock post, tremors wracking her frame.

Without asking for permission, he tugged the sweatshirt over her long-sleeved T-shirt and swept her into his arms once more.

She didn't protest, simply turned her face into the side of his neck and clutched his shoulders.

---

Emily used the towel to clear the steam off the mirror and tried to calm her shaking. The hot shower had chased away the bone-deep cold, but the horror of what she'd just lived through wouldn't loosen its hold. She'd thought she was going to die.

Tears dripped down her cheeks as the images flashed in her mind.

A knock on the door made her jump, and she pulled the plush white robe tighter, then swiped the tears from her cheeks. "Yes?"

"You okay? I've got some sweats and a dry sweatshirt you can put on while your clothes and shoes dry if you want."

She opened the door and looked up into the kindest blue eyes she'd ever seen. The gentleness she found there eased her pounding pulse. "Thank you." She took the clothes from him.

"There's a hair dryer under the sink too. If you need to use it."

"I do. Thanks."

"Anything else you need?"

"No. I'll be out in just a moment."

He nodded and she shut the door.

After drying her chin-length chocolate-colored hair, she changed into the clothes, for once doing so without studying herself in the mirror and judging. She had to roll the waistband to shorten the length, then roll a thick cuff around her ankles. The sweatshirt hung midthigh. Once she had on the wool socks, she took a deep breath.

She was alive and finally warm.

Only now she had to go explain to the man who'd just saved her life why someone wanted her dead and that he was now in danger as well. Which meant she should probably leave quickly.

Gathering her nerve, she stepped out into the hall and followed it into the spacious den area. Her rescuer sat in one of the wingback chairs facing the warm flames from the logs. His right hand worked a cloth over the weapon held in his left hand. Probably the gun he'd fired at her captor.

"Excuse me while I take care of this," he said. "It went into the lake with me and I need to get it dried out just in case we need it."

"In case they find me here, you mean?"

"I would think that whoever was in the boat would be long gone, but you never know about people—or how desperate they are." His eyes locked on hers for a moment.

"He seemed pretty desperate," she said. He'd showered and changed into jeans, warm socks, and a red-and-blue flannel shirt. She stepped up next to him and held her hands out to the fire. "This is lovely."

He gestured to one of the chairs to his right. "Have a seat. Your clothes and shoes are in the dryer."

"Thanks." She lowered herself into the chair and curled her legs under her. "I should probably leave as soon as my clothes are dry. I don't want to put you in danger."

He went back to cleaning the gun. "I'm not worried about it."

"But I am."

He glanced up again. "Don't. I can take care of myself. And you."

"But—"

"Seriously. Okay?"

She sighed. "Okay. For now." She took in her surroundings for the first time. "This is a nice cabin. Big, but still cozy."

"I think so. It's got three bedrooms and three baths." He shot her a smile. "Too much room for one guy, but the people who own it are friends and gave me a deal I couldn't refuse."

"Good friends if they let you undo all their winterizing."

He laughed. "Yeah, they are. And I promised to leave it like I found it." He studied her.

With a deep sigh, she shook her head. "Thank you for saving

me. I probably would have drowned if you hadn't jumped in." She paused. "Actually, I might not have made it to the drowning part. He was going to shoot me."

His hands stilled. Those blue eyes met hers. "You want to tell me what that was all about?"

She shrugged. "It's complicated."

"I've done complicated before."

"That's cryptic."

His lips curved, but the slightly haunted expression that slipped into his eyes said he'd seen things better left alone.

"I'm a financial crimes investigator for a bank," she said.

His hands paused in their cleaning and he looked up. "I've worked with a couple of those before. Cool job if you like numbers."

"It can be. Apparently, it can also be quite dangerous," she muttered.

"After your late-night swim adventure, I'm inclined to agree." He set the cloth aside and put the parts of the weapon back together, then wiped it down once more. "So, you think your job had something to do with all this?"

"Pretty sure."

"Why's that?"

"I think someone didn't like what I was investigating, decided to grab me as I was walking out of work, throw me in the trunk, and bring me here to kill me."

Finished with the weapon, he set it aside and turned his full attention on her. "I know that was scary for you."

"A bit of an understatement, but yes. It was definitely scary. And they would have gotten away with it too, if not for you."

"Did the guy on the boat say anything? Give you any clue about why he wanted you dead?"

"No. That was the weird thing. He never said a word. Even when I was begging him to tell me why." She shuddered and looked away, the fear washing over her once again.

"You said they grabbed you as you were leaving work. How did they do that?"

"They drugged me."

"They?"

"There were two of them, I think. Could have been three."

"So they got you after work. Did you yell? Try to grab someone's attention?"

"I never had a chance. And even if I had, it was late and there wasn't anyone around." She rubbed her eyes. "It all happened so fast. They stuck me with a needle and whatever was in it made me feel weird and lethargic. I remember being in the trunk, but I must have passed out, so I have no idea how long they drove or what happened until I woke up in a shed, tied to a boat ramp."

"What time did you leave work?"

"I don't know, sometime after midnight?" She shook her head. "I'm a night owl. I don't have anything to rush home to." She grimaced. "That sounds pathetic, but nevertheless, as long as I'm doing my job, my boss, the bank manager, Calvin Swift, lets me flex my hours so they're convenient for me." She paused and stared at the flames. "I fought them, but—" Goose bumps pebbled her arms even though she wasn't cold. "What lake are we on anyway?"

"Lake Henley."

"I've heard of it but don't know much about it."

"It's private. Mostly second homes people rent out. I think there are about five year-round residents, which means during the winter, it's a ghost town." He shrugged. "That suited my purposes."

An interesting comment she'd like to follow up on but had a feeling he wouldn't say anything more. "And probably why my kidnapper thought it would be a good place to dump a body," she muttered, then sighed. "So, what day is it? Is it still Wednesday night? Early Thursday morning?"

"It's Thursday night." He glanced at his watch. "A little past nine."

Her shoulders slumped. "So you're saying I lost a day?"

"Looks like it. Anyone you need to call and let them know you're okay?"

"I probably should call Heather. She's got to be wondering where I am."

"Who's Heather?"

"My best friend."

He handed her his cell phone and she dialed the number. It went straight to voice mail. "Heather, call me when you get this. Only call me on this number because I don't have a phone right now. I was kidnapped and almost killed and I need to talk to you ASAP." She paused. "And no, this isn't a bad joke." She hung up and rubbed her forehead.

"Are you okay?" he asked. "Or is that a stupid question?"

"Not stupid at all. I'm just a little worried. Heather always answers her phone and the fact that she didn't . . ." She shrugged. She fell silent, then shook her head. "Heather will call me back when she can. I guess I need to go to the police and report this."

"I called it in while you were warming up. They're sending an officer to take your statement, but unfortunately, there was a big wreck nearby with fatalities and this is a small town. The majority of officers will be responding to that first until help from other counties arrives. I told them you were safe for now and the guy in the boat was probably long gone. Which means they'll get to you when they can."

She blinked. "Oh. Okay."

"Who was he? The one in the boat?"

She shook her head. "I've never seen him before."

"How'd you get loose from the railing?"

"Dumb luck? The grace of God? I was struggling pretty hard and he'd been in a hurry when he tied me to it." She pulled her sleeves back just far enough to reveal the rope burns. Blood had flowed from them before her dip into the lake but had washed away during her impromptu swim. They stung like fire, but it was better than the alternative.

"If I have to choose between the two, I'll go with the dumb luck," Brady said.

"Hmm." She paused. "What is it you do exactly?"

"I'm a detective with the Columbia Police Department. I work with the dive team when they're shorthanded, but my main job is criminal investigation."

She gaped, then snapped her mouth shut. "Wow. Okay, then. You might not be very happy with God right now, but I'm thrilled with him for sending you my way."

He barked a short laugh and rose to grab his pack by the door. He rummaged through it and she watched, curious. He returned to kneel in front of her. "Let me see those wrists."

"They're fine."

He took her right hand in his anyway. The feel of his warm fingers wrapped around hers chased some of the horror away.

"You don't believe in God?" she asked, sliding her hand out of his grasp and pulling her sleeve down over the wound.

"I believe in him." He nodded to her wrists. "And they're not fine. Let's wrap them for now. Give them a chance to heal and keep the germs out. You don't want them to get infected."

With no energy to argue—and feeling uncharacteristically compliant—she let him bandage her wrists. When her sleeve rose a little too high to reveal a multitude of white scars crisscrossing the inside of her forearm, she said nothing, just adjusted the sleeve to hide them. He glanced up and caught her gaze, a question in his eyes she had no intention of addressing.

"Why are you mad at him, then?" she asked.

He blinked. Then shrugged. "Who says I'm mad at him?"

"A number of little clues you've dropped."

"Like?"

"Like choosing dumb luck over divine intervention. Body language when I mentioned God. Changing the subject to my wrists." Should she push him on that or leave it alone? It really wasn't fair to expect him to answer deep personal questions if she wasn't willing to respond in kind, was it?

Then again, she knew firsthand that life wasn't fair.

He raised a brow, then focused on her wrists. When he was finished, he replaced his supplies and returned to his chair.

So, he wasn't going to answer. Alrighty then. "You always carry bandages and antibiotic ointment?" she asked.

"I do when I'm going to be fishing."

"Ah, smart."

"I try."

A pause. "So, are you going to tell me why you're mad at God?" she asked.

"No."

"Okay. Then what are you doing out here all by yourself?"

He tilted his head as though surprised she'd not pushed. "I'm on vacation. Where are you from?" he asked.

"Sicily. The city in South Carolina, not Italy, much to my regret."

"Is that where you were kidnapped from?"

"Yes."

"I know that city well. It's about fifteen minutes from where I live. I have some good friends who work out of the Midtown Region police department."

She offered him a small smile. "I don't even know why they had to make it a separate city. It might as well be Columbia."

"True, but the family who founded it missed Sicily—the other one back in Italy."

"You know your history."

"Yeah. I do."

She smiled. "The Italian influence is one of the things that I love about Sicily. One of the reasons I fell in love with it and decided to move there." She yawned. "Apparently, the low crime rate report was a big old lie, though."

They fell silent and her eyes lowered to half mast. She was warm. She was safe. She was sleepy. She let her eyes shut all the way and stayed there, close to dropping off, but vaguely aware of Brady moving in the background.

The window behind her shattered. She dove out of the chair to the floor. Brady's body covered hers. He had a weapon in his hand before she could blink. Flames spurted from the floor in front of the fireplace and the sharp sting of gasoline burned her nose.

"What's going on?" she cried.

He yanked her to her feet and grabbed his pack. "We've got to get out of here."

Smoke curled around her. "How?"

"The back door. Through the kitchen. Laundry room first. We need to grab your shoes from the dryer on the way out."

Another explosion shook the cabin as Brady led her to the kitchen's laundry room. The heat intensified. Moving fast, he grabbed her shoes and stuffed them into his pack. A quick look at the kitchen door said they weren't going out that way.

"Stay here." He ran to the front window. A few seconds later, he returned and pulled her into the laundry room. "Saw two guys out there. If we go out the front door, we'll be picked off."

"What are we going to do?" she gasped.

He grabbed the string connected to the attic stairs and yanked. Once he had the steps down, he pulled her in front of him. "Climb!"

# 4

Pack slung over his shoulder, Brady scrambled up behind her. The flames roared close on his heels, and he knew they wouldn't have a lot of time, but if things worked like he hoped, they wouldn't need too much.

In the attic area, he turned on the light and was actually surprised when it worked. Electrical wasn't totally fried yet. "You okay?"

"Yes." He heard the tremor in the word.

"Come on."

The light flickered.

"Where are we going?"

Another explosion rocked the cabin and he stumbled but kept his balance. Heat seeped through the floor. Most likely they'd tossed another cocktail into the kitchen. There was no going back now.

He gripped her hand and pulled her with him as he walked the length of the house. "There's a balcony off the master bedroom with steps that lead down to the deck surrounding the cabin. If we can climb out the vent, I can lower you down."

"The vent? Won't that be a little small?"

"It's a large rectangular vent. I know you'll fit."

"What about you?"

"It'll be tight, but I think I will. We're going to find out." He found the vent and quickly assessed it by giving it a tug. It was screwed in nice and tight.

"Move back." He stepped back and planted his foot in the middle of it.

It loosened but didn't drop. Four more kicks did the trick.

Brady grabbed it with both hands and yanked it off, then tossed it aside. The smoke grew thicker, the air now pressing against his lungs, but fresh air blew in, and for a brief moment, the smoke cleared around them.

Only to quickly return.

At the opening, he looked out and didn't spot anyone. Probably still waiting at the front door. The balcony was small but directly below. It was going to be a drop, but a broken ankle was better than being fried to a crisp. "It's not too bad a drop if I lower you, okay?"

Steps led from there to the deck that ran around the perimeter of the cabin, stopping at the screened porch where he'd enjoyed his home-cooked dinner only a couple of hours earlier.

"Come on." He gestured her over. "It might be a bit of a rough landing."

"As long as I'm alive at the end of it."

"That's the spirit—and the plan. Climb out and place your feet against the side like you're going to walk down, and I'll lower you as far as I can before I let go." She followed his instructions and he leaned as far as he dared while getting her as close to the balcony as possible. "Ready?"

"Yes."

He released her hands and heard the thud when she hit the wooden porch floor. Her knees buckled and she landed on her hip. For a moment she sat there, then scrambled to her feet looking up at him. The smoke in the attic now choked him. Heat pressed in on him, flames licking behind him. The floor shuddered and part of it caved into the room below.

Coughing, he tossed the pack out and pushed his lower body through the vent. The flames continued to advance toward him.

A gunshot echoed through the crackling chaos, and for a second he froze. "Emily?"

The metal edges scraped his ribs, but he ignored it and shoved on through. When he was hanging by his fingertips, he let go. His left knee protested the jarring stop and a sharp pain shot through his left leg. He went down, slamming his shoulder against the wooden planks. Sucking in a breath, he rolled to see Emily huddled by the edge of the balcony.

"Are you okay?" she asked.

"Yeah." With his eyes probing the dark shadows, he stood, carefully testing his weight on the knee. It throbbed, but it held. "Where'd the gunshot come from?" he asked. He pressed the knee further and grimaced.

"I don't know. From the front, I think."

He slung the pack over his shoulder and limped to the edge of the deck with her right behind him. A quick glance didn't reveal anyone who might spot them or where the gunshot had come from.

Heat seared his back and he grabbed Emily's hand. "Down the steps to the lower deck. I spotted them near my truck out front, so we're going to avoid that area."

"I think that's wise. You think they stuck around?" she asked as she hurried down the steps.

"Yeah. That gunshot came from somewhere, so that's the way we're going to play it."

"What would they be shooting at? We're the only ones . . ." Her eyes widened. "Oh no. The officer who was on his way here. We need to check on him."

"I know. I'll do my best to get to him and find out how bad he is after I make sure you're safe."

They kept their voices low, but he wasn't sure it mattered. The roar of the cabin burning would drown out any sounds they made.

At the bottom of the steps, he pulled her across the yard to the copse of trees about ten yards away, and they huddled behind them while he waited to see if he could spot anyone watching.

He'd seen two attackers. The cocktails had been strategically thrown. One into the hall, the second through the back-door window to prevent their exit from that end. The third in the kitchen. They obviously wanted them to go out the front door.

From his vantage point, Brady couldn't see that anyone was watching—and the cop had probably called in the fire before he'd gotten to the cabin. But their best option was to get away from the property so he could call for help for the downed officer.

Movement to his left paused him. Emily tensed.

"Go that way and watch the door," a voice said. "The cop won't give us any trouble. Now, let's make sure this is over tonight."

The order came so close to him that for a moment Brady froze, certain the person could see him. Beside him, Emily went still. Brady reached for her hand and gripped her fingers, willing her not to breathe, not to move.

A dark figure passed in front of them, stirring the breeze, ruffling the leaves. Her fingers dug into his, but she never made a sound.

Once the man was out of sight, Brady tugged and she fell into step behind him. He moved as quickly as his throbbing knee would allow, putting some distance between them and the burning cabin.

A hiss escaped her and she jerked, pulling him to a stop. "What is it?" he asked.

"I stepped on something. Can I put the shoes on?"

"Oh, man, yes. I'm sorry." He pulled them from his pack and handed them to her.

She dropped onto the nearest fallen tree trunk and slipped on the shoes, then stood. "Okay. What now?"

"We keep going and find a way to call for help. One of these houses will have a landline, I just have to find it."

She brushed her hair out of her face. "Do you think the cop's okay?"

"I don't know. These guys are professionals, though, so . . . I would say his chances aren't great."

"Right. I'm sorry." The words were thick, her grief tangible. "He shouldn't have been out here."

"The best we can do now is find a phone and call for help. You're my first priority. And if he's the kind of cop he should be, that's the way he'd want it."

He continued to lead her through the trees away from the burning cabin.

"Won't someone call 911 when they see the fire?" she asked.

"Hopefully, the officer who was called out here reported it before they shot him, but there's no telling if he did or not. If not, it could be hours before someone realizes what's going on. I left my phone in the cabin, so it's deep fried at this point. We need to find a landline ASAP."

She stayed behind him. "How far away is the nearest house?"

"About half a mile. Can you do that?"

"Yes."

The question was, could he? His knee pounded with pain, but the fact that he could still walk was a good sign.

"Do you know where you're going?" she asked.

"Somewhat. I studied a map of the place before I decided to rent the cabin. There's a house along the road that is just on the other side of these woods. If we keep going, we should come out in the backyard."

"I'm following you."

Together, they hurried down the path that wound through the trees with Brady constantly looking over his shoulder, his weapon held tight.

"Do you think they know we escaped?" she asked.

"No idea, but when the fire trucks and police arrive, they'll figure it out quick enough."

Emily gritted her teeth against the pain shooting up from her foot. She wasn't sure what she'd stepped on, but the center of her arch throbbed with an intensity that was making her sick.

When the house finally came into view, she gave a relieved sigh that might have actually been a sob.

"This way." He led her around the back of the home and floodlights came on.

"Is someone here?"

"I don't think so. Probably motion activated. But just in case—" He knocked.

Nothing.

Pounded once more on the wood.

Still no response. "Guess that answers that." He pulled his sleeve over his fist and punched the lights. Darkness engulfed them once more. He tried the knob. "We're going to have to break in."

She wasn't going to argue, she just wanted a chance to get off her foot.

He used the butt of the gun to break the glass on the kitchen door, then reached in and released the lock on the knob, then the dead bolt. He pushed the door open. "If people have a landline, they're usually in the kitchen on the wall or by a recliner in the den."

"Or on a nightstand in the bedroom."

He glanced at her. "Yeah. True."

"What if they don't have one?"

"Then we move on to the next house, but I'm hoping that's not going to be an issue. A lot of these are rentals and will have a landline. The crispy cabin had one." He stepped inside. "Let's see what we can find."

"I need to check my foot while you find a phone." She limped into the chilly home, glass crunching under her shoes, and shut the door behind her. She took a step, then turned back to lock and dead bolt the door. At least that would buy a few seconds if anyone tried to get in.

Brady was opening and closing drawers in the kitchen. "Aha."

"What?"

"A flashlight."

"I need that for a second." She sat in the nearest chair and pulled her shoe off. Blood spilled to the floor.

"Whoa!" Brady hurried to kneel before her, pulled the sock off, and shined the light on it. "That looks painful. I can't believe you walked this far on that."

"Well, I didn't really have a choice, did I? I think there's glass or something in it." She waved a hand. "Check for a phone."

"Just let me look."

"Brady, go. Find a phone."

He hesitated a fraction of a moment as he took another look at her foot, handed her the flashlight, then bolted into the den. Shortly after, she heard his footsteps on the stairs heading to the second floor. She probed the wound with a shaky finger and felt something hard just on the inside. Her nail scraped the edge of it and she grimaced. "See if there's a first aid kit, please," she called.

Brady returned shortly, a small box in his hand. "No phone." He shook his head. "Of course I pick the one house on this lake that's not used as a rental." He knelt in front of her again. "I found a first aid kit, though. If I leave it with you, can you handle it? I'd help, but we still need a phone and it may take me some time to reach the next house."

"I can take care of it. It won't be the first time I've doctored myself." She'd been taking care of herself for a long time. Pulling a piece of whatever out of her foot would be a minor thing. The thought of staying here by herself didn't appeal, though, but she'd keep that to herself. He had to go.

"Okay, stay low. I promise I'll be back as soon as I can get help on the way. Keep the light to a minimum. We're at the back of the house, so it's probably okay to use the flashlight to doctor your foot."

She nodded and he slipped out the door, leaving her sitting in the kitchen. The sudden quiet engulfed her. But the pain in her foot demanded her attention.

Inside the first aid kit she found tweezers, alcohol wipes, Band-Aids, and antibiotic cream. By the light of the small beam propped on the chair next to her, she cleaned the area as best she could, then used the tweezers to find the piece of glass. Breath whooshed between her teeth when she probed, but finally, she got a grasp on it, pulled it out, and held it in front of the light.

"Whoa." At least an inch long and half that in width, the piece must have come from one of the lower windows in the living area.

Using the alcohol wipes, she cleaned the area one more time, then used the antibiotic cream and bandages. She left the bloody sock off, but used paper towels to clean the shoe, then pulled it back on. She flipped the flashlight off. For a moment, she simply sat, trying to catch her breath and process what had just happened and why.

Although it didn't take much processing to know that someone had tried to kill her. Twice. She'd told Brady she thought the attack on her had something to do with what she was investigating. The more she thought about it, the more it made sense. Actually, it was the *only* thing that made sense.

A large shadow passed by the big bay window to her left, moving fast toward the kitchen door.

It couldn't be Brady, he hadn't been gone long enough. Had he? How much time had elapsed since he'd left? She'd been working on her foot for at least twenty minutes.

Heart thudding, she slipped out of the chair to the floor and waited, watching the window. The figure stepped up to the door and tried the knob. The broken glass pane was a dead giveaway that she and Brady had taken refuge here. With a gloved hand, he reached through the broken glass pane and flipped the dead bolt off. Then pressed his masked face to the window as though making sure he should enter.

Emily sucked in a breath and tried to slow her runaway pulse. Only a sliver of moonlight illuminated the outdoors, and while she could see his outline, she didn't think there was any way he could see her.

With the table and chairs between her and the door, she army crawled her way out of the room, trying to figure out how she was going to defend herself if it came down to it. Beneath the panic, doubts niggled at her. How would he know to come to this house?

Because it was the closest one? Had he seen the beam of the flashlight before she'd turned it off?

Or had he seen the floodlights come on before Brady snuffed them? Or . . .

. . . was Brady working with them?

A shudder swept through her. No. He'd saved her. Twice. What was the point in rescuing her only to turn her over to the people after her?

In the den, making sure she was out of the line of sight from the kitchen door and windows, she stood and limped to the fireplace. No tools. The owners probably never used the place when it was cold enough to need a fire. "Rats," she whispered. "Now what? Think, Em, think."

A knife from the kitchen?

The back door creaked open and shut.

No way was she going back in there.

Her only option was to stay hidden until Brady returned. If he returned. "Please come back, Brady," she whispered.

Emily's pulse pounded. She darted up the stairs, down the hallway, and ducked into the farthest bedroom. She started to shut the door, then stopped and left it open. Shutting it might clue him in.

Emily hobbled to the window, unlocked it, and tried to shove it up. Only to find it was stuck.

Footsteps in the hallway sent her pounding pulse skyrocketing. A king-sized bed dominated the room, and she slid under it. So cliché. He was going to find her and—

The footsteps stopped at the entrance to the room.

Then continued inside.

The light flipped on.

Feet encased in black army boots moved closer and stopped at the edge of the bed. Emily shoved her palm into her mouth to keep the scream from escaping.

———

The broker crumpled the picture in his fist and let out a yell that rattled the rafters of his home office.

Within seconds, the door opened and the cleaning woman stared at him with wide brown eyes. "Are you all right?" she asked in a soft southern accent.

He glared at her and she backed up, pressing a hand to her chest. *Get it together.*

He shut his eyes for a good five seconds before he opened them to find her still there, frozen. Afraid to move, afraid to stay. "I just got some really bad news, Gretchen, and it's going to affect me in ways I'd rather not talk about."

Her eyes instantly softened. "It must have been awful news."

"It was."

"Then I'm so sorry. I will pray for you." She backed out of the office, and within seconds, the vacuum roared to life. He liked Gretchen. She was innocent and soft. And a hard worker who kept her nose out of his business. And she never, ever entered his office, following his explicit orders to stay out. He knew this because he checked the camera each time she was in his home. And even if she did pray too much, she'd never once disappointed him.

He wished he could say the same thing about Jeremy Hightower. It was time for the man to die.

The door opened and his friend stepped in. "Gretchen seems to think you need someone to talk to."

"He sank it."

"What?"

He shoved the picture at his friend. "He sank the *Lady Marie*."

The man studied the picture and his eyes narrowed. "I'll take care of this."

"He needs to die."

"You should have paid him."

The broker turned his chilliest stare on the one person he trusted most in the world. Second only to himself. "And then he would just keep coming back for more."

The room was silent while his friend considered the inevitable. "I hate to admit you might be right. And maybe this isn't such a tragedy after all."

"What do you mean?"

"Well, we both know he didn't get into the safe, so that means the pictures are at the bottom of a lake somewhere. No one's going to get their hands on them. At least not easily."

The broker fell silent. "That's true. I can't believe you can't get the combination."

"Unfortunately, he changes it regularly, but I'm working on him."

The broker raised a brow and noted his blood pressure already leveling out, thanks to his friend's calm demeanor. "Well, work harder."

His friend sighed. "If only that were possible."

"Fine. We'll let the boat sit on the lake floor for a while. Let things cool off. Kill the man who caused all these problems. Then find it and retrieve the flash drive and all will be fine."

"All right. Sounds like a reasonable plan."

"Of course it is. Let me know when you have Hightower at the place. I want to do the honors."

# 5

**B**rady moved at an awkward half run, half jog, ignoring his knee's full-blown protest at the weight he was insisting it endure.

But he'd found a house closer than he expected and had called for help. For him and Emily and for the officer he was certain had been shot. Now, he had to get back to Emily.

At the driveway to the home where he'd left her, he paused. The light in the bedroom on the second floor sent his internal alarms firing. Had she not listened?

Or did that mean she was in trouble?

Brady picked up the pace, bypassing the driveway and hooking around to the back of the house where he'd left Emily. The kitchen was dark. Nothing moved. Nothing said anything was wrong.

And yet he felt it.

Brady slipped up to the back door and noticed it was cracked open. Okay, there could be an explanation for that other than something bad. Unfortunately, he couldn't think of anything. Heart pounding, he nudged the door open and winced at the slight creak.

The dark kitchen was silent with no sign of Emily. Stepping inside, he slid his gun from the back of his waistband and shut the door behind him.

Weapon held ready, he stepped around the broken glass and into the kitchen. The chair where he'd last seen Emily was still pulled out. The bloody sock still on the floor. He continued his careful trek past the table and into the den.

Nothing.

A heavy thud followed by a short scream from above sent him racing for the stairs. He took them two at a time, still doing his best to be as quiet as possible. He didn't want to tip off whoever might be in the room, but a desperate need to find Emily unharmed pushed him.

At the top of the stairs, he paused. Checked right.

Heard a grunt to his left.

He followed the carpet runner to the end of the hallway and paused just outside the open door.

A muffled scream came from under the bed and a hand flew out to grasp at the rug.

"Let me go!"

Emily's voice.

Brady stepped into the room. "Stop! Police!"

A figure rose from the opposite side of the bed and, keeping his back toward Brady, took four steps and threw himself out of the window. Glass rained down behind him.

Brady raced to the window and saw the man clinging to the gutter. The groans coming from the metal said it wasn't going to hold much longer.

"You okay?" Brady threw over his shoulder at Emily, who'd emerged from under the bed, face red, eyes flashing.

"Yes! Don't let him get away!"

Brady bolted down the steps and out the front door, hitting the porch steps hard enough that his knee violently protested. And on the last step, buckled under him. Brady rolled to his feet and limped-ran around the side of the house in time to see the man disappear into the woods.

Giving chase wasn't an option. He'd never catch up with his knee throbbing and begging for an ice pack. With a growl of frustration, Brady turned back to see Emily standing on the front porch, brandishing a cast-iron skillet like a baseball bat.

He hobbled over to her. "That's a little cliché, but I suppose it would get the job done."

"That's all I cared about," she said.

"Well, you can put it back. He got away thanks to my bum knee." He forced the last three words past his clenched teeth, then tilted his head as the sirens reached him. "Sounds like help's almost here."

She disappeared into the kitchen, then returned to go into the den. He followed her, using the railing to keep some weight off the knee. He dropped into the recliner with a grunt and lifted the footrest.

"What happened?" she asked and took a seat on the sofa. She sat opposite him and ran a shaky hand through her hair.

"It's an old football injury. I haven't had any trouble with it for years, but I landed wrong jumping out of the attic. It'll be all right with some ice and rest. And probably a brace."

"Ouch."

"A little bit."

"I'll be right back," she said.

He sat forward. "Wait, stay away from the windows."

"I'll be careful."

He heard her rummaging in the pantry, then the freezer.

When she returned, she handed him a plastic bag full of ice. "Try this."

He settled it over his knee and let out a low breath. "Thanks."

For a moment, they simply sat in silence until a police cruiser turned into the drive. Then another, and finally, a third. "The cavalry is here."

He stood and hobbled to the door, opening it with the sleeve of his shirt. Brady's jaw dropped when his brother Derek stepped inside, followed by Linc and three uniformed officers. He snapped his mouth closed and raised a brow. "How did you guys get here so fast? No. More importantly, how did you even know to come here?"

"We were already in the area," Linc said. "Heard the call come over the scanner."

"In the area?" He frowned. "Never mind," he said before they had a chance to explain. "First things first." He showed his badge to the officers.

The nearest one, who looked to be in his midfifties, raised a hand. "Your brothers filled us in on who you are."

"They did, huh?"

A faint smile curved the man's lips. His dark skin glowed onyx in the kitchen light. "I'm Officer Beau Schaffer. These are Officers Mia Hansen and Terrance Montague." He pointed to the broken glass. "What happened here?"

"I broke in looking for a phone because we had a killer after us. And he found us. The guy came in this door, so you'll want to dust it, but I'm guessing he had on gloves."

"He did," Emily said.

Brady introduced her, then said, "The bedroom up the stairs and down the hall to the left is a crime scene. Tell the crime scene unit to be sure to check under the bed. It was where she was hiding."

"And fighting," she muttered.

"Yeah. Might find a stray hair or something."

"We'll take care of it. This is a small town. There's no CSU. They'd have to come from Columbia." Officer Schaffer offered another crooked smile. "But I'm well-trained in collecting and bagging evidence and I have the tools in my cruiser. Why don't you all hang out in the den and we'll let you know if we need anything."

"Works for me," Brady said. He limped into the den.

"What'd you do to your knee?" Derek asked him.

"He hurt it when we jumped out of the attic," Emily said.

Derek blinked. Linc simply sighed.

"Of course he did," Linc said. "Now that's a story I'm ready to hear."

Once Brady was settled on the couch, Emily handed him the ice pack and he placed it back on his left knee with a wince. She sat in the chair next to the mantel.

"Is that the one you hurt in high school?" Derek asked him.

"That's the one."

Emily gasped and Brady raised a brow. "What is it?"

"I pulled his ski mask off. It's under the bed." She popped to her feet. "I need to tell Officer Schaffer."

"They'll find it." He frowned. "So, did you get a look at his face?"

"No, I was under the bed and too busy trying to get away from him to get a good look."

"Okay, but he might not know that. We'll have to be even more careful."

"Of course."

Brady turned to his brothers. "Back to my original question. What are you guys doing here?"

"We were kind of on the way up here to join you," Linc said.

Brady narrowed his eyes and cleared his throat. "Emily, in case you haven't figured it out, these two lunatics are my brothers, Linc and Derek."

"Yes, I figured as much. Hi," she said.

"Hello," Derek said. "What kind of trouble did our brother drag you into?"

She huffed a low laugh. "Actually, it's more what I dragged him into, I believe—I have to give him credit for dragging me out of the lake and saving my life. Several times over actually." Her eyes flickered with remembered fear and Brady found his protective instincts surging once more.

"Saved your life several times? How?" Derek asked.

"He pulled me out of the lake so I didn't drown because I was too shocked to swim. And then when someone bombed the cabin, he dropped me out of the attic vent so I wouldn't burn alive. Then he jumped out so we could run into the woods and hide from the guys who were still hanging around to make sure we were dead. And I was almost dead, thanks to the man who came after me, but Brady got back in time to save me from him too." She finally took a breath. "I think that covers it."

Linc and Derek stared at her, then turned as one to look at Brady.

He gave a grim chuckle, followed by a shrug. "Well, that's a pretty accurate summary, I guess."

Emily found herself comforted by the presence of the brothers. Granted, fear from her narrow brushes with death still had a tight grip on her nerves, but the obvious camaraderie the three of them shared distracted—and fascinated—her.

Derek quirked a brow at Brady. Then her. "You want to fill us in with the details? Summaries have their place, but details are better in this case."

Emily deferred to Brady, and the telling of it didn't take too long, as there wasn't a whole lot to add to what she'd already said.

"That's what I call a really bad night," Derek said.

Emily gave a light snort. "No kidding."

Derek shot a look at Linc. "Guess you're going to want to get involved in this one."

Linc raised a brow. "I only get involved when I'm invited to do so."

"I think this case may be one where you can invite yourself," Derek said. "Someone just tried to blow up your big brother and you're saying you're not interested in being a part of the team that catches them?"

"Well, sure, but—"

"Wait a minute," Emily said. "What are you talking about? Why would someone invite you to the investigation? You're a detective like Brady?"

Derek shook his head. "He's FBI."

"Oh."

"Look," Derek said, leaning forward. "You were kidnapped, thrown into a trunk, and the man in the boat most likely would have killed you had Brady not intervened."

"Yes."

"Right, so it's only fitting that Linc step in and help figure that out."

"No," Linc said.

"Yes," his brother insisted.

"How many times do I have to say it? She was kidnapped in Sicily. If the local police want some help, then fine, but I'm not going in and asking for them to hand me the case. You know as well as I do that's not how it works. We only step in—"

She let them argue and turned her attention to Brady. He was watching his brothers with a partly amused, partly irritated expression. There was no doubt they were related. The three of them could almost pass for triplets except for the subtle differences. Linc was taller than Brady and Derek, a little stockier through the shoulders.

But to her, Brady was just about perfect. He'd saved her life and she supposed that might sway her emotions a bit. He could easily be her hero. A man she could seriously fall for if she'd let herself. Which she wouldn't. For various reasons she refused to think about at the moment. She slipped over to him. "Are they always like this?"

"Yes."

"Oh."

She turned to Derek and cut him off midsentence. "What area of law enforcement are you in?"

"I'm—uh—with OCN—organized crime and narcotics. But I also do a lot of undercover stuff. And SWAT. Mostly SWAT lately."

"It's a family business then."

The corners of Brady's lips lifted slightly. "You could say that."

Her eyes widened. "Wait a minute. St. John. Is the chief of police your mother?"

"Guilty," Brady said.

Before she could respond, Officer Schaffer stepped into the room carrying several evidence bags in his gloved hands. "All right, I think we've gotten everything we can. Found a ski mask."

"I pulled it off of him," Emily said.

"Good job. I know you said he was wearing gloves, but we dusted for prints just in case. I've also contacted the owners and they'll be on the way in the morning to assess the damage, give us their prints to rule out, and file an insurance report."

Officer Hansen took the bags from him and noted the change of custody on the log. "I'll just put these in the car. We'll have to send them off to the lab and it'll take a while to get anything back. If the DNA's in the system and we get a match, we'll know who we're after. If not, then I'm afraid your guy may be long gone."

"No," she said softly, "he might be gone for the moment, but he'll be back." The men fell quiet and Emily sucked in a deep breath. "Any news on the officer who responded to the call before they blew up the cabin?" she asked.

"Last I heard he was on the way to the hospital. Not sure of his status at the moment, but he was alive when they got to him."

"I'm so very glad to hear that. What about the cabin and the other homes near it?" she asked.

"Firefighters are on the scene and making sure it doesn't spread to any of those. It's probably too late, but we've got teams looking for the boat in case he ditched it and questioning anyone we can find who might have seen something."

"Excellent," Brady said. "Sounds like you've got it all under control. Thank you."

"Sure thing. Now it's time to vacate the premises," Schaffer said.

Linc nodded. "One more question for Emily."

She turned. "Yes?"

"You were kidnapped as you were coming out of the bank."

"Right."

"Where did they snatch you?"

"On a side street. I was parallel parked against the curb. No garage."

"Any security cameras?"

"Yes, of course. On the streetlamps, I think."

"I can see if our tech person, Annie, can get the footage. And we need to bring in the Sicily police on this so they can start looking for whoever nabbed you."

"You will?" Brady asked. "I thought you were going to stay out of it and let the Sicily guys handle it."

Linc scowled. "Just trying to be helpful. Now, get the woman's statement and stop being annoying."

Emily couldn't believe she felt a smile pulling at her lips. "What do I need to do?"

"You just have to tell your story while one of us writes it down. Or you can write it yourself and we'll witness it."

"I can do that."

"As soon as we find a safe place for you," Brady said.

Emily drew in a shaky breath. "A safe place. That would be nice. I'm pretty sure that's not going to be home, though."

# 6

**B**rady raised a brow. "I'm pretty sure I would agree with that. At least not without protection. We'll make sure you have that."

"We will?" Derek asked. Brady scowled at his younger brother and Derek held up a hand. "We will."

"No, no," Emily said. "I don't want to put you out."

"You're not putting us out," Brady said.

"Absolutely not," Derek agreed. "I wasn't protesting, I was just surprised he was offering. He's not usually so quick to do something like that."

Brady snorted. "Thanks, Derek."

His brother flushed. "That's not what I meant. You're a nice guy who likes to help people. I just meant you're not an impulsive kind of guy. You usually take thirty minutes to order at a restaurant because you think through each choice on the menu. Offering protection for someone you just met is so out of—" Linc punched him in the arm. Derek winced and glared at his brother. "What'd you do that for?"

"Shut up," Linc said.

Brady shot Derek a dark look but could feel the heat climbing into his cheeks because he didn't have a good argument. "Yeah, good time to stop talking. Why don't you go call Elaine or something? Come on, let's go."

They loaded into Linc's King Cab pickup. "Who's Elaine?" Emily asked.

"Derek's on-again, off-again fiancée."

"Ouch. Which one's afraid of commitment?"

"Elaine. Surprisingly enough."

"So are they on or off right now?"

"On. I think."

Linc drove them back to the smoldering cabin and Brady climbed out, wincing at the sight of the blackened shell. "So much for returning it the same way I found it," he muttered.

Firefighters continued to monitor the area, making sure the fire was truly out. He flashed his badge and his brothers did the same. Allowed access to the area, Brady led Emily to his truck. She reached for the passenger door handle, but he laid his hand on top of hers to stop her. "Let me have a look first." His hand lingered a second longer than he'd intended, triggering the thought that he liked her. A lot.

*You don't know her. Keep her safe and move on. Just like you should have done with Krystal.* It was a good plan. He just hoped he stuck to it.

The side of the truck facing the cabin had been scorched but, other than that, looked like it had survived relatively unharmed. "My dive gear."

He moved quickly to the storage box that ran the width of the truck behind the window and spun the combination lock. Inside, he found his gear untouched and apparently unharmed. Relief pounded him and he was grateful he'd put it back into the box once he'd finished diving instead of leaving it in the cabin bedroom. But it was habit. Always be prepared for a call no matter what. Thankfully, that had paid off tonight.

Further inspection showed the contents of his glove compartment had been scattered over the front seat. Using the hem of his shirt, he opened the door.

Linc stepped up beside him. "They searched your truck."

"Just the glove compartment."

"Looking for your address," Linc said.

"No doubt."

"They find it?"

"I don't know. Registration card is still here, but they could have snapped a picture of it." He raked a hand through his hair. "The fact that they left everything out on the seat means they don't care if I know they now know where I live."

"Not just you, but Ruthie and me too," Derek said.

"And considering these guys like to play with explosives, I'm not real comfortable with that," Linc said.

"I'm going to put Ruthie on notice that she's not to go home until we have coverage on the house," Derek said. "I'll arrange that too."

"I'm so sorry," Emily said. "This is my fault you all got dragged into this."

Brady turned to find Emily with tears swimming in her eyes, deepening them into a shade of purple he couldn't quite name. "Aw, Emily. Don't." He pulled her into a loose hug. She stiffened and he almost lowered his arms. After all, they'd just met a few hours ago. It felt like longer than that. Then she wilted and dropped her head to his shoulder. "It's going to be okay," he said. "Don't forget that the guy shot at me. I have a bit of a personal stake in this as well."

"You're just saying that to make me feel better."

"Maybe a little, but I still mean it."

A tiny laugh escaped her. At least he thought it was a laugh. Whatever it was, it seemed to lighten her burden slightly. He'd take it. He caught Linc watching and the speculative, albeit slightly worried, look in his brother's eyes had him giving a mental grimace. He rolled his eyes and Linc simply raised a brow.

Emily stepped back and swiped the tears. Then lifted her chin, narrowed her eyes, and gave a sharp nod. "All right, if these guys want to play dirty, then that's what we'll do. Tell me what I can do to help."

The change that swept over her made him blink. The helpless victim was gone. A woman with focus in her gaze and determination in her stance now faced him.

"Um . . . okay. What just happened? It's like you went through some weird mutant transformation. What do you know about fighting dirty anyway?"

She let out a short, humorless laugh. "As a teen, I lived on the streets for a year and managed to survive. Part of that survival involved fighting dirty. The other part was pushing down emotions that aren't productive for survival, because being perceived as weak can have really bad consequences. Fighting these guys is going to require much of the same skill set, I would suspect."

Brady's jaw dropped a fraction and Derek stared while Linc's brows rose. Then his brothers turned their gazes to him.

Brady cleared his throat. "Hopefully, we'll be able to keep you safe and you won't have to do much of the fighting. Now, stand back while I check for anything that might go boom." When he found nothing that concerned him, he helped her into the front of his truck and handed her the keys. "Start it up and get the heat going if you want to."

He shut the door, heard the engine growl to life, and turned back to Linc and Derek. "Okay, that was interesting, and I have even more questions that I want to ask her."

"Be careful," Derek said, "you might not like the answers."

"I'm a big boy, I can handle it," he said. A glance at Emily's firm jaw and narrowed eyes had him amending that. "Maybe. That being said, I still want you on my side and at my back. I want y'all on this investigation with me."

Linc hesitated. "Not that I'm not willing, but you guys and the

Columbia police department are more than capable of handling this without FBI input. The kidnapping took place in Sicily, so that's where the investigation is going to start. Since you know so many of the cops over there, you shouldn't have any trouble working it."

"I do know the cops in Sicily," Brady said. "They're not going to mind if I butt in."

"Nope. But they *will* think you're crazy," Derek said. "Every detective on the force is overworked."

"I know, but this is something I have to do."

"Then they'll probably hand the case to you on a silver platter," Linc said. "I'd check with your captain, though."

"Of course."

Derek shrugged. "I'll do what I can to help. OCN is busier than ever and it took a lot of negotiating to get the next few days off so we could come babysit you."

"Babysit me?" He laughed. "Seriously? So, that's what you guys were doing so close to the cabin and how you got there so fast?"

"Guilty," Linc said. "But, I have to admit, I was looking forward to it."

"Yeah, me too." Derek sighed. "But now we've got an attempted murder to figure out."

"If you count arson," Brady said, "it's essentially another attempted murder."

Linc nodded. "And Emily's kidnapping. As soon as I hear something back on the security footage, I'll pass it on to the locals and they can take it from there."

"Right. Keep telling yourself that."

Derek laughed and Linc scowled. Brady sobered. "It's about to get busy, boys," he said. "But first order of business is to get me a phone. Mine is fried to a crisp."

"I need one too," Emily said.

He looked over to find she'd rolled the window down. "We'll get you one," he said.

"I'm afraid I don't have any money or anything on me. Most of my belongings were in my purse when I was snatched."

"We'll take care of everything," Brady said and headed for the driver's door. "Ready when y'all are."

---

Emily rode in the passenger seat of Brady's truck while Derek and Linc followed. The events of the last few weeks blipped across the screen of her mind. It had all started with seeing Jeremy Hightower walk into the bank and into her boss's office. Pure rage and a white-hot hate had nearly taken her to her knees. The emotions had shocked her, as she'd thought she'd come so far in putting him out of her mind—her life. Guess not.

"What are you thinking about?"

She jerked at Brady's question then cleared her throat. "A lot of stuff. Why?"

"You looked really intense."

"I was just thinking how life can be so fickle. That just when you think you have it mostly figured out, it throws you a curve ball that takes you by surprise and before you can react, you get slammed right between the eyes. Or taken down at the knees. Either way, it's not good."

"I was right. That's intense. Is that what the kidnapping did to you?"

"No, that happened a couple of weeks *before* the kidnapping."

He slid her a sideways glance. "You've had a rough time of it lately, sounds like."

"I'll admit I've had better weeks." She tugged on the sleeves of the too-large sweatshirt and let the cuffs cover her fingertips. Then stopped and pushed them back to her wrists. She would not revert to behavior she'd overcome years ago.

"So, what happened before the kidnapping?"

"I saw someone I haven't seen in a long time."

"And?"

"I didn't know he was back in town and it was a shock to see him. Especially walking into my bank."

"A shock, huh?"

"Yes." She frowned. "Why?"

"You didn't say 'surprise.' In this instance, shock has bad connotations here. So, I'm deducing that he hurt you once upon a time."

Emily sucked in a breath. "That's just scary."

"It's my job. Sometimes I'm wrong, but not often."

"Well, don't do that anymore, it's creepy."

"Does he have something to do with those scars on your arms?"

She fell silent. Then rubbed her forehead. "Yes," she finally said.

"I'm sorry."

"Me, too." She sighed and gave a small shrug. "It was years ago. I've done a lot of healing since then." And a lot of helping other teens just like the one she'd once been. She'd told her story many times over in an attempt to encourage others that they, too, could overcome whatever bad stuff life handed them. But for some reason, she didn't want to tell Brady.

He glanced at her. "I'm glad."

She shot him a faint smile. "Thanks."

"How are your wrists?"

"They sting, but they're fine. How's your knee?"

"Sore, but at least it's my left one and I can drive."

"This is some pretty stilted conversation. What is it that you really want to ask me?"

He raised a brow. "You're kind of good at reading between the lines yourself, aren't you?"

"Call it survival instinct."

"I want to hear about that later." Fingers tapping the wheel, he pursed his lips and shook his head. "For now, tell me what happened the day your past walked into your bank."

"You're not going to let that go, are you?"

"Not if it will help us figure out if it had something to do with you—and me—almost getting killed."

She groaned. Did she even want to get into it? Then again, her past walking into her bank—as Brady put it—was the reason she'd found the whole suspicious money trail in the first place. "His name is Jeremy Hightower. I went to high school with him. Basically he was a jerk to the nth degree and I never wanted to have anything to do with him ever again. And didn't think I'd have to when I heard he went to college out west."

"Ouch. High school bully?"

"To put it mildly. Anyway, when he came into the bank, he had a meeting with my boss, Calvin Swift. He went straight to Calvin's office, so he didn't see me cowering in the corner."

"I have a hard time picturing you cowering."

She wanted to laugh but couldn't quite manage it. She had cowered—and that shamed her. Never again. "Thanks, but . . ."

"So, he didn't see you, but you saw him."

"I did. It didn't take long for the shock to wear off and the rage to start boiling. I was going to speak to him. Be very controlled and professional just to prove to myself that I could, that he had no power over me anymore. So I walked over to Calvin's office. The door was cracked and I could hear them talking."

"About?"

"I . . . I don't know. As soon as I heard his voice, I ran to the bathroom and threw up."

"Emily," he whispered.

She held up a hand. If he got all nice and compassionate, she'd never finish. The fact that she hadn't been able to face Jeremy without getting sick frustrated her. Shamed her. "Once I was sure he was gone, I looked him up to see if he was in the bank's system. And he was. Five weeks prior, he'd opened four new accounts, each with an initial deposit of around nine thousand dollars—all under different business names."

"Not so weird in and of itself."

"No, but . . . something just didn't set right with me, so I kept digging. He had all the paperwork, ID, addresses, et cetera that he needed. The business addresses are all post office boxes or apartment complexes. The Articles of Incorporation were from Florida and New York."

"I see where this is going. Those are two high-volume human trafficking states."

"Yes. And he kept the deposits under the required cash reporting threshold."

"Funnel accounts?" Brady asked.

"That's what I was thinking. And then two days later, large sums went out to different accounts, withdrawn from towns not too far from Sicily. One in Columbia, one in Lexington, one in Irmo, and one in Richland County."

"Now I'm really not liking where this is going."

"Exactly. Over the course of the next week, cash deposits between nine thousand and ninety-five hundred went in each day. I couldn't leave it alone. I continued to research the deposits and withdrawals. Most deposits were made between 10:00 p.m. and 6:00 a.m. at various branches around the city, and then within two days, the funds were withdrawn and moved."

"Whose names are on these accounts?"

"Corporations and businesses with Jeremy as the contact person, but I don't think he was the head of the organization. I think he was simply the dispatcher—and the one who's being set up as the fall guy. I think he's the one who takes the calls and sets up all of the appointments." She grimaced at the word. "And I think he has someone who is doing the actual money laundering for him. Purchasing property, cars, and other things."

"What were the businesses?"

"Two cleaning companies, one restaurant, and two travel agencies. I've been trying to track down where the money winds up—to see who the head honcho is, but it's almost impossible. When I call the companies, I do get a receptionist. She said she was part of a call center for the companies and would pass along any messages. I asked her to have someone call me but never heard from anyone. And there was a lot more that made me sit up and take notice, such as all of the transactions on the accounts were never for anything related to cleaning or restaurants. The travel agency did have some travel expenses, but because it was opened by Jeremy on the same day as the others, it was still on my radar. Anyway, I was trying to tread carefully, but"—she shuddered—"obviously I left some footprints somewhere. Like with the receptionist."

Brady pursed his lips. "All of that raises some serious red flags for me. Especially the deposits made late at night and early in the morning. That's classic human trafficking funds movement."

"I thought so too. I was trying to get more information before taking everything to law enforcement, only I didn't have a chance."

"Someone didn't like you looking into the transactions."

"Yes. But I can't figure how they found out—unless it was the message I left with the receptionist."

"Did you tell anyone what you were doing?"

"Just a close friend, but she wouldn't say a word because she's helping me look into everything."

His eyes narrowed. His skeptical expression tightened her nerves.

"She wouldn't."

"Who's this friend?"

"The friend I told you about back at the cabin. Heather Gilstrap."

Again his eyes cut toward her. "What does this friend do for a living?"

"Why?"

"Humor me."

"She's . . . a writer."

He snorted. "For which paper?"

Emily jerked. "You've really got to stop doing that."

"I wouldn't have to if you'd be straight with me."

"She's an investigative reporter and works for the *Columbiana*. She's the friend I tried to call back at the cabin before it blew up. I need to try her again."

"A reporter? You trusted a reporter?"

She narrowed her eyes. "Of course. We've been working on this for weeks."

"And you think she's going to keep her mouth shut?"

"She will if she wants the exclusive. We have a deal. She waits on me to complete the investigation before she writes a word."

He shrugged. "Maybe."

"No maybe about it. We've been friends since fourth grade. I trust her."

"I hope that doesn't come back to haunt you."

"It won't."

He grunted. But she didn't care. She knew her friend.

"Sounds like we need to talk to Jeremy Hightower."

"I know, but not yet. I just need a little more time to gather more evidence about the transactions, then I can turn everything over to whoever will be in charge and they can run with it."

"I don't think you need anything else. It sounds to me like you have enough for a grand jury subpoena or even a search warrant for those records. You probably shouldn't wait much longer."

"But I don't know where the money finally lands. I don't know who the ringleader is."

"The feds can figure that out. I'm going to let my boss put some surveillance on Hightower and see what they can find out. Is that okay?"

"If he knows you're on to him, he'll disappear. And trust me, he has the money to do it. I mean, he's not a millionaire or anything— he's not that high up in the organization—but he's well paid."

He gave her a half smile. "Hightower won't even know they're there." She waited while he set up the surveillance. When he hung up, he asked, "What about your boss? Did he know anything?"

"No, I never said anything to him."

"Why not?"

She rubbed her eyes. "Because when I present something to him, every *t* has to be crossed and every *i* has to have its dot. I learned that the hard way a couple of times and I wasn't about to make that mistake again, especially when we were dealing with millions of dollars. I was also talking to other banks to see if they were having some of the same activity as we were. And they were."

"Only none of their investigators were kidnapped."

"As far as I know, I'm it."

She fell silent until he pulled into the parking lot of a twenty-four-hour all-in-one superstore.

"Wait here, okay? I'll be two minutes in and out. Derek and Linc are right behind us, watching out for you."

She nodded. "I'll be fine."

True to his word, he returned quickly with two phones—and a pocketknife. "I hate these packages. They're impossible to get into."

"I think that's the point. Shoplifters, you know."

He shot her a smile and cut into the plastic. "Right." He gave one phone to her. "Go ahead and program my number in there." He recited it and she punched it in. "And Linc's and Derek's." He rattled off their numbers.

"Anyone else?"

"Probably, but that'll do for now."

Emily dialed Heather's number. And just like before, it went straight to voice mail. "Heather, ignore the last number I left you and call me on this one as soon as you get this." She hung up and dialed her voice mail for the phone that had been lost.

"Emily? This is Heather's mother." Emily jerked and sat up straight. Brady shot her a concerned look as she listened to the message. "I need you to call me when you can. I'm afraid something terrible has happened to Heather and I need to know if you've heard from her. And if you're safe. The police came by and said they had a 911 call from Heather's phone. They think she was attacked in the parking garage outside of her work and are looking into it. But no one's heard from her and she said you were in danger too!" Mrs. Gilstrap's voice wobbled. "I really need to hear from you."

She turned the speakerphone on so Brady could hear. Three more of the same type of messages.

Emily dialed Mrs. Gilstrap's number and got her voice mail. "It's Emily, Mrs. Gilstrap. I didn't know about the 911 call. Give me a call back when you can. I'm fine at the moment, but now I'm very worried about Heather too." She gave her the new number, hung up, and closed her eyes. "Something's wrong," she said. "Something's very, very wrong. What if they got her too? Only she didn't have someone around to rescue her? The 911 call certainly seems to indicate that, doesn't it?"

"We can try to find out. Where does she live?"

"In the same apartment complex that I do. She's on the first floor, I'm on the third on the other side of the same building."

"Give me the address. We'll head that way and check out her place first. I'll call Derek and get him to look into the 911 call."

Emily gave him directions and then logged in to check her email while Brady spoke with Derek. When he hung up, she glanced at him and frowned. "I have a full inbox, but nothing from Heather. That's completely out of character for her on so many levels." She signed out and set the phone in the cup holder. "This isn't good. Those messages from her mother combined with me not hearing from her? She's in trouble. Big trouble."

"Let's not worry too much until we know something for sure, okay?"

She cut him a glance. "Didn't you hear her mom's message? Heather made a *911 call*. The police went by *their* house looking for her. They went by *her* place and she wasn't there. None of this is adding up to anything good."

"I know, but I was trying to be encouraging."

Chills danced over her skin and she rubbed her arms. "I appreciate it."

"But it's not working?"

"Sorry."

"Okay. Then, I'll admit, you're right. It's not sounding good."

"Could have kept that to yourself."

He huffed a short, humorless laugh and fell silent, the tense set of his jaw saying he found the situation anything but amusing. Emily leaned her head against the window and closed her eyes. *Please, God, let Heather be all right.*

# FRIDAY, OCTOBER 25

# 7

Brady pulled to a stop at the address Emily had provided before she'd dropped off into a restless sleep. He hated to wake her, but he needed the code to access her complex. A gentle shake popped her eyes open and she sucked in a breath as she looked around. "What? We're here?"

"You dozed the last hour."

She shoved a hank of dark hair behind her ear and blinked a few more times. "I'm so sorry. I haven't been sleeping well and then after the last few hours . . ." She shrugged. "I guess I'd had it."

"Understandable."

She scrubbed her eyes. "Um. You need the code, I'm guessing."

"Yes. Or I would have let you sleep a little longer."

"No. Let's go to Heather's place first." She rattled off the numbers. "Did Derek get back to you on the 911 call?"

"Not yet. It may take him a bit." He punched in the code and the gate swung open. "Can you text the code to Linc? They're about five minutes behind us."

"Sure." She sent the text. "Turn right here," she said. He drove slowly, scanning the area, taking note of anything that might spell trouble. Nothing alarmed him. The parking lot was quiet at this time of the morning. Just before dawn, the first orange and gold rays of the sun were starting to sneak into the horizon. "Do you see her car?" he asked.

"No. And that's her spot right there." She pointed.

A young man exited the apartment nearest them and hurried to a packed silver BMW. Brady thought about telling him he needed to move a few of the boxes so his view wouldn't be obstructed, but that wasn't his priority at the moment.

The man's gaze met Brady's, then slid to Emily's. He gave a double take, but lifted a hand in a wave. Emily returned it and rolled down her window. "Paul. Hey, Paul!"

Paul paused, then walked over to the vehicle. "Hi, Emily. What's up?" He nodded to Brady. "I'm Paul Bailey."

"Brady St. John." Brady held out a hand and the two men shook.

"I'm looking for Heather," Emily said. "Have you seen her?"

"No." He frowned. "Did you try her cell?"

"Of course. She's not answering."

"That's weird. She didn't say anything to me about being gone. Is she all right?"

"I don't know. When was the last time you saw her?"

"Wednesday morning, I think. She was in a hurry to get to the office. Why all the worry?"

"She called 911 late Wednesday night and no one's seen her since."

"What!"

"I know."

"That's not good. What's being done to find her?"

"Everything possible," Emily said. "Will you ask around and tell me if you hear from her—or anyone who might have seen her before she left work that night?"

"Of course."

"Thanks." She gave him her number and the man climbed into his car, backed out, and headed toward the exit.

"That was Paul," Emily murmured.

"I gathered." A spark of jealousy flamed for a nanosecond,

making Brady catch his breath. *What in the world? Just because you saved her life doesn't mean you get to stake a claim.* He'd saved lives before and had never once had a flash of jealousy when he'd reunited them with friends and loved ones. His reaction made no sense. "Who's Paul?" He couldn't help it. He had to ask. A few seconds' worth of conversation hadn't told him much.

"A friend. Sort of. He's a realtor and occasionally comes into the bank where I work when he's in town. He mostly works in Columbia and deals in commercial real estate, but he and Calvin are friends and have lunch once or twice a month. He's loaded. He's been living here for about two weeks."

"I see. You said he was loaded. Not to diss your apartment complex, it's actually very nice, but someone who's loaded doesn't live in a place like this. At least I find it odd."

She frowned. "But his cousin, Claire, isn't loaded. He's having his home renovated and moved in with her. He said she insisted he stay with her and get to know each other again. Apparently, they'd grown apart over the years and had recently reconnected. When Paul needed a place to stay, Claire convinced him it would do his character good to 'live like a normal person.'" She wiggled air quotes around the last few words. "I've only talked with her a handful of times. I think I've seen more of Paul in the past two weeks than I have of Claire in the past two years."

"Seems like he would offer to help her out with a fancier place."

"He did. She said no. He said she refuses to let him help her out, that she wants to make it on her own."

"Admirable."

"Hmm."

"You sure do know a lot about him for having only known him for two weeks."

"I got all that from Heather. He's been trying to get her to go out with him from the moment he met her, but she keeps turning him down. I think she really likes him, and if she wasn't working so hard on this story, she'd go."

"Oh. Heather, huh?" He refused to acknowledge the fact that he was relieved. But he also couldn't help wondering why he was so drawn to this woman he'd rescued. She was very similar to Krystal in a lot of ways, but there was also something very different about her. He thought it might have something to do with the way her eyes expressed every thought she had and yet managed to remain mysterious at the same time.

She raised a brow. "Yes, Heather."

"And she keeps turning him down?"

"Yes, why?"

"Just curious." He made a mental note to look into the guy's background, then nodded at the apartment next door to Paul and Claire's. "Is that hers?"

"Yes. I know where she keeps her spare key."

"All right. Stay here and call me if you see anything suspicious or if anyone starts doing drive-bys—"

"Actually, why don't I just come with you?"

"Emily—"

She opened the door and climbed out, ignoring his protests. Brady scowled and she met his gaze over the hood of the Chevy. "I need to go with you."

He nodded. He'd do the same thing in her shoes. "Fine, but stay back."

"You think someone's in there?"

"No, but just—"

"Then you think she's dead?"

"Emily . . ." Planting his hands on his hips, he sighed. "I don't know if she is or not, but it's better if I take a look by myself." He paused. "That way, if it's a crime scene, there's not two of us trampling around in there, okay? If it's all clear, I'll call you in to take a look."

She gave a slow nod. "All right. I'll hang back."

"Thank you."

"But not far."

"Of course not." She was stubborn. Probably why she was still alive. Besides, the 911 call came from the parking garage. If someone took Heather . . . or had killed her . . . he seriously doubted they'd bring her back here. But he'd keep that to himself.

"Heather keeps the key in a magnetic holder on that small plant stand," Emily said. "Behind the right rear leg."

He found it with ease, but if he hadn't known it was there, he never would have spotted it. "Clever."

"She is."

Brady inserted the key in the lock and turned it. And frowned. "It's unlocked."

"What?" Emily stepped forward and reached for the knob. He caught her wrist and she yelped.

"Sorry." He released his hold immediately, knowing he'd grabbed the area the ropes had rubbed raw. "I didn't mean to hurt you, but don't touch that. We may need to see if there are any prints on there."

"Right. Of course. I wasn't thinking. I'm sorry." She held her wrist with the other hand and pain glittered in her eyes. Regret arced through him. He'd have to be more careful. And in that moment, the reason for his attraction clicked.

There was no pretense about Emily. What you saw was what you got. He blinked and shook his head. "It's okay. No apology necessary. Stand to the side out of the line of fire. Should there be any shooting. I'm hoping there won't be."

"You haven't learned to wait for backup?" Derek said from behind them.

Brady jerked to see Derek and Linc hurrying toward them, hands on their weapons. "Didn't know I was going to need it, but backup is always welcome." He nodded to Emily. "Make sure she stays behind you."

She frowned, but didn't argue. Once she was positioned so that if someone started shooting she'd be out of danger, Brady pulled his weapon and used the hem of his shirt to turn the knob. He pushed the door inward.

When nothing happened, he rounded the doorjamb and into the small foyer, favoring his throbbing knee. Empty. But the place had been ransacked. His nose twitched at the combined smell of cinnamon and other spices he couldn't identify while he took in the destruction. Satisfied no one was going to shoot him immediately, he glanced back and found Derek and Linc just inside, weapons held ready, and Emily peering around the edge of the doorjamb.

"Someone's been here," he said, "and it's not pretty."

"What do you mean?" she asked, trying to see around his brothers. "Heather?"

"No," he said quickly. "Sorry. I simply meant someone broke in and trashed the place. Stay put for just a minute until we can clear it, okay?"

She stepped inside next to Linc and moved to the left of the door. Linc shut it behind her and Brady let her take in the destruction. Her gaze went to the sofa on the far wall. Then cushions on the floor and the lamp next to the sliding glass door.

"Don't move," he said. "If she's here, we'll find her."

Her furrowed brows dipped farther, but her gaze met his and she nodded. He glanced at his brothers who stood ready to help and gave them a nod. Derek covered his back. Linc stayed slightly in front of Emily.

Hip to hip, Brady limped and Derek walked down the hallway, Brady with his weapon pointing ahead and to the left and Derek pointing ahead and to the right. They passed the kitchen to his right. Silverware lay scattered on the floor with the drawer resting on its side next to the refrigerator. The broken spice bottles identified the source of the smell he'd noted upon entering the apartment. Together, he and his brother continued on down the hall, clearing the bedroom and bath to his left and then the master and en suite bath at the very end.

"All clear," Derek said.

"Same here." Brady turned and walked back to find Emily standing where he left her. Apprehension held her stiff while her gaze searched his. "She's not here," he said.

A puff of air escaped her lips and her shoulders slumped. "Oh, thank goodness."

"For now."

She nodded. "I know. I'm still worried she hasn't gotten in touch with me—or you. I'm worried about that 911 call. But she has both numbers in her voice mail. Maybe she'll call soon."

Brady wasn't so optimistic, but he wasn't going to take away the hope the empty—if trashed—apartment had given her.

"We good here?" Derek asked.

"We're good," Brady said. "Thanks for the backup."

Linc stood next to the door. "So, what's next?"

"Can we go check my place?" Emily asked.

"Absolutely." Brady gestured to the door. "Derek can lead. You follow him, and Linc and I'll bring up the rear."

Together, the four of them walked up to the third floor, and this time Emily held back while Brady took the lead. "Key?"

"Same place as Heather's. We found the matching plant stands on a shopping trip about a year ago."

He found it and he wished he had a way to ease her worry. But only finding Heather would make that happen.

Derek placed a hand on his arm. "You want me to take the lead on this? I can tell your knee is hurting."

"Thanks, but it's fine." He retrieved the key and, without touching the knob, unlocked the door and pushed it inward.

Only to have something slam into him, knocking him off his feet.

---

Emily let out a low scream when Brady went down with the person on top of him. Linc grabbed her arm and jerked her away from the two men scuffling in the open doorway. Derek reached in, grabbed the intruder by the back of his collar, twisted, and yanked him away.

The man gasped, swung a fist, and connected with Brady's cheekbone just as Derek yanked.

Emily blinked. It was over that fast. And she recognized him. "That's the guy from the boat! The guy who tried to kill me!"

Brady rolled to his feet, breathing hard, wincing when he put weight on his left leg, then patted the man down while Derek held him. "The guy from the boat, huh?" He pulled a gun from the man's waistband and gave it a slight shake. "What were you going to do with this? Do you have permission to carry it?"

The man was turning an alarming shade of red and Emily was about to protest when Brady said, "Loosen up a little, Derek. I want to hear what he has to say."

Derek relaxed his hold on the collar slightly, and the intruder gasped, then gulped in air.

Brady touched the reddening area under his eye and winced. "Okay, I guess it's clear you're under arrest." He read him his rights. "Now, who are you and why are you in Emily's apartment?"

The man's rugged features tightened even as his right hand hovered over his throat. Emily took a closer look. His green eyes met hers and the flat look there sent shivers dancing over her skin. "Who are you?" she asked.

Again, he said nothing, simply continued to stare and take in deep breaths.

"Maybe a little time downtown will help loosen his tongue," Brady said.

Green eyes flashed and Emily swallowed. She doubted much of anything was going to make him say a word if he didn't want to. He hadn't said two words to her when he'd tied her to the rail of the boat.

"No matter," Linc said. "We'll run his prints and see what shows up." He flashed his badge and the intruder's eyes widened, then his face dropped into a scowl.

"Great," he muttered.

"You have something you want to say now?" Brady's words were soft, but lacked nothing in intensity.

"You're a cop?" he asked Linc.

"Better," Linc said. "I'm a fed."

"Hey now," Derek protested. "I don't know about better—" He snapped his lips shut when Brady glared at him.

Brady then returned his attention to the intruder—whose shoulders had wilted a fraction. "He's FBI," Brady said, pointing at Linc. "We're with the CPD. Detectives."

"And SWAT," Derek said. "Don't forget that."

Their captive laughed. A harsh sound with an edge that raked across Emily's nerves. "So that's just great," he said. "Three cops. Of course."

"Nope," Linc said. "Two cops and a fed."

"Whatever."

"Feel like talking now?"

With a tight jaw, he gave a short nod. "Maybe. If I talk, I want some protection."

"From who?"

"The people who hired me. Who do you think?" He lunged at the door and Derek yanked him back.

Brady shook his head. "Derek, do you have cuffs on you?"

"Never leave home without them," he said with a glare at the man. He passed the cuffs to Brady.

Once he had the man's hands secured behind him, Brady shoved him into the nearest chair at the kitchen table.

"Come on, man," their prisoner said, "I'm serious. Look, I got a rap sheet, I'm not going to try to deny it."

"I'm shocked," Derek murmured.

"But I don't know who's got it in for her," he said as though Derek hadn't spoken. "I'm just a hired hand."

"You're also an ex-con. Which means you're not supposed to be carrying a firearm," Linc said, holding the weapon he'd already unloaded. "I guess you forgot that when you decided to slip this into your waistband?"

The man scowled. "Yeah. That's it. I forgot."

"Dude," Derek said, "you're going away for a good long time. Why don't you just cooperate and make things easier on everyone?"

Their intruder sighed and shook his head. "I know it won't take you long to find my record, but the guy I work for isn't someone you play games with." He paused, then shrugged. "However, I have no loyalty toward him. Like I said, I'm just a hired hand, but if I talk, I want protection."

"Your name?" Brady asked.

"Owen Parker."

"What do you want with Emily?"

He hesitated. "She's a job. There's nothing personal about it, understand?"

"Yeah, I understand. What does the job entail?"

"Someone wants her to disappear," he said. "I was hired to make that happen."

Brady turned to Emily. "You recognize this guy from the kidnapping?"

She frowned. "I can't tell if he's one of the men who tossed me in the trunk or not, but he's definitely the guy from the boat."

"Did you help toss her in the trunk?"

The man glared.

"I'll take that as a yes," Brady said as his fingers clenched into a fist. "Who was your partner?"

"Another hired hand."

"And who did the hiring?"

Parker's eyes hardened. "Someone she's managed to make very

angry." His gaze swung to Emily. "Trust me, whoever hired me is not a nice person. I don't know how you ended up on his radar, but you did. And it's a deadly place to be."

"Whose radar?" Emily asked with a shudder.

"Actually, I have no idea. Every contact I've had with him has been via secure emails or text messages from burner phones. He—or she—" he shrugged—"never uses the same number or email twice."

"How'd they find out about you?"

"Word of mouth, probably. Now, I'm done talking until I get some guarantees that I'll be safe."

"You don't get any guarantees on that until you've convinced us that you're worth keeping safe," Brady said.

Parker started to answer when his phone vibrated. He stiffened. The phone sounded again. Brady swiped the screen and put it on speakerphone.

"No!" Parker's harsh whisper echoed. "Don't!"

Brady glared. "Hello?"

"Parker?" the voice said.

"Yeah."

A pause. "Who is this?"

"Parker." Brady practically growled the name.

*Click.*

Emily didn't like Parker's color. He'd turned an alarming shade of red without Derek's help this time. "You don't know what you've just done," Parker growled. "Now he knows I got caught. You've just signed my death warrant."

"You're in custody," Derek said. "You'll be fine."

Parker gave his head a violent shake. "You're cops. You know there are ways. If someone wants me dead, I'm dead."

"Should have thought about that before you became a hit man and targeted Emily," Brady said. "We all have consequences due to our actions. If you happen to get dead while in prison, it's no skin off my nose."

Emily wouldn't have thought it possible, but the man's face darkened more and his eyes actually frosted over. "You're all dead. You better make sure I don't make bail."

"You kidnapped her," Linc said. "She can ID you as the guy on the boat who was about to shoot her and dump her in the lake. You broke into her home. You're carrying a weapon, which is a violation of your parole. You assaulted a police officer. I don't think you making bail is going to be something I lose sleep over."

"I didn't know he was a cop!" Parker surged out of the chair and struggled briefly against Linc's firm hold before giving up and dropping back into the seat. "I want a lawyer."

"Fine," Derek said. To Linc, he said, "Let's get this bozo out of here. I'll call someone to come get him." He dialed and was soon on the line with the local police, requesting an officer come pick the man up to file formal charges of attempted murder, burglary, and assault—at the very least.

Once the local officers had arrived and taken custody of her attacker, Emily walked to the sliding glass doors and watched the officers load the man in the back of the cruiser. Linc and Derek returned.

"Well, he's taken care of until we can question him," Derek said. "Now what?"

Emily rubbed her arms and shook her head as the cruiser pulled out of her parking lot with the man who'd planned to kill her. "I don't believe this. Someone hired a hit man to kill me?" She gave a low humorless laugh. "That doesn't even compute."

Brady stood behind her. Somehow she knew it was him and not one of his brothers. A fact to process later.

"Come on, take a look around," he said. "See if anything stands out to you as missing or messed with or whatever."

Emily ran a shaky hand over her hair and sighed. "Who is doing this? The people I was investigating?"

She took in the familiar surroundings. It felt like she'd been gone a week instead of two nights. And she'd never feel comfortable sleeping in this place again. Her lease was up in two months. She'd start house hunting as soon as it was clear she was going to live to do so.

In the kitchen, she noted the overturned drawers and the open pantry that mimicked the way they'd found Heather's home. And every picture she'd had on the refrigerator had been swept to the floor. Except one that was held in place by a small black magnet. All in all, it looked innocent enough—a woman and child laughing at something they found amusing. But she hadn't taken the photo and she hadn't put it on the refrigerator.

She pulled it out from under the magnet and stared at it.

"Emily?"

She jerked and turned to stare at him. "What?"

"You okay?"

"Not really."

"Yeah. Sorry. Dumb question."

"No, it wasn't. It's okay." She rubbed her arms and turned the picture over. Nothing.

"What is it?" he asked.

She showed him the picture. "This wasn't here when I left for work on Wednesday. I didn't take this picture. I think someone left it on my refrigerator on purpose."

"Who are they in the picture?"

"My mom and little sister."

"And you've never seen this before?"

"No. That's what I'm saying. Why leave all of my pictures on the floor and this one stuck right in the middle? It's like a message." She paused and bit her lip, then shook her head. "I think this means they're in danger."

# 8

"C all your mom," Brady said.

She pulled her phone from her pocket and touched the screen to bring up the number pad. Her finger hovered and she closed her eyes. A tear leaked down her cheek.

"Emily?"

"I don't know her number," she whispered. "I had it programmed in my other phone, but I don't have it memorized. I can't believe I don't know her number." A sob slipped out.

"It's okay." He rubbed her shoulder and resisted pulling her into his arms. "Derek?"

His brother stepped into the kitchen with a frown. "What is it?"

"Need you to check on someone," he said as Emily swiped tears from her cheeks. "What's her address?"

She told him.

"That's not too far from here," Derek said. "I'll have someone swing by."

"Yes, do. But I want to go." She sniffed. "I *need* to go. But I want to change into some other clothes first." Clothes that fit.

"This is a crime scene," Brady said. "And while we have the guy who broke in, we'll still need CSU to do their thing. So, try to touch as little as possible."

"Here," Linc said. "Put these on." He handed her a pair of gloves.

"Grab an overnight bag too," Brady said, "just in case."

"Okay. Give me three minutes."

As Brady watched, she went through the apartment in record speed, even while favoring her sore foot. When she returned, she'd changed into jeans, an oversized long-sleeved T-shirt, a zip-up fleece. Her pink tennis shoes matched the fleece. She held the handle of a small rolling suitcase. "I'm ready."

"Great." Brady grabbed the suitcase.

"Oh! Wait, I need my laptop. It's in my safe in my closet. I'll be right back." When she returned, he took her bag and led her outside and to the truck.

Once they were on the way, she chewed on a thumbnail while he drove. "If he just wanted to kill me," she said, "why trash the place? It's like he was looking for something here too."

"Could be. You have any clue what that might be?"

"No."

His eyes landed on her laptop. "You keep that in your safe?"

"Yes. I don't take any chances." She paused. "Do you think that could have been what he was looking for?"

"Could be."

"But how would he even know about it?"

"Most people have technology in their homes. You're a workaholic. That means you most likely work from home. And chances are you work on a laptop. Probably a work-issued one." He slid her a sideways glance. "Right?"

"You baffle me."

"Why?"

"You just seem to know too much about me. It's weird. And creepy."

"Not so weird or creepy. You're the one who said you were working late the night you were snatched and—"

"And I said I didn't have anything to hurry home to."

"Yeah."

A small smile curved her lips and she shook her head. "Do you remember every single detail of every conversation?"

"Just the ones that interest me."

"Oh." She seemed to find that intriguing, even though her frown deepened.

"What is it?" he asked.

"Just thinking about Heather."

"What about her?"

"When I gave her the information I'd found and asked her to look into it, she came back and said something was definitely not right and to give her a couple of days to see what else she could discover."

"What'd she find?"

"She followed the trail of the deposits, noting the branches and times they were going in. Based on that information, she picked one branch and waited until she saw the guy making the deposit."

Brady frowned. "That could have been really dangerous."

"I agree and I told her so, but she insisted she was perfectly safe sitting in her car and watching an ATM. Anyway, she followed him home and figured out his name was Martin Burnett. We looked him up and he is a bad, bad, very bad man."

"So you went to the police with your info, right?" he asked.

"Not exactly." She sighed. "Heather convinced me that we could get more. She wanted to stay with this Martin Burnett guy and see if he would lead her to someone higher up."

"Higher up?"

Emily pressed her fingers to her eyes for a moment. "She was convinced we were dealing with a money trail for human traffickers and wanted to bust the ring and whoever was at the top of the chain. Burnett was just an errand boy. I was still following the money and not liking the activity I was seeing on the accounts of some of our well-established clients. I planned do a little more digging, then turn everything I had over to the police after I talked to my boss about it on Monday. The next thing I know, I'm waking up in a boathouse with Owen Parker standing over me." She shuddered.

"I'm sorry," he said.

She bit her lip. "And now my mother and sister could be in danger and Heather's missing—or worse."

"I'll admit I'm concerned. I think it's time to file a missing person report if her parents haven't already done so."

She nodded.

"And," he added, "we don't know your mom and sister are in danger."

She met his gaze when he briefly glanced at her before turning his attention back to the road. "You may not, but I do." She raked a hand through her hair. "Can't we go any faster?"

"No, sorry." His phone rang and the Bluetooth activated. "What is it, Derek?"

"Had an officer drive by the house and it appears to be empty. No sign of any disturbance. Should they knock or go in and check it out?"

"No, don't do either one," Emily said.

"Why not?" Brady frowned at her.

"My mother is . . . she's . . . well . . . if the cops are wearing uniforms, it could set her off. She hates cops."

"I see."

"Tell them to see if anything looks off. If not, wait for me. Again, I know where a key is if she hasn't changed where she put it."

In a few seconds, Derek came back on the line. "Everything looks quiet. No sign of anyone at home."

She rubbed her forehead. "Could I be wrong about the picture?"

"We're here, so let's go find out."

Emily shot out of the car and raced up to the front door where she reached above the door and pulled the spare key down. Brady stayed right with her just in case. Telling her to wait on him would be useless.

"Her car's not here," she said. She sounded slightly breathless. "That could be a good sign."

"Maybe." She opened the door and pushed it in. "Mom?"

No answer.

She started forward, but Brady caught her arm, pulling her to a stop. He noted Derek and Linc right behind them. "Let me clear this," he said to her. "Just like the last couple of times. Only stay on the porch with Linc, okay?" He shot his brother a look and Linc nodded while Derek stepped inside.

Brady raised a brow and she nodded, wrapping her arms around her middle. Knowing she was safe with his brother, Brady gave his knee some test weight and decided he would be all right. He followed after Derek into a small living area. The kitchen was to the left. The hallway to the right.

"Clear in here," Derek said. "Hall bath is clear too."

Brady kept going through the home. It was neat. Nothing out of place. At the end of the hall, the bedroom door was cracked. He caught Derek's eye and his brother nodded, raised his weapon.

Using his elbow, Brady nudged the door all the way open.

And found the room empty.

---

Emily stepped inside once Brady gave the all clear. She sat on the sofa and lowered her head into her hands. What did the picture mean? Anything? She still couldn't call her mother and ask because she didn't have the number—or her phone with the number in it. So stupid. So utterly stupid. She knew Heather's number. Could recite it as fast as her own. But not her mother's. Shame curled through her, but she pushed it aside. She'd had her reasons for staying away. Good reasons. Real reasons. However, at this very moment, she wished with all her heart she'd found a reason to come home.

"You could get my mother's number, couldn't you?" she asked Linc, who'd walked to the porch door to look out. "Her cell number?"

"I could."

"Would you?"

"Is it unlisted? I'd have to get a subpoena if it is."

"Oh. Right. Of course."

"What about on your old phone?"

She hesitated. "I'm not sure."

"Okay if I request the records? All I need is your permission."

"Yes, please."

He pulled his phone from the clip on his belt.

Emily let her eyes roam the room, touching on the family photos on the mantel, then the collection of mugs on the first shelf of the bookcase next to the television. Her gaze traveled into the kitchen, noting the table, the pictures on the refrigerator. Wait. She froze and homed in on one, rose from the couch, and walked into the kitchen.

It was the same picture that had been left on hers. With a glance over her shoulder, she noted that Linc was on the phone. Derek and Brady had moved into the living room and were talking about something. Now that they weren't worried about someone jumping out and grabbing her or concerned they were going to walk into a hail of bullets, they'd relaxed a fraction.

While they hadn't noticed the picture, it had been right in her line of sight from her seat on the couch. She took it from under the magnet and had a moment of déjà vu. Then she flipped the photo over and found very small printed words. "We have them, but we want you. If you don't want them to die, you'll be waiting for our call in one hour for instructions on how the exchange will happen. Be alone. We are watching. No cops. If we see cops, your loved ones die. If you follow the instructions, they will be released. It's that simple."

A smartphone lay on the counter next to the refrigerator. It wasn't her mother's. At least she didn't think it was. She swiped the screen and found no password needed. A tap to the phone app showed no contact information, no dialed numbers, and no incoming calls.

Swallowing against the nausea and fear clawing at the back of her throat, she slid the phone into her pocket. Was that the phone they planned to call on? Or her cell phone? No, if these were the same people who'd kidnapped her and tried to kill her, they were the ones who had her cell phone. At least she assumed they did. It hadn't been in her pocket where she'd had it when she'd awakened in the trunk.

They'd know she'd need a phone if they wanted to call her and wouldn't know about the new phone she had in her possession. So, they'd left her one.

And now she had to fight through the terror clogging her thinking and make a decision. Did she tell Brady and the others or try to handle this alone? They'd said no cops, but how would they know?

*We are watching.* Well, if they were watching, then they knew she'd entered the building with three cops. Or—at least three men. They wouldn't necessarily know they were cops. Then again, a police cruiser had come by the house and an officer had checked it out. But it had left.

Indecision swirled and she pressed her fingers against her forehead as she debated.

Regardless, she was still confused. On the one hand they seemed to want her dead. On the other, they just seemed to want to grab her—keep her alive. They took her family to get to her. For what? So she would be easier to kill and they could stop hunting her down and just have her come to them? Most likely.

Keeping the scream that wanted to escape stuffed down took effort, but she managed. *Think. Think.*

"Emily?"

She startled, then cleared her throat. "Yes?"

"Anything else seem out of order?"

"Uh. No. Nothing." *Everything! God, please, tell me what to do.*

When she got no answer either in feeling or spirit, she kept her mouth shut. She couldn't take the chance that whoever had her mother and Sophia would know. No, they wouldn't, and she couldn't do this alone. "Someone's taken them."

"We don't know that."

*Show him the note!*

"Yes, we do." Tears leaked against her will. She uncurled her hand and passed him the picture that matched the one from her apartment.

Taking it, he frowned. "What's this?"

"It was on the refrigerator. Read the back."

He did. "This is not good."

"No, it's scary."

He raked a hand down his cheek. "That too. Linc?"

"Yeah?"

"We're going to need a little more help." He showed his brother the note.

Linc sucked in a breath. "Okay, what phone are they going to call?"

It was all she could do not to pull the phone from her pocket, but . . . no, she'd done enough. If she gave them the phone, it was possible she would be sealing her mother and Sophia's deaths. "Maybe they don't know that my original phone is at the bottom of the lake?" It was possible, but she wasn't sure how.

"I'll get on this." Linc tapped the screen and walked away, the device held to his ear.

"While Linc's making arrangements to find your mom and sister," Brady said, "we're going to work on a different angle."

"What angle?"

"We probably just ruined any evidence or fingerprints on this, but I guess what we need to do is ask Parker about it. If he left the one at your place, he left the one here as well."

"But why leave the pictures? Why kidnap my mom and Sophia? I thought he was just there to . . . uh . . . make sure I disappeared for good. What's the point in leaving the pictures for me—or someone else—to find?"

"That would be a question for him."

"Then let's ask him," she said.

He turned to Derek. Linc was still on the phone. "Let's go down to the station where they've got Parker. I need to ask him a couple of questions." He shook the picture. "They said they were going to call in an hour. What phone do they think they're going to call?"

Her mind went to the device in her front pocket. They said she needed to be alone when they called. She almost showed Brady and the others the phone, but she'd already shown them the note. If she showed them the phone, they'd want to listen in on the call. "Not sure," she said.

The lie wasn't easy, and guilt immediately hammered her. These guys had been nothing but kind and helpful. Then again, it wasn't an outright lie. She *wasn't* exactly sure which phone they would call. She was just *assuming* it was the one in her pocket.

She glanced at the picture again. Her mother smiled down at the little girl with a look of love Emily had never seen on her face before. Ever. It shook her more than she wanted to admit. And Sophia laughed up at her mother, obviously happy, with everything right in her world. At least at that particular moment.

Against her better judgment, she decided she'd take the phone call and then figure out what to do from there. She couldn't put her family's lives in danger. She couldn't take a chance—any more chances—that the people holding them would follow through on their threats if she didn't do as instructed.

"Let's just go see if that guy Parker knows anything—or will say anything—about the pictures," she said. "He was nervous—or maybe just plain scared—about the fact that the people who hired him to kill me knew that he'd been caught. Maybe he'll be more inclined to talk now that he's had time to think about it."

"It's not a bad idea," Derek said.

Brady nodded. "We'll add that to our list of questions when we interrogate him. I, for one, am anxious to start grilling the guy."

Linc clapped Brady on the shoulder. "Fine. We'll follow you."

"I can handle this from here," Brady said. "You guys don't have to stay."

"Right," Derek said. "We'll meet you there."

Brady shook his head and didn't argue. Emily had a feeling he knew it would be futile and that his brothers would do as they pleased. He cupped her elbow and escorted her out the door. She started to walk to the passenger side when a sharp crack pierced the air.

Just as the pain in her arm registered, she found herself on the ground next to Brady's fire-scarred truck with his body hovering over hers. Another bullet slammed into the side of the vehicle and Emily flinched, swallowing her scream. He had his weapon in his hand, but his eyes were on her. "Are you okay?"

"Yes."

"Stay down."

He really didn't have to tell her that. Fire arced through her arm and she gasped. She slapped a hand to the area and wetness coated her palm. The coppery smell of blood reached her. A glance at her hand confirmed her suspicion. She'd been shot.

## 9

**B**rady scanned the area and couldn't see where the shot had come from. Derek and Linc had scattered at the initial pop. "Derek?" he hollered.

"Going after him!"

"Linc?"

"Calling for backup!"

With everyone accounted for, he turned back to Emily. Only to pull up short at the sight of her right hand clasping her left upper bicep. Blood covered both. "I thought you said you were okay."

Her pain-clouded eyes met his. "I just kind of realized I'm not."

"Linc! Call for an ambulance too!" Favoring his aching knee, he knelt beside Emily. "How bad is it?"

"It hurts, but I don't feel like I'm going to pass out from lack of blood or anything."

"That's a good sign. I'm assuming anyway."

She huffed a short laugh, then squeezed her eyes shut. A tear leaked down and he swiped it away.

"Just be strong a little longer, okay?" He heard the sirens screaming in the distance but didn't figure it would take them long to arrive. "Help's on the way."

"I heard. I'm fine."

Brady waited and finally heard the tires of the first cruiser roll to the curb. He peered around the front of his truck. Two more cruisers. He saw Derek slip out from behind a car and hold his badge in front of him. Linc did the same.

Brady stayed put and waited with Emily, using his hands to keep pressure on the wound. And finally, the ambulance arrived.

Derek hurried over to him and he frowned when he spotted Emily's arm. "She okay?"

"I think it's just a graze, but she'll need to be seen. Did you see the shooter?"

"No. He shot and ran."

"You see where the shots came from?" Brady asked.

"Briefly." Derek pointed. "I'm pretty sure he was on the roof of that service station across the street. By the time I got up there, he was gone. I lost him, I'm sorry."

"Don't be," Emily said. "We don't need anyone else getting shot." She shifted and grimaced.

Brady tightened his hold and she jerked. "Sorry," he said.

"More help is coming," Derek said. "We'll have cops start canvassing the area. I spoke to the officer in charge and told him I didn't hear a car or anything to indicate anyone was in a hurry to leave, so hopefully, the guy is on foot."

Brady helped Emily to her feet as a paramedic rushed over. "What do we have?"

"Gunshot wound," Brady said.

"It's just a graze, it's fine," Emily said.

"Let me take a look anyway."

"No, we need to—"

"The faster you let him look," Brady said, "the faster we'll be done."

Emily sighed and held her arm out. The paramedic led her to the back of the ambulance and proceeded to cut the sleeve of her shirt away from the wound. Emily sucked in through clenched teeth and turned her forearm facing down, hiding the scars.

"You're really taking a beating, aren't you?" Brady said softly. She blinked at him. "What?"

"Between your foot and your arm, you've got to be hurting."

"I am, but that's okay. It means I'm alive."

"You're a glass-half-full kinda girl, aren't you?" Derek asked.

A low laugh that might have been more of a snort escaped her. "Not really, but I'm working on it."

"She needs to go to the hospital and get this cleaned up," the paramedic said. "I don't think it needs any stitches, but the doc might disagree. Let's get this going."

Emily shook her head. "No, I don't want to go. I . . . I need to stay here. I need to—"

"You're going, Emily," Brady said. He wasn't quite sure why she was resisting so much.

Her eyes flashed. "I don't have to go."

"You're worried about the phone call."

She nodded.

"I'll get your mother's number from Linc and have it forwarded to my phone. If they call on that number, I'll pass the phone to you." He turned to Derek. "In the meantime, do you mind questioning Parker and see if he knows anything about the pictures?"

Derek nodded. "Sure. After we finish up here, we can do that. But I don't like you two going off on your own. You need someone watching your back."

"We're going to the hospital. Have some uniforms meet us there."

"We may need to form a task force," Linc said. "This just keeps getting bigger and bigger." He turned to Emily. "Agents are already working on finding your mom and Sophia."

"Good," she whispered. "Thank you."

"The Sicily police are also questioning your boss, Calvin Swift, about your kidnapping. They're gathering all of the bank's security footage as well as the footage on the street you were taken from."

"Okay."

"Also, when I spoke to Izzy, I asked her to find out the status of Jeremy Hightower. No one's been able to track him down. There's been no activity on any of his accounts in the last three days. He's not at home and none of his neighbors even seem to know who he is."

Emily's lips tightened, but her jaw lifted even while her eyes flashed. "He must not feel like they're worth anything. Trust me, if he needed something from them, they'd know who he was."

"We'll have some answers soon, I hope," Linc said.

"I hope so too. Thanks."

Linc nodded to Brady. "I'm going to join my partner and see if we can make some more progress on this. You take care of Emily."

"I will. Let me know what you find out." Brady climbed into the back of the ambulance with Emily and turned to the driver. "Head to Providence in Columbia."

"But Kershaw Health is closer."

"My sister doesn't work at Kershaw Health."

"Ah. Gotcha." He shut the door and Brady turned to Emily, who was looking pale and washed out.

"Close your eyes," he told her.

The fact that she didn't hesitate worried him.

The other paramedic continued to monitor her vitals while Brady texted his sister, Ruthie.

> Are you working tonight?

> Ruthie
> On call.

> Coming in with a patient for you. Probably not surgical, but can you check her out?

Yes. Who is she? Do I know her?

She's a new friend. Her name is Emily.

Want to hear more.

Of course she did. And he'd fill her in later.

I need a knee brace too.

What'd you do?

Jumped off the roof of a building.

Pause. Then,

I'm not even going to ask. I'll have a knee brace
waiting on you.

Thanks.

When the ambulance pulled to a stop at the emergency entrance, Brady stepped out of the back and waited for them to lower the gurney wheels to the ground.

Cold fingers clutched his and he looked down to find Emily's eyes on him. Trusting eyes. Wary eyes. Eyes he couldn't look away from.

Until someone made him.

A nurse shoved past him. "Let's go. Room 4," she said.

When they wheeled her into the room, the door hadn't quite shut before it was pulled open by his sister. "Ruthie."

"What do we have?" She shoved the knee brace at him, and he stuck it in the back pocket of his jeans, although he'd like nothing more than to sit on the floor and pull it on.

"GSW," Brady said.

Ruthie shot him a shut-up-right-now look and turned to the nursing staff surrounding Emily. "Vitals?"

Brady stepped back while Ruthie evaluated. His heart thundered in his chest while Emily was hooked up to an IV. She looked pale, but alert. He stayed quiet and in the background so he wouldn't get kicked out, but every so often her eyes would catch his and he got the feeling she was glad he was there.

Ruthie removed the stethoscope from her ears and let it hang around her neck. She then discarded the gloves into the red bin behind her and patted Emily on the shoulder. "It's just a nice groove in your bicep. Bleeding has slowed and almost stopped. Whoever kept pressure on it did a good job."

"That was Brady," Emily said.

She shot him a look of approval. "Nice job."

"What about her foot?"

"It's fine," Emily said.

Ruthie raised a brow. "I'll take a look."

Emily sighed and raised her foot. It didn't take Ruthie long to declare it healing well. "We'll get this arm cleaned up and bandaged. I'll put you on an antibiotic as a preventative, but while you'll be sore for a while, it should heal up nicely."

"Thank you."

"It could have been a lot worse. You got lucky."

"I think I'll chalk it up to God looking out for me," Emily said softly. "I'll take him over luck any day."

"Me too," Ruthie said. "Me too."

Brady gave a light snort and Ruthie lasered him with another one of those "shut up" looks. He held up a hand and she turned back to Emily. "Just sit tight while we get your discharge papers ready. Are you allergic to anything?"

"No. Nothing."

"Perfect. I'll write you a prescription for a few pain pills just in case that wound makes sleeping difficult."

"No pain pills. I don't do narcotics. I've beat an addiction and I'm not going back there."

Ruthie raised a brow, then gave a slow nod even as her gaze locked on Brady. He ignored the question in her eyes. "All right," she said to Emily. "Will you at least take something that's not addictive and won't make you sleepy, but will cut the edge off the pain?"

"Yes."

"I'll write the script for those and the antibiotic and we'll get it filled at the hospital pharmacy if you don't mind waiting for it."

"I'll wait, but while we're here, you need to do one more thing, if you don't mind."

Ruthie's brow lifted. "What's that?"

"Make Brady get his knee checked."

Brady blinked. "My knee is fine."

Emily huffed. "It's not fine. I'm no doctor, but even I can tell he probably needs an X-ray or an MRI or something."

Ruthie headed toward the door. "I'll get that taken care of," she said over her shoulder.

"Good. Thank you." That seemed to lift Emily's worries about him, and she dropped her head to the pillow and closed her eyes.

Ruthie eyed him. "Want to step outside for a minute?"

"Why?"

"Brady . . ."

He gave a short nod. "I'll be right outside the door," he told Emily.

"I'll be fine," she said without opening her eyes. "As long as you get your knee looked at."

Brady followed Ruthie into the hallway. "What is it?"

"Who is she?"

"A woman in trouble."

"I can see that. Who shot her?"

"I'm not sure, but I'm working on finding out. Derek and Linc are aware of the situation as well." He narrowed his eyes. "Don't worry, this isn't like Krystal."

Her stance softened. "Are you sure? She just said she was addicted to narcotics."

"Used to be. You just saw her refuse them—and admit she had a problem. Do you think Krystal would have done that?"

"No."

"So, yeah. I think I've learned that lesson." His jaw tensed in spite of his efforts not to let it. "And I refuse to not help people because of Krystal's choices. I'm trying to move on, put her in the past, but it's hard to do that when other people won't let me." She flinched and he sighed. "I'm sorry. That was harsh. I know you've got good intentions." He gripped her fingers. "I'm healing, Ruthie. The bitterness and guilt are fading, the hurt isn't quite so sharp. But it was a lesson I won't soon forget. Or be able to let go of." His eyes landed on the door that led to Emily's room. "And I'm not about to be a repeat offender."

"It's been eight months."

"I'm aware."

"I know," she said softly. "I'm just not sure you can be objective." She sighed. "Seeing you hurt makes me hurt too."

He hugged her. "I love you, sis, but you've got your own life to worry about right now." He stepped back.

"Doesn't keep me from praying for you, though."

"Well, that's fine, but God doesn't always answer prayers like we want him to."

"I know, but sometimes he does." She crooked her finger at him. "Follow me."

"Where?"

"To that room right there." She pointed to the one opposite Emily's. "It's empty and I want to take a look at that knee."

"Honest, it's—"

"I can see you're in pain. You're limping, too, even though you're trying not to. And you asked for a knee brace. That raises all kinds of red flags for me. Now, in the room or I'm calling for backup."

"Backup?"

"Mom."

"What? No!" Brady groaned. "Fine, but leave the door open so I can see Emily's room."

Within seconds, she was palpating and pressing his swollen knee and it was all Brady could do not to come off the table. "Okay, I'm no ortho doc," Ruthie said, "but I think your friend is right. Let's get an MRI done and see what you've done this time."

"I don't have time for an MRI."

Ruthie pulled her phone from her scrubs pocket.

"What are you doing?" he asked.

"Calling Mom."

"Ruthie . . ."

His low growl stopped her and she raised a brow, then sighed and tucked the phone away. "I can't force you to do it, but I think you should."

Brady raked a hand through his hair. "Fine, fine. You can order it, but let me check on Emily. You can find me in her room."

"Great." She spun on her heel and was out the door before he could blink. Probably worried he'd change his mind. He remembered Paul Bailey and shot a text to David Unger.

> Can you do a background on Paul Bailey? See
> if he has any previous issues of stalking or
> harassment?

He waited for an answer, but when David didn't text him back right away, he decided to check on Emily. He stood and crumpled back onto the examination table with a pained grunt. Letting out a growl, he pulled on the brace and tried standing again. Still not comfortable, but definitely better.

He stepped across the hall and raised a hand to knock on the slightly open door when her words reached him. "Well, if you want me to meet you, don't shoot at me!"

Emily's entire body quivered. Rage and fear battled it out inside her and she bit her lip to keep from demanding things she knew they wouldn't give her.

"Shoot at you?" The voice on the other end of the line laughed. "No one shot at—"

"She's in the hospital." Emily had to strain to hear the second voice.

Someone cursed, then a crash sounded. She flinched. "I want to speak to my mother," she said. "I need to do that. I need proof that she and Sophia are really alive. You have to understand that, right?"

"Hold on."

A rustling in the background gave her hope that she would actually hear her mother's voice. "Emily?"

The absolute terror in the woman's voice drove the spear of pain and fear deep into her heart. "Yes, Mom."

"What's going on? What have you gotten yourself into?"

"Is Sophia okay?"

"For now."

"Okay, I'll do whatever they want, Mom, I prom—"

"Good choice," the hard voice said. "Get rid of the cop. I'll text you the instructions." *Click.*

Emily opened her eyes and found Brady standing in the doorway, watching her. "Guess you heard that?"

"Where'd you get the phone? It's not the one I bought."

"It was on the counter at my mother's house."

"Why didn't you tell me?"

She sighed and rubbed her face with her good hand. "You read the note. They said not to."

He frowned. "But you told me about the note."

"I was scared. Terrified. I didn't know what to do. So, I showed you the note. And by the time I got my thoughts together, I was afraid I'd done too much by showing you what I did and . . ." She shrugged.

"If I had known they were going to call that phone, I could have set up a way to trace the call."

She shot him a sad smile. "It's a burner phone."

"Wouldn't hurt to try."

"Okay, they're going to text me what I need to do." She gave him the number. "Can you figure out where the text comes from?"

"Possibly." He paused. "You've mentioned your mother and a sister. Where's your dad? Is he in danger as well?"

"No. He's dead." The phone pinged and she glanced at the screen, then met his gaze. "That's them. Is it too late to trace it?"

"Maybe. What does it say?"

She ran a shaky hand over her eyes. "That I need to meet them."

"They say where?"

"Not specifically. Just to start walking at the corner of Rabon and Two Notch Road in three hours."

"Not exactly the best area."

"I don't care what area it is, I'll be there." She paused. "The guy on the phone said he wasn't the one shooting at me outside my mom's house."

"And you believe him?"

"I don't know. He actually sounded confused. And a guy in the background told him I was in the hospital. Part of me thinks they just got tired of me not dying and decided this was the easiest way to get to me."

He nodded. "Could be."

"Then again, it doesn't really make sense that they'd leave the note with instructions to follow and then shoot at me with the intent to kill me as I come out of my mother's house."

"I agree." He frowned.

"So, if you think about it," she said, "it sounds like there are two different people involved here. One who wants me dead and the other just wants me—for whatever he thinks I can do for him."

Brady stood and paced the length of the small room. He finally stopped. "No matter, I'm going to get this set up to intercept these people. We'll get an officer to be your double and take it from there."

"What? No!"

He frowned. "What do you mean, 'no'?"

"What if they know you're there? They'll hurt my mom and Sophia. They may realize that the person isn't me. No. Absolutely not. I can't take that chance."

"Emily . . ." He sighed and stepped closer. "You can't go meet this person by yourself. That's not happening. This is an investigation that extends farther than just you. Right now, we've got your kidnapping, your family's kidnapping, attempted murder, and the list goes on."

"And Heather," she whispered. "Don't forget about Heather."

"Yes, and your friend. The police are going all out trying to find her."

"But no word?"

"No, I'm afraid not."

"And her parents haven't called me back," she said. "What's up with that?"

"I don't know, I'm sorry. I've asked Derek to arrange for me to listen to the 911 call and talk to the officers who responded to the call. Hopefully, he'll get back to us soon with a time to do that."

"Okay. Thank you." At least something was being done to find Heather.

His phone pinged and he glanced at the screen. "I need to take this. I'll be right back."

"Sure."

He left and Emily dropped her head back against the pillow and closed her eyes. For a moment, she let her mind spin, then focused on the fact that her life had fallen apart and she didn't know how to put it back together again.

The phone buzzed and she jumped. On the second ring she answered. "Hello?"

"Now that your cop is gone, ignore the previous texts and get dressed. You have new instructions. Go out the back door near the cafeteria. An Uber will be waiting. Keep the phone, but if you pull it out of your pocket at any other time than to respond to my texts, they die. I'll be in touch."

"What?"

"If you want your mom and little sister to see dinnertime, leave the hospital now. And don't let anyone see you do it."

"How am I supposed to do that?"

"Figure it out."

*Click.*

She stayed frozen to the bed for a split second before swinging her legs over the side and standing. Dizziness hit her and she grabbed the rail until the feeling subsided. Then shoved her feet into her shoes that someone had kicked under the chair. While she readied to leave the room, her mind raced. They knew when Brady had been in the room. They knew when he left. They'd deliberately sent her the first text message because they'd predicted that she'd pass the information on to Brady. Her gut clenched. Someone was on the floor watching and monitoring her actions. Would her family pay the price for that?

Breaths coming in close-to-panic pants, she looked around. She couldn't do this alone no matter what orders she had. Because she had no doubt if she went alone, she and her mother and sister would all three wind up dead.

She needed to leave a message. And a trail. She had no idea where she was going or if they could track one of the phones she had on her. Emily grabbed a pen and paper from the nightstand and scribbled as fast as she could, then tossed the note into the middle of the bed. She snagged her jacket from the foot of the bed and headed for the door.

# 10

**B**rady shoved the phone into his pocket and pressed his fingers against his eyes for a moment. Linc had just called and said Annie was working on getting security footage of Emily's kidnapping, but so far hadn't been able to pull any. He'd also had Brady's truck delivered to the hospital emergency parking area. Thank goodness for brothers who went above and beyond the call of duty.

He started toward Emily's room when his phone vibrated.

A glance showed he had a text from David:

I'm on it. Stay tuned.

Thanks.

Brady walk-limped to Emily's room and pushed open the door. "Emily, I've got—" The bed was empty. Her coat and shoes were gone.

He checked the bathroom. Also empty.

Doing a one-eighty on his good leg, he headed for the door but stopped when he caught sight of a paper on the bed. He grabbed it. "He called. Threatened Mom and Sophia if I didn't obey. Disregard previous instructions. Knew you were here. Told me an Uber would be waiting. Don't know destination. Find me, please."

Heart thumping, Brady crumpled the note and called Linc. "I need your help again."

He limped out of the room as fast as his knee would let him and headed straight for hospital security. When the woman answered his knock on the door, he flashed his badge and nodded to her monitors. "I need you to find someone for me."

Within seconds, he was watching Emily leave her room and head for the elevator. Another camera picked her up exiting the hospital and climbing into a cab. "Thank you for not being an Uber," he whispered.

"Why?" the woman asked.

"There's no GPS system on an Uber, but there is on a taxi. Can you get that license plate number?"

"Sure."

Would they really be that stupid? They'd know he could trace a cab. Emily's note had said Uber. She'd taken a risk so he could follow her. "Good girl, Emily," he whispered.

The frame zoomed in and he got a clear view of the plate. Brady called the company. "I need to know where he dropped the passenger he picked up at Providence Health approximately eight minutes ago."

Once he had the address, he sent it in a text to Linc, then called him. "Meet me there with the cavalry."

"Don't go in all gangbusters. Wait for us."

"Then move fast." He hung up and turned to the security officer. "Thanks."

"Anything I can do?" she asked.

He paused. "Yes. Can you get a plate off the car behind the cab? The driver got out when the cab drove off. His gesture indicated he wasn't happy." It might have been the Uber she was supposed to take. "Also," Brady said, "can you get a shot of every person on that hall and send me the pictures? I want to put the faces through a facial recognition software and see if we get a hit." He paused one more time. "And if you pray, you can pray." Ignoring the fire coursing through his knee, he ran from the office. Bolting down the hall and the stairs, he burst through the exit door to jump into his truck, thanking Linc for his thoughtfulness. He was sure he hadn't known Brady would need his truck this fast.

---

Emily stood still, ignoring the fact that the cab was gone and she was all alone. And unarmed. Using the coping skills she'd learned from her year of living on the streets, she shoved her terror to the back of her mind and focused on the fact that her mother and sister were probably being held somewhere in the building in front of her.

With a glance behind her, she slid her hand into her coat pocket and curled her fingers around the phone the kidnappers had left for her. In her other pocket, she had the phone Brady had gotten for her. She'd thought about calling Brady from the cab, but the voice's order to keep the phone in her pocket or her family would die had kept her still. If someone had seen her get in the taxi instead of the Uber, he could be following, watching. She'd left the phone alone, hoping the fact she'd taken the taxi instead of the Uber would allow Brady to follow. She'd just have to play dumb if those giving her orders were angry she'd gotten in the cab.

Now she found herself at the back of an office building that looked deserted in the midafternoon sun. It sat away from the main road, set apart and lonely on the block of warehouses. Hidden in plain sight.

She shivered.

Snowflakes started to fall and a lump formed in her throat. She loved the snow, and it so rarely happened in Columbia that she always took a moment to enjoy it when she could.

But now she found herself hoping it would stop. She needed her mother and sister safe without the possibility of the weather making that more difficult than it was already going to be.

The phone she'd found in her mother's home buzzed. She looked at the text.

That was a dumb move getting in the taxi. No
more mistakes or they'll suffer, you understand?

Yes. Sorry. Uber, cab, I'm not thinking clearly.
Sorry.

Just get in the car and drive.

A second delay, then—

Now.

She spotted the lone vehicle in the parking lot. She hurried over
to it, climbed into the driver's seat, and slammed the door. In the
cab, she'd received a text for the address to give to the cab driver.
Obviously, they'd given her one to throw off anyone who might
be trying to track her. She texted back,

Drive where?

An address popped up on her screen.

Can I use the GPS?

Yes.

She tapped the address in, her mind whirling, trying to figure
out how to leave Brady an idea of what was happening.
The phone buzzed again.

Drive!

They had to be watching. But how close? Could they see inside
the car? She started the engine and put her seat belt on and lowered
her head to the wheel, holding the phone in front of her.

IT'S TIME TO DRIVE, NOT SLEEP!

The all caps shouted at her. She typed back.

Dizzy. Hold on.

With her body still doubled over and hopefully blocking any cameras or high-powered binoculars aimed at her, she removed the phone Brady had gotten her from her pocket and pulled up his number. It was awkward holding the two phones, but she managed to type the address into the other phone along with the words,

Find me here.

Did she dare? What if they were somehow monitoring the text messages? No, there was no way.
A text flashed.

Restricted
If you're not driving in five seconds, I'm going to hurt the little girl.

A picture of Sophia followed, her eyes wide, tears hovering on her lashes.
With shaking fingers, Emily hit send, then erased the text. On the other phone, she texted,

I'm driving. Don't hurt her.

She left the phones on the passenger seat beside her, then drove, following the GPS directions that led her to the front door of a building that was almost identical to the one where the cab had dropped her. The drive took all of three minutes. At a stoplight, she had immediately disabled location services on both phones just in case someone checked. And she had no doubt they would. Then she'd slipped her phone into her pocket.

The burner phone vibrated.

Restricted
Come inside.

With a deep breath, she climbed out of the car and forced her legs to carry her to the door while she took in the surroundings. More office buildings lined the street. If she didn't know better, she'd never suspect anything dangerous about the one she was approaching.

Tremors shook her and she wiped her palms on her jeans. She could do this. But what if Brady couldn't find her? What if these people knew she'd sent the text?

She'd have to cross that bridge when she came to it. At the door, she turned the knob and pulled it open.

A hard hand clamped down on her arm and yanked her inside. She let out a scream before she could stop it, then clamped her lips together.

Her captor stood slightly over six feet tall, had hard green eyes, a goatee, and dark brown hair. "Give me the phone," he said. She did. Without releasing her, he checked it, then dropped the device to the cement floor and stomped on it. Then he turned back to her. "Stand still."

Hard hands patted her down and she flushed at the violation, resisting the almost overwhelming desire to slam a knee into his face. Instead, she endured it, taking comfort in the fact that the act was impersonal and he was simply looking for a weapon.

Or her other phone. When he found the second one, her heart dropped, but she kept her fear to herself when he scanned through it, then crunched it under his boot. Finally satisfied she had nothing else on her, he pointed to the back corner of the warehouse. "That way."

She hesitated. "Where are my mother and sister?"

"Still alive since you followed instructions relatively well. Keep up the good work and move it."

Emily obeyed. Her eyes roamed the space, looking for anything that could be used as a potential weapon—or escape route. The building had been opened up so that it had one central area. Metal support posts interrupted the open flow. There were several closed doors that lined the back wall that could be additional offices or storage space. She noted the back door in the right corner with the EXIT sign above it.

"In there." She was yanked to a stop at the first door, and she hissed at the arc of pain in her bicep but bit her tongue as she entered. Computers and monitors dominated the area, and the lone man seated in front of them watched surveillance video of the perimeter of the building. Video that showed no sign of rescue. Her spirits plummeted and despair gripped her.

The man behind her gave her another shove and she stumbled forward. The one facing the monitors spun to face her, eyes hard, a blue vein pulsing in his bald head. A large snake tattoo slithered down his left cheek, over the side of his neck, and disappeared beneath the collar of his long-sleeved T-shirt, only to emerge on the back of his hand, mouth wide, fangs exposed.

Two other men with various snake tattoos stood against the wall, arms crossed, eyes hard and watchful.

She shuddered and took a tight hold on her nerves. The tats said they were gang members. Just like when she'd been living on the streets, when the terror had threatened to engulf her, she straightened her shoulders and stared her fear in the face. "Where are they?"

"I see you're pretty smart and followed my clues."

"You left the pictures and trashed my place and Heather's?"

"Of course."

"What were you looking for?"

"Information, but since you weren't very accommodating in leaving anything useful for me to find, we're now forced to do this the hard way."

"What kind of information?"

He studied her as though trying to decide if she really didn't know or was playing ignorant. "The information you received Wednesday night."

"I didn't get any information Wednesday night. Look, where are my mom and sister? Did you kill Heather?"

"Your mother and sister are safe. For now."

"And Heather?"

His jaw tightened and eyes narrowed. The slight flare of his nostrils said she'd touched a sore spot. "I had nothing to do with her."

"But you know who she is."

"I know, but since she can't help me—or your family—looks like it's up to you."

"Fine. I'm here. Let them go. Please."

"That's the plan." Snake Man crossed his arms and his biceps bulged, straining the material of the shirt. "And as soon as you give me what I want, they'll be released."

Emily frowned. "What is it you want?"

"I need to know the location of the *Lady Marie*."

"What is the Lady Marie?"

"The houseboat that went down! I want to know which lake and where on that lake it sank."

"Why would you think I know anything about that? I have no idea what you're talking about."

He slammed a fist on the desk and Emily jumped back. "Then I have no reason to keep you alive, do I?"

---

Brady pulled to a stop in the parking lot next door to the warehouse where the cab driver had said he'd dropped Emily. Linc and the others were right behind him, being careful to stay out of sight of the windows in the building.

With no time to get set up with COMMS, he had to use his phone. Linc was on the other end. "Note the cameras on the front," Brady said.

"Noted," Linc said. "Probably some on the back too. I've got the blueprints on my phone. Forwarding to you. We've got a command truck on the way and a drone in the air. I'm sending you the link so you can watch it as well."

His phone buzzed. He glanced at it expecting to see the text from Linc. Instead, Emily's number popped up.

With an address and the words *Find me here.*

"Hold on, hold on!" His heart thudded. "We're at the wrong place."

"What?"

"She managed to text me. We need to move out. Head for this address." He sent it to Linc. "Send the drone there. Get new blueprints. Fast!"

His phone buzzed again and he ignored the useless prints and pulled up the link so he could see what the drone saw. Two sedans, a Jeep, and a black Honda sat in front of another warehouse. With orders to move out, they took off for the second address Emily had provided, coming in slow and sleek into the next-door parking lot while hidden from the other building. His nerves itched with the impatience to get to Emily. He didn't know how she'd managed to send the text, but he'd find that out when he located her. And he *would* locate her.

# 11

"Where's the *Lady Marie*?" Snake Man growled.

Emily's insides shook. He'd asked her the same question three times and the fact that she didn't change her answer infuriated him. "I'm telling you I don't know! I don't know anything about a houseboat sinking on any lake, and you repeating the question isn't going to make me know it." When his hand hovered over the weapon resting on the desk, she drew in a deep breath. "But I . . . I can try to find out for you."

Snake Man reached for her and she stumbled backward into a hard chest. The man behind her shoved her forward and her thighs hit the edge of the desk. Snake Man picked up his weapon and aimed it at her head. Emily shut her eyes and wondered if her heart would explode from the frantic beat. Was she going to die for information she had no way of giving even if she wanted to?

Another man entered the office. "Boss? Got something you need to see."

Emily opened her eyes to see Snake Man stiffen. "What?"

"Not sure. Looks like some movement next door. Might not be anything, but I think we need to check it out."

Snake Man jabbed a finger at Emily. "We're not done."

"I want to see my mother and sister."

He jerked his head at the man with the goatee who'd met her at the door. "Lock her in with them. The rest of you check the area." Goatee gripped her bicep in a bruising grip. At least it wasn't the wounded arm.

"You don't have to hurt me," she said, keeping the tremble from her voice through sheer effort. "I'll go where you want me to go." Especially if it meant her mother and sister were there.

He didn't bother to acknowledge her—or loosen his grip. Instead, he drew to a stop at the room next to the office, pulled a key from his pocket, and unlocked the door. He shoved Emily inside, and her ears registered the dead bolt clicking into place even as her eyes landed on the woman and child huddling on a wooden bench in the far corner.

"Emily?" the woman asked.

"Mom?"

Emily's mother held a young girl against her. Sophia. Eleven years had passed since she'd been in the same room with her mother. Eleven long years.

"What's going on? What do they want?" her mother whispered.

"I'm not exactly sure." Emily answered automatically, but for a moment, she was suspended in time. Her gaze never left the two on the bench. Her mother's never left her.

"You look good," her mother said.

"Still on the heavy side, though, right?" She snapped her tongue with her teeth. *Keep your mouth shut and the past in the past.*

With a flinch, her mother pushed her gray-flecked brown hair from her narrowed eyes. She still wore it in the same style Emily remembered from her teens. "They kept telling us not to be afraid, that they were going to let us go."

Shocked—yet relieved—that her mother didn't acknowledge the jab, Emily crossed her arms. "Let you go?" She wasn't sure she believed that. Neither her mother nor Sophia wore any kind of blindfolds and their captors hadn't worn masks.

119

In fact, she was quite sure that as soon as the men got what they wanted, they were all three going to die. "Of course they'll let you go," she said. "And as soon as they tell me what they want, I'll give it to them and then we'll all go home."

"I know you," Sophia said.

Emily smiled and walked over to squat in front of the girl. "I'm Emily."

"I've seen your picture."

"And I've seen yours."

"Mom said you're my sister. Why don't you ever come to visit?"

Her mother stiffened and Emily swallowed. "It's a long story. Right now, I need to focus on getting us out of here, okay?"

Sophia gave a nod. "Okay. Please. I really want to go home."

"Yeah, me too." Emily stood and examined the room. As far as she could tell, it was 10′ × 10′ with Sheetrock walls and tile drop-ceiling panels. Further investigation revealed a bathroom and another small office attached on the other side. "We're trapped," she murmured.

"I know. I've already checked," her mother said.

Of course she had. Emily closed her eyes and pictured the office building and the surroundings. Located at the edge of Columbia, the building was one of many separated by alleyways and streets, and it blended well with the others. Even the bars on the windows wouldn't be suspect in this area of town.

She walked back into the room where her mother still sat holding Sophia's hand and studied the girl. Sophia had been just barely four weeks old when Emily had left after that horrible night.

*"Get out! Get out! This is your fault! You killed him!"*

So she'd run and never looked back. Much.

As far as Emily was concerned, she needed to put that out of her mind and let the past stay in the past for now. "Can you two get up for a minute?"

They stood. Emily examined the bench and gave a satisfied grunt. "That might work," she whispered to herself.

"What might work?"

The bench rocked slightly under her hard shake. "This. As a weapon of some sort. It's not very sturdy. I think I can pull it apart and use one of the pieces as a weapon."

Her mother hadn't taken her eyes from Emily, tracking her every movement. "A piece of wood against a gun?"

Emily shot her a hard smile. "I'm counting on the element of surprise."

"They used us to get you to come here. Told you they'd hurt us if you didn't."

"Yes."

"And you came."

Emily blanched. "Of course."

Her mother blinked and looked away. Emily's heart hurt at all the unresolved issues, but she had to focus—and pray there would be time later to talk. She slipped her jacket off and ripped the sleeve of her T-shirt from her unwounded arm.

Her mother gasped. "What happened?"

Emily saw she was staring at the bandage around her other arm. Blood had seeped through. Probably from all of her activity.

"Just a little incident." Emily strode to the window and gave it a shove. To her surprise, it opened. "Guess they're not too concerned about us crawling out of here with these bars."

"Guess not," Sophia said. "What are you doing?"

Emily tied the shirt sleeve around the bar at the lowest point, hoping no one would be able to see it when they opened the door—or notice it on a security camera. She shut the window. "Leaving a signal in case my friend was able to follow me." She turned to Sophia. "Now, how good are you at climbing and hiding?"

---

"Anything at the back?" Brady asked. The drone moved and he narrowed his eyes. "What's that? In the window?"

"Not sure. Looks like a piece of material. We need eyes on the inside more than anything," Linc said. "SWAT—and Derek—are on the way."

"Can you take care of the cameras on the back of the building where that piece of cloth is?"

"Why? You think it's something significant?"

"I don't know, but Emily's done really well leaving us a trail to follow. She left me the note, then made sure she took a taxi that I could trace. She even managed to get me a text where they were rerouting her to." He nodded at the window. "And now there's a piece of material hanging on the bars of the window. I think she's trying to tell us she's in that room."

Linc pressed a finger to his earpiece. "Cameras are out in the back," he said. "It'll cause some concern when someone notices."

"I don't plan for this to take long. Can we get a thermal image of the room?" With that equipment, he'd be able to detect if someone was inside the building in the room signaled by the material tied to the bar on the window. If that was Emily sending him a message, they needed to know—and act. Linc walked over and Brady tucked his phone into the front pocket of his jeans.

"SWAT's going to approach," Linc said. "They've got the thermal imaging equipment."

Brady shook his head. "I'm going with them."

"Your knee—"

"Is holding up. I'm going." He rubbed his eyes and sighed. "But I promise, if I think it's going to interfere or cause a safety issue, I'll stand down."

"Ruthie said you ran out on the MRI."

"Didn't have a choice. She gave me a brace. It's helping."

"Then suit up. You're not going in without a vest on."

By the time Brady slipped on the combat gear, law enforcement had the entire building surrounded. And it was confirmed there were three people inside the room. "Two adults and a kid, right?" Brady said. He shoved the earpiece Linc had provided into his left ear.

"Yeah. Looks like the kid is in the ceiling," Linc said. "They can see inside the room with the binoculars, but whoever's in there is staying to the side."

"Smart." Brady paused. "Don't breach until I'm in position."

"Stand by," Linc said to the men and women waiting for his command to go. "They've got the cameras at the front on a loop too, so it looks like everything is okay out there. Also thermal imaging is picking up five people in the main area. They're all gathered in a room off the main floor."

"So, they're distracted?"

"Yeah. For now."

"I'm going to knock on the window where I think Emily is."

"What if it's not her in there?"

"Then I guess I'm going to figure out who it is. But I think it's her."

Brady took one more look at the blueprints and drew in a deep breath. He could let SWAT do this, but for some reason he . . . couldn't. He'd rescued Emily several times already and he wasn't going to entrust her safety to people who didn't know her.

Which made absolutely no sense and he knew it. The people he worked with were more than skilled in hostage negotiation and rescue.

But he wanted to be there. He *had* to be there.

He held his weapon in his right hand and made his way to the side of the building. Fortunately, the window was low to the ground. Unfortunately, the bars were solid. He had to find a way to get her out of there. If it was her.

He lifted a hand and knocked.

———

Emily heard a yell from outside her door the same time she heard the noise at the window. Her fingers gripped the bench leg she'd yanked off and planned to swing like a bat at the next person who entered the room. "Was that a knock on the window?" she asked.

Her mother stood in the bathroom doorway, looking at the window. "Yes."

Still gripping the wooden leg, Emily moved to the window and stood to the side to peer out. One thing she'd learned on the streets. Don't be seen until you know who's looking. "Get in the bathroom, Mom, and shut the door. No matter what you hear, don't come out unless I yell for you or law enforcement does. Okay?"

"What about you?"

"I'll be all right, but you need to protect Sophia. Please?"

To Emily's amazement, the woman nodded and obeyed. Emily turned her attention to the window and could see a man in law enforcement gear. Hope leaped. With her free hand, she pushed open the window and recognized the eyes under the baseball cap. "Brady?"

"Are you okay?"

"Yes."

"Is that Sophia in the ceiling?"

She blinked. "Yes."

"Good move." His eyes traveled the small room. "Where's your mother?" She'd been in the room just seconds before.

"In the bathroom guarding Sophia's hiding place."

"We're going to work on getting these bars off without them realizing it. Then we'll—"

The door slammed open. Brady jerked to the side out of sight and Emily spun, the piece of wood hidden behind her.

The man who'd shoved her into the room stood in the doorway. "Get away from that window!" His eyes flicked around the room. "Where's the old woman and the kid?"

Old woman? Her mother was only forty-eight. "In the bathroom."

He shut the door behind him and strode toward the bathroom.

124

As he passed her, Emily swung the bench leg with all of her strength. Pain shot through her wounded arm as the wood connected with her captor's head, but satisfaction flowed when he slumped to the floor.

She darted to the door, twisted the knob, and opened it a crack. Three of the remaining four men were focused on the front window. Snake Man still sat behind his monitors. "See what's taking Chico so long," Snake Man called.

The man closest to the office headed toward her. "I don't like this, boss. Something's going down."

"The monitors don't say anything, but yeah, I think you're right. Get the Chastain woman and kill the other two," he said. "Dump them in the lake. We've got to get out of here."

Emily shut the door, wishing she had a way to lock it, and ran to the window. "Brady!"

"I'm here."

"They're coming to get me and I heard one of them say to kill my mom and Sophia and dump them in the lake." She couldn't help the edge of hysteria in her voice.

"Stand to the side of the window," he told her.

She stepped aside as the latch clicked on the door.

"Breach now!" Brady's sharp whisper came through the window, then the door opened.

"Chico, what's going on in—" The man's eyes fell to his unconscious comrade on the floor, then shot to her. "What'd you do?"

She hefted the wood and dropped into a defensive stance. "I hit him and I'll hit you too."

"You're dead." He lifted his weapon. One shot came from outside the window.

Her captor dropped. His weapon clattered to the hardwood.

Emily screamed and jumped back, heart pounding. She ran to the doorframe to peer out in the large area. All she could think was two down, three to go.

The front door burst open. Law enforcement swarmed the building. Gunfire sounded and Emily slammed the door.

The bathroom door opened and her mother appeared.

"Go back," Emily said. "Shut the door."

Her mother's eyes landed on the man with the bullet hole in his head. She turned and retched but slammed the bathroom door.

The other door opened and Emily turned to see Brady enter. His gaze went to the two men on the floor and she gestured to the dead man. "Was that you?"

"No, SWAT." He hurried to cuff the unconscious man on the floor and pat him down. He removed two more guns.

"That's why you wanted me away from the window."

"Yes." He moved to the dead body, cuffed him, checked for a pulse, confiscated another weapon, then stood. "Get Sophia and your mom and stay in the bathroom until I come back for you. It's the safest place at the moment. They're not all in custody, but will be soon. Be ready to move fast." He nodded to the men on the floor. "Cover Sophia's eyes. She doesn't need to see that."

Emily bolted into the bathroom. Her mother leaned against the sink, rinsing her mouth. Emily stood on the toilet and removed the ceiling tile closest to the wall. In her desperation to find a hiding place for her sister, she'd pushed the tile up and discovered a small "shelf" that jutted from the wall just above the toilet. "Sophia?"

"I'm here." The child's voice wavered and Emily's heart clenched.

Her mother stood next to her, arms reaching up. "Come here. Lower yourself down and I'll help you."

"I heard some loud noises," Sophia said. "Like shooting. I don't want to come down if someone's shooting."

"The cops are here now," her mother said. "You're going to be fine."

The girl's legs swung down and Emily helped her mother lower her to the toilet, then jump down. The little girl looked up at her. "I want to go home."

"I know." She wanted to offer a hug, but Sophia didn't know her. Not like she should. She was a stranger to the child and she had only herself to blame for that. Yes, her mother had kicked her out, but it had been Emily's choice to stay away for so long. Sophia ran to her mother and buried her face in the woman's stomach.

Shouts, gun blasts, and screams echoed from the outer room.

"Stay here," Emily said. She ran out of the bathroom.

"Emily! Get back here!"

For a moment she froze. Her mother actually sounded concerned, but she ignored the order, cracked the door, and peered out. Law enforcement swarmed the warehouse floor, weapons raised, shouting orders to the scattering men with the snake tattoos.

Another shot rang out, followed by three more.

Emily pressed her back against the wall until the shooting stopped, glanced at the now-closed door of the bathroom, then took another look at the floor.

Controlled chaos reigned. The man she'd slammed with the piece of wood was awake and in the grip of a SWAT officer, being led from the building.

Another man lay on the floor, hands cuffed, three dark holes in his chest. An officer held a hand to a bleeding bicep but didn't look too concerned. Where was Snake Man?

And where was Brady?

"Clear!"

"Clear!"

"All clear here!"

The shouts came from all directions. Men and women in their gear, rifles and other weapons held ready.

And then Brady was in her line of sight. He caught her gaze and frowned at her as he hurried toward her. "Thought I told you to stay back."

"You did. Did you get them?"

"Two of them. There were five in all, right?"

"Right."

"We got all but one. Two are dead and two in custody. Their other buddy escaped somehow, but we'll get his face off a camera from somewhere and put him through the recognition software. It won't take us long to find him."

He sounded more hopeful than she thought he should. Not everyone was in the system. Although Snake Man didn't exactly look like he was new to a life of crime, so maybe they'd get a hit. Brady looked over her shoulder. "Everyone okay?"

Emily turned. Her mother and Sophia stood in the bathroom door, watching wide-eyed and scared. She didn't blame them. "What now?"

"Officers will want to get your mother's statement and talk to Sophia."

"Of course. Then what?"

"Then we make sure your mother and sister are safe while you help us figure out who is so desperate for what you have that they're willing to pull this kind of stunt."

## 12

Emily sat on the grass outside the office building with her mother and sister close by. Once the paramedics had checked them out and deemed no hospital visit necessary, they'd left and the medical examiner had arrived shortly thereafter.

Half an hour ago, Sophia had stretched out, laid a head on her mother's thigh, and promptly dropped off to sleep. Emily envied her. Neither she nor her mother had spoken in the last twenty minutes and the silence was straining Emily's nerves to the breaking point. She sighed and rubbed her eyes. "I'm sorry about all this," she said softly, not wanting to disturb the child.

"I see trouble is still showing up wherever you land. At least this time no one died except the people who deserved it."

The jab nearly decimated the fragile hold she had on her emotions, but what could she say? "Yeah," she whispered. "At least there's that." She fell silent again since that seemed to be the least painful option. She refused to revert to her childhood ways of snapping off whatever she thought, regardless of the consequences. It almost surprised her that she had no more desire to cause as much hurt as possible to the woman who'd given birth to her.

"What happens now?" her mother asked, keeping her voice low while she stroked Sophia's dark hair.

Emily's heart stumbled at the sight. Her mother had never touched her like that. Ever. She cleared her throat and looked away. "They catch the people who did this." She paused, then nodded to Sophia. "She's beautiful."

"Yes."

"She's happy?"

"Unlike you as a child, you mean?"

Why was she even trying? But . . . "Yes."

"I think she is. After all, it's just the two of us."

"I know." Emily swiped a hand across her eyes and refused to let the tears come. It was just the two of them and that was Emily's fault too. At least in her mother's eyes.

"Why did you come?" her mom asked. "Risk your life for us? I never would have—"

"What?" Emily asked. "Thought I'd do it?"

"Yes. I even told them you wouldn't."

"Wow." Of course she'd had no reason to think otherwise. Old pain became new. "It's been a long time. Things have changed. I've changed. You don't know who I am now."

"I never knew who you were."

"Unfortunately, that is very true." But she wasn't sure who got the blame for that one. Probably her father. Emily drew in a deep breath and stood. "I'm going to find Brady and ask him what we're supposed to do now."

"I'm sorry, Emily. For a lot of things."

She wasn't going there. Not right now. "I know, Mom. I am too."

"Who is Brady to you?" her mother asked.

What a loaded question. Emily gave a small shrug and shook her head. "I don't know. A friend." And that made her sad because while she wanted more, there was no way that was going to happen. The fact that she was sad about that made her mad.

"He's a cop."

"I'm aware." She wasn't getting into this now. "I'll be back."

As she walked, she took inventory. Her foot throbbed, along with her arm. She had the beginnings of what was shaping up to be a pounding headache, and she was hungry.

She found Brady near the entrance to the warehouse talking to Linc.

". . . secret door that led to an underground tunnel."

"What underground tunnel?" Emily asked.

"It's how one of them was able to escape. It leads to a basement next door. He simply climbed down and walked away."

"So, he let his guys fight it out while he ran?" Emily shook her head. "Nice."

"Yeah."

"He was the one who broke into Heather's and my apartment and trashed them."

"Did he say what he was looking for?"

"Just information. Something about a boat that sank. He wasn't exactly clear, but I'll fill you in later. When can we go?" she asked. "My mom needs to get Sophia home and get her something to eat."

"Soon. We're going to have to transport them to the station to get their statements. We'll have someone trained in interviewing children question Sophia to make sure she's not traumatized further. We'll also feed them and do our best to make sure they're as comfortable as possible."

"Okay. Who's we?"

"Well, law enforcement. I also think we need to put them in a safe house," Brady said.

"Because they can identify the guy who escaped?"

"That, and because these guys didn't get what they wanted from you. They got you here using your mom and sister once. They know your weakness. There's nothing to stop them from trying again."

Her stomach twisted at the thought. "All right. That makes sense." Because he was right. She'd do it all over again if they were snatched a second time.

"You should go with them."

A harsh laugh escaped before she could stop it. "Um, no. That's not going to happen."

"Em—"

"Not going to happen and nothing you can say will change my mind."

He studied her a second longer before he frowned and nodded. "All right. You said she hates cops. Why?"

"Because a cop shot and killed my dad."

He stilled, his eyes soft, yet wary. "I'm sorry."

"Don't be. He deserved it."

She could tell she'd rendered him speechless. He cleared his throat. "Okay, I see we have some more topics to talk about later, but for now"—he nodded toward her mother and Sophia—"do you want to tell them or do you want me to?"

Which would be better? She glanced over her shoulder at the pair. Her mother's eyes were closed and Sophia had rolled to her left side. "Actually, I think at this point she probably hates me more than she hates cops." Emily looked away from the instant concern in his blue eyes. "Which vehicle should I wait in while you tell her?"

"I have my truck across the street, but don't leave yet. I don't want you to be anywhere alone."

Emily waited while Brady walked over to her mother and broke the news. The woman's shoulders slumped, then straightened. Emily heard her say something but couldn't make out the words. Brady responded and her mother's mouth shut. With snapping eyes and a hard jaw, she nevertheless was gentle when she woke Sophia.

Unable to figure out the emotions rolling through her, Emily pressed chilled fingers to her burning eyes and did her best to keep the memories at bay.

"Emily?" Brady placed a hand on her shoulder and she opened her eyes. "You okay?"

"Not really, but that's not important. Did she agree?"

"She did."

"Wow. What did you say to make that happen?"

"That if Sophia died because she refused police protection, then that was on her."

Emily's jaw dropped and she quickly snapped it shut. "Impressive."

He shrugged. "Whatever works. You want to say goodbye for now?"

Emily spotted her mother and a now-awake Sophia talking to another officer. "No."

"You're sure?"

"I'm sure."

He waved to someone behind her, then took her hand. "All right then, let's get out of here."

"Where are we going?"

"You might not want to go with your mom and sister to their safe place, but we're going to find you one you can live with."

---

Brady stood at the island in the middle of the kitchen he shared with his sister and brother while Emily sat on the couch and let Ruthie change the bandage on her arm. She'd borrowed a long-sleeved T-shirt from Ruthie, tossing her torn, bloodied one in the trash. "Check her foot again while you're at it," he said. "Please."

Ruthie raised a brow, then nodded.

"Come on, Brady," Emily said, sounding half amused, half irritated. "The paramedics at the warehouse said I was fine."

"Yeah, well, I'd rather have Ruthie's word for it."

The kitchen bar faced the den, the open concept allowing him to raid the refrigerator and participate in the conversation taking place on the couch. He set a couple sodas on the counter.

"Are you sure Mom and Sophia will be all right?" Emily asked Linc, who stood near the mantel. She took a sip of her water. "I could tell Mom wasn't real happy about being sent to a safe house. And when Mom's not happy, heads can roll."

"They'll be fine. Better to be unhappy than dead."

Emily flinched and Brady rolled his eyes. "Smooth, Linc."

"Sorry. I'm afraid Derek is influencing me, as I seem to be having trouble with tact these days." He sighed. "But really, Emily, I promise, they're better off there for a bit while we track down who snatched them—and you."

"I know. I understand—and they do too, I hope."

Ruthie pressed the last strip of adhesive to the bandage. "Do you need anything stronger than what I prescribed at the hospital to help you sleep tonight?"

Emily recoiled. "No."

Ruthie frowned. "Just asking."

"I know." Emily cleared her throat. "Sorry. I . . . used to have an addiction to painkillers, and I prefer to just suffer rather than risk getting addicted again."

Ruthie's features softened. "I understand. I wasn't really talking about painkillers per se. You can go a natural route with some melatonin or something."

"I'm okay right now."

If the tight set of her jaw and pale cheeks were any indication, she was lying through her teeth.

Linc paced in front of the brick fireplace, phone pressed to his ear. "Can you threaten him with something to get him to talk? Uh-huh. Right. Yeah. Got it." He hung up and rubbed his eyes. "That was Derek. He said Parker isn't speaking other than to request a burger and to leave him alone so he could think. So, Derek said they've given him an hour to think. Said normally he'd push, but there was something about Parker that made him think backing off would be the better move."

"For all his lack of tact, Derek's good at reading people," Brady said. "If he thinks that's best, then it probably is. Did Parker make any phone calls?"

"Not yet. His request for a lawyer still stands, so we're waiting to hear that we can go question him."

"Good." Brady slid a glance to Emily. Gas logs gave off a warm glow, and all he could think about was that he wanted to send his siblings away so he could sit on the couch with Emily and ask her how and why she'd become addicted to painkillers. But now wasn't the time for that. Priorities.

He stepped into the den and sat on the love seat across from her. "I know you told the lead investigator everything, but could you go through it again? I didn't get to listen like I wanted to and Linc didn't hear any of it."

"Neither did I," Ruthie said.

Emily raked a hand through her dark hair and the T-shirt sleeve slid up—revealing the rope burns she'd acquired yesterday. As well as the older white crisscrossing scars. She lowered her arm and pulled the sleeve down. "The first text I got in the hospital was to throw you off," she said to Brady. "Once you were gone, they knew it."

Brady looked at Linc. "Any word on the faces on her hall at the hospital?"

"Not yet."

Back to Emily. "Go on."

"Anyway, after you were gone, I got the next text telling me they were watching and that I was to leave or else. I wrote the note, made sure I stayed in view of the hospital cameras, and grabbed a cab."

"Are you a cop?" Ruthie asked.

Emily raised a brow. "No. But I lived on the streets long enough to figure out how to think like one—and how to make sure someone can follow me. Or not." She scowled. "At least when I know someone plans to do so. I had no idea someone planned to grab me as I walked out of my office building and throw me into the trunk of a car."

"Of course not," Brady said. "Just to satisfy my own curiosity— why were you living on the streets?"

She looked away from him. "It was after my dad was killed.

My mom told me to get out, so I did. It's a long story. I . . . can tell you about that another time. As for today, from what I could tell, the cab driver was innocent in all of this, but I knew someone was watching at the hospital and I was afraid they could still see me somehow. That's why I didn't try to call or text once I got in the car." She rubbed her arms and shivered.

"We've already tracked the driver down," Linc said. "He's being questioned as we speak. As are the other two who were rounded up at the warehouse. The Uber driver's in the wind, but we subpoenaed the Uber records. There's a BOLO out on him right now."

Brady's phone buzzed and he glanced at the screen. "Well, looks like it's time for a chitchat."

"Who's that?"

"The lawyer has arrived, so I'm going to head over to question Parker about the break-ins and the pictures," Brady said. "Since we connected on such a personal level, maybe he'll open up to me."

"Sarcasm?" Linc asked.

Brady rubbed a hand over his bruised jaw. "I owe the guy a punch in the face."

"I want to see him," Emily said.

"No, you need to stay here and rest," Brady said. "Linc and I can take care of this. But I promise we'll let you know what we find out as soon as possible."

"But—"

"They're right," Ruthie said. "Let them do their job."

Emily's shoulders wilted, and Brady was surprised she didn't argue further. Probably a good indication of her fatigue. And pain.

"Is there anything else you can tell us?" Linc asked.

She rubbed her forehead and nodded. "They wanted me to find the *Lady Marie*."

"The what?" Brady crossed his arms and frowned.

"It's a houseboat that sank. They wanted me to tell them which lake it sank in and the location on the lake."

"Did you tell them?" Brady asked.

"No, because I didn't know what they were talking about."

Frowning, Linc tapped his pen on the notebook. "And yet, they think you do."

"Apparently." She sighed. "He said he wanted the information I received Wednesday night. The only thing I can think of is that Heather may have had some information that she hadn't passed on to me yet. I don't know how they would know what she was working on or that she was going to send it to me, but it's obvious they did. So maybe they think she emailed me and that information was in there. Only she never emailed, which means I don't have a clue."

"Makes sense," Brady said.

"Have you been able to find anything at all that might tell us what happened to her?" Emily asked.

Linc shook his head. "We haven't been able to locate her car even with the BOLO on it. No credit card usage or ATM withdrawals. Nothing. And the security camera in the parking garage where she made the 911 call was disabled, so there's no way we can see what happened." His eyes met hers.

Emily winced and stood. Paced to the entrance to the sunroom, then to the fireplace, where she stood in front of the flames. "I don't understand. Where could she be?"

"Emily . . . ," Brady said.

Her gaze met his and he wanted to reassure her that her friend was probably fine and just hiding out. But . . .

He didn't think so.

The 911 call, the lack of activity on her accounts, the missing car . . . all added up to the fact that it was probable they just hadn't found her body yet. Or she was being held somewhere.

She looked away.

"They've already pulled her records and pinged her phone, but there's nothing to indicate her location now." Linc glanced at

Brady. "If you ask me, our best lead is sitting in the interrogation room. You ready?"

"I am."

Linc headed for the door and Ruthie gestured to her medical supplies. "I'll just put these away."

"I'll be there in a minute," Brady said to Linc.

Linc turned. "I'll be in the car."

Once they were alone, Brady placed his hands on Emily's shoulders. "Are you going to be all right?"

"I don't really have a choice, do I?" She sighed. "As long as my mother and sister are okay, then yes, I'll be able to function. I just need to know about Heather." She bit her lip. "One way or another. I'm going to try to reach her parents again. I just don't understand why they haven't called me back."

He pulled her into a hug even as part of him asked himself what he thought he was doing—and why he was doing it. He kept telling himself she was a victim, that she was emotionally fragile, and that he needed to tread carefully. Then again, her emotional state really shouldn't matter to him.

Because he wasn't interested. At least not any more than he would be interested in—that is, *concerned about*—someone who was having as much trouble as she.

*Which is why you're standing there with her in your arms, right?*

He let her go and she stepped back, the confusion in her gaze zinging his heart. "Uh. Okay then," he said. "I'm going to leave you here with Ruthie. Derek plans to come over as well to keep an eye on the place. Izzy and/or Chloe, my sisters, may join him."

"Your sisters. Who are also police officers?"

"Izzy made detective last year and Chloe is in the K-9 unit."

"Got it. You have an amazing family, don't you?"

He smiled. "Yeah. I really do." And then he slipped out the door to join Linc in the vehicle.

# 13

Emily locked the door behind him and leaned her forehead against it as fatigue battered her. But she couldn't sleep. As long as she didn't know who was after her, her family was in danger. And Heather. Heather was as much a sister to her as Sophia. More so. And she w.as so very afraid she was never going to see her again. Tears gathered, prayers formed. *Oh please, God, please . . .*

"You're not going to help yourself if you let your body wear down," Ruthie said from behind her.

Emily turned. "Mentally, I know you're right. However, my heart is pushing me to keep going, keep thinking, and keep working until I get it all figured out."

"Hmm. Sounds like you fit in just fine with the St. John crew."

A laugh huffed from Emily and she followed Ruthie to the couch. Ruthie took one end, Emily took the other. She closed her eyes. "I can't think straight."

"It's called 'you need sleep.'"

"Yes, probably."

"They'll call if they find something or hear something."

"Not if they think it will wake us up."

Ruthie's brow lifted. "That's probably true. And impressive."

"What's impressive?"

"How long have you known them?"

"Just met them last night."

"And you've already got a good read on them." Ruthie nodded. "Like I said, impressive."

"They're good guys," Emily said. "Rare ones."

"Indeed. And one of them thought to get your overnight bag and bring it here. Oh, and they bought you a phone and filled your prescription. Just in case." She handed Emily the phone.

"Thank you. They did all that, huh?"

"They did."

"I was right," she said. "They're good guys. Special."

Ruthie gave a short laugh. "Yeah, well, let's keep that between us. As special as they are, they still have the ability to be insufferable if their heads get too big."

Emily laughed and stood, doing her best to ignore all the aches and pains. It was going to be hard to sleep tonight. Not just because someone wanted her dead and she was massively worried about Heather, but because of the throbbing in her arm. "I think I'm going to have to eat my words," she told Ruthie. "What do you have that will knock the edge off the pain but isn't addicting?"

Her new friend smiled. "The stuff I prescribed at the hospital."

"Right. I think I'll take one."

"I think that's a really good idea."

"I've decided it's stupid not to take advantage of your expertise. I'm going to need to rest if I'm going to be any help in this case." She paused. "Whatever this case winds up being."

"I agree."

"Where are the pills?"

"In the room you'll stay in." Ruthie stood. "Sit tight, I'll get them for you."

"Thank you."

Ruthie left, pulling her phone from her pocket, and Emily spotted her laptop sitting on the kitchen counter. Brady must have set it there so she'd see it easily. She walked over and opened it. Then shut it. Would someone be able to trace her if she logged in?

The possibility had her backing away. But what about her phone? If she logged in to her email through her phone, which she'd done earlier in a different location, would someone be able to track her here?

And she'd like to check her text messages, but again, she hesitated. She'd have to transfer all of her information onto the new phone in order to access everything.

Which, again, might allow someone to track her.

But she could call Heather's parents and give them yet another new number to reach her. She dialed Mrs. Gilstrap's number.

"Hello? Heather?" the frantic voice cried.

"No, Mrs. Gilstrap, it's—"

The distinct click of the line disconnecting stopped her. She checked the screen and frowned. "Great." When she called again, it went straight to voice mail. "What?" Maybe the battery had died. She left a message, begging for a return call, then set the phone on the counter and went back to the couch to close her eyes.

Moments later, the sound of footsteps opened them. Ruthie stood in front of her with a glass of water and a pill. "Here you go. Nonaddictive, I promise."

Emily downed it. "Thanks."

"Why don't I show you to your bed and you can rest awhile?"

"I think that sounds like a lovely idea."

Now she needed her brain to shut off. Just for a few moments. Please. Then she'd call Heather's mother.

---

Brady led the way into the police station. Although it wasn't his home turf, it was still the same atmosphere. The familiar smells and ongoing activity washed over him, offering him a strange comfort that the peaceful little cabin at the lake—before it was blown up—hadn't been able to compete with.

"Brady?"

Detective Andy Kirkpatrick strode toward him and Brady smiled. "Hey, good to see you." Brady shook his hand. "This is my brother, Linc St. John. He's an FBI agent. Not sure if you two have met."

"Nope, but welcome. Good to meet you."

"Likewise," Linc said. "Thanks for letting me sit in on this."

"Absolutely. I never turn down help. Come on back to the interrogation room. Your guy, Mr. Parker, is not a very nice fellow."

"Surprise, surprise," Brady muttered. "Has he said anything?"

"Nothing worth noting. He lawyered up."

"Who's representing him?"

"A court-appointed attorney. Ms. Sarah Downs?"

Linc raised a brow. "Now that actually does kind of surprise me. In his line of work, I'm sure he's got money to afford private representation." Hired killers didn't come cheap.

Andy shrugged. "Said he wasn't going to be inside long enough to worry about it."

Brady frowned and pulled his phone from his pocket. He'd taken a snapshot of the photo from Emily's refrigerator. The original had been entered into evidence. "When's Ms. Downs due to arrive?"

"She got here about twenty minutes ago. They've been talking ever since."

"All right. Lead me to him. I want to see if we can get a name out of him. I want to know who hired him."

"Let's get your weapons locked up and you can have at him." After securing their weapons, Andy motioned for them to follow. Brady's phone rang. "Just a second, let me take this if you don't mind."

"Of course."

The two men talked while Brady turned his back and pressed the phone against his ear. "Hey, David, what's up?"

"I found out who the building belongs to."

"Who's that?"

"A guy by the name of Nicholas Raimes. He bought it about three years ago. Probably because it looked like that area was going to make a comeback, but then deals fizzled because the crime rate soared."

"Gangs protecting their turf?"

"Yeah."

Brady frowned. "What does Mr. Raimes do for a living?"

"Flips houses and some commercial properties. That office building cost him a pretty penny, and he doesn't appear to have made any efforts to do anything with it. Although someone did something with it. Looks deserted on the outside and high-tech on the inside."

"So, how did these guys gain access?"

"Still working on that one," David said. "I've got a call in to Mr. Raimes to be in contact with you."

"Perfect. Thanks for going above and beyond." Brady hoped David knew how appreciated he was.

"Anytime. Also, I've some information on your Paul Bailey, Heather Gilstrap's neighbor."

"Anything to be concerned about?"

"Not really. No run-ins with the law. The only thing that's kind of a red flag for me is that he was sued by Ralph Jenkins, the CEO of Jenkins Corporation, about a year ago."

"What for?"

"Looks like Bailey renovated an office building, then turned around and sold the property to Jenkins and part of the building collapsed, injuring several employees. Including Jenkins's wife, who's now in a wheelchair. Jenkins sued, accusing Bailey of using substandard materials in the renovation. Bailey fought it and won. A week later, Jenkins was hauled out of Lake Murray sans his head."

"Whoa."

"Of course, Bailey was questioned, but he had an airtight alibi and no other connection to Jenkins. And besides, he argued that he won the lawsuit, what reason would he have to kill Jenkins?"

"Out of pure revenge for Jenkins dragging him through months of proceedings?"

"Well, yeah, I guess there is that, and while he was questioned in detail, there wasn't any evidence to connect him to the killing. Other than that, his nose is squeaky clean."

"Okay, thanks, David. Appreciate it." He paused. He had to admit he thought it interesting Raimes and Bailey were in the same business—or at least similar. Probably a coincidence, but . . . "One more thing?"

"Name it."

Brady's phone beeped. He glanced at the screen. "I've got another call, but can you see if there's a connection between Bailey and Raimes? There's probably not, but . . ."

"Sure."

Brady hung up and switched to the other line. "Brady St. John."

"This is hospital security. You'd requested photos of everyone on the hall of the lady who was threatened and eventually left the ER room?"

"Yes."

"I included hospital employees as well as anyone who looked like they were on their phone shortly before and a few minutes after the time your friend left the room."

"Perfect."

"I'm sending those by email now. I was only able to pull four or five good ones. There's one guy with a baseball cap who keeps his head down for the most part. He looks rather suspicious to me. However, if he's the one you're looking for, there's no way to know his identity. I think he also followed her out of the hospital."

"Great. Thank you. Include them all. We'll go through them. I appreciate your help."

"Of course. Have a good day." He turned to find Linc and Andy waiting. "Sorry." He filled Linc in on what David told him about Raimes.

"Sounds like we need to have a chat with Mr. Raimes," Linc said.

"Sounds like. Possibly right after our chat with our buddy in there," Brady said with a nod at the door. His phone chimed and he gave them a tight smile. "And now we've got more pictures to show."

"Our buddy? He's your buddy. You were the one he was hugging."

Brady gave his brother a shove. "He tackled me, dude." He looked at Andy and frowned. "Trust me, there was no hugging involved."

Andy held up a hand and did a pretty good job of keeping his grin under control. "Come on, you jokers." At the interrogation room, he knocked and opened the door. "Excuse me, I have someone here who'd like a word with you two."

Brady slipped inside, his aching knee causing his fingers to fist. Linc followed.

Parker looked up and scowled. His lawyer wore a similar expression. Brady nodded to the lawyer. "I'm sorry to interrupt, but I have a few questions and some pictures for your client to look at, if you don't mind."

"And if I do?"

"Then I guess I'm out of luck."

"I'll look," Parker said. "Sit down."

"Only if Ms. Downs says it's okay," Brady said without taking his eyes from the woman.

She never blinked. "What's the connection between the photos and Mr. Parker?"

"They're of some people we'd like identified. I'd like to know if Mr. Parker recognizes them."

"I said I'd look," Parker said.

"Mr. Parker, please refrain from speaking unless I direct you to do so," Ms. Downs said, her mild tone laced with a hint of steel.

Parker's scowl deepened, but he snapped his lips shut. Brady took a seat opposite the man. Linc settled in the chair beside him. "We know you were hired to kill Emily Chastain. She's identified you as the man who put her on the boat, held a gun on her, and was going to shoot her, then dump her in the lake."

"Yeah? So?"

"Mr. Parker—"

The prisoner slapped the table and Ms. Downs blinked but didn't move. Brady stepped closer just in case he needed to intervene— although he had the distinct impression she could take care of herself.

"Shut up, lady," Parker said. "I'll answer the questions if I see no reason not to."

Sarah Downs's furious gaze lasered her client and Brady thought she might simply get up and walk out. But she sat back, crossed her arms, and stayed put. Probably wanted to see how this played out.

Since Parker seemed inclined to disregard his lawyer's advice anyway, Brady continued. "Who did the boat belong to?"

"Dunno. I was told it would be waiting at the dock. My instructions were that once I had her, I was to take her out to the middle of the cove, shoot her, and dump her."

The casual, cold, matter-of-fact recounting of how he was supposed to end Emily's life turned Brady's stomach.

"Really," Ms. Downs said, "I have to insist that you not say anything else until—"

"And I said shut up. It's well established that I was in the apartment and the boat. You're not going to get me off on either of those."

"But it's possible you could get a reduced sentence if you'd listen to me."

"Or, you could keep talking. Cooperate," Brady said, "and I'll make sure the judge knows you did so."

This time Parker's gaze slid to his lawyer. "He can do that?"

"Oh, now you want my advice?" she said. Parker scowled and she sighed. "Yes, sure, he can note that you cooperated. Might make a difference, might not."

Parker nodded. "There you go then."

"So you were supposed to kill her, but I came along and ruined that."

"Yes."

"Who was the other guy with you?"

Parker froze. "What do you mean?"

"There were two of you there. I heard you talking while we were hiding in the woods."

"Naw, man, it was just me."

"Now you're lying. I was there, remember?"

Parker didn't deny it but wasn't going to admit anyone was there with him, either. "Fine," Brady said. "Let's move on to another topic for a second." He turned his phone around to show the picture to the man. "This is one of the men who was watching Emily at the hospital. She was ordered to follow instructions or her mother and sister would die."

"Whoa, I didn't have anything to do with that."

"Not saying you did. Just giving you some background."

The man shrugged. "Okay. Go on."

Brady looked at Ms. Downs. She still had a pinched look around her mouth and her narrowed eyes would probably wind up with permanent wrinkles, but she was paying attention. Brady almost felt sorry for her. What was she supposed to do when her client wouldn't listen to her? As long as it helped him figure out where the picture came from, he didn't care. He looked at Parker. "She went to the place where her mother and sister were being held. Fortunately, we managed to rescue her. Unfortunately, one of the five involved in her second kidnapping escaped. This one, however, we've got in custody along with one of his cohorts. Do you know him?" Brady held his phone out.

Parker examined the photo. "No, I don't know the guy."

"Come on, Parker. Bald guy, snake tattoo."

Parker snickered. "I said I didn't know him. I didn't say I've never seen him before." He pointed at the tat. "Just never done business with him or that gang he's with."

Linc frowned, and Brady scowled. "How do we know you're telling the truth?"

With an exaggerated eye roll, Parker nodded. "I've got no reason not to. I don't know the guy."

"Like you don't know the guy you were with the night you tried to kill Emily?"

Parker's jaw tightened and his eyes narrowed. "I told you I was working alone."

"Right. I've got pictures of three other guys I need to know about. Here's the first one. You know him?" He turned his phone and showed the man the first picture of one of the dead men from the office building.

"Nope."

Brady swiped to the next one. "Him?"

"Nope."

"The third."

"Huh-uh. I don't know who they are, sorry."

"You're lying."

Parker spread his hands. "Like I said, I've got no reason to lie. Never seen 'em before."

Brady met Linc's gaze and his brother shrugged. Brady sighed. "All right. Anything else you want to say?"

"Yeah. Watch your back. I'm not the only one on the payroll."

# SATURDAY, OCTOBER 26

## 14

Emily rolled over to find herself trapped in the comforter and part of the sheet. She kicked her way free, then lay still for a moment as she tried to figure out where she was. She took in the tastefully decorated bedroom. Light blues and golds gave the room a warm aura, and she offered a mental thumbs-up to the decorator.

Then remembered. She was in Ruthie, Linc, and Brady's guest bedroom because her home had been broken into and someone wanted to kill her.

Right.

A glance at the clock almost made her scream. 7:45? A.m. or p.m.? She squinted. It was a.m. That meant she'd slept the entire night. She ran a hand down her face and grimaced as she stumbled from the bed to the en suite bathroom.

She'd only meant to close her eyes a few minutes—or at least until Brady and Linc came back—because she'd wanted to hear what they'd found out. Apparently, her body had had enough.

Fabulous.

Once she'd brushed her teeth and showered, she made her way back into the bedroom to find the jeans and fleece she'd tossed in the bag before leaving her apartment. As she dressed, she couldn't help but wonder if Linc had heard anything more about Heather's

911 call or if he'd gotten her phone records. He'd had to get a subpoena, she knew that much, but how long did it take to get one anyway?

And she needed to check on her mother and sister. Since seeing them shuttled off to a safe house, she'd managed to put them from her mind. Mostly. She'd reverted to the days when she'd had no choice but to stuff down emotions and feelings or she'd have never survived. The fact that she'd managed to do so almost effortlessly bothered her. But she comforted herself with the knowledge that they were safe and she had other things to worry about.

But still . . . she hadn't even told them goodbye yesterday. Why? Because she'd been scared to look into her mother's eyes. The woman had been angry, and Emily simply couldn't handle the blame that she knew would be thrown at her. More blame. The never-ending blame.

She closed her eyes and pictured the day she'd left home almost eleven years ago. At seventeen years old, when her mother screeched and railed that her father's death was all Emily's fault and told her to get out, Emily had worn her pride, guilt—and hurt—like a mantle, and had done just that.

She stood in front of the full-length mirror, brushing her hair as she studied her reflection. She could admit now that while she didn't like the number on the scale, she did like *herself*. She liked who she was and who she'd worked hard to *become*. Did she wish she'd done some things differently? Of course, but overall, there was a small kernel of pride that she'd come this far from the hurting, self-destructive teen she'd once been.

Pulling the sweater away from her midsection bloused it out a bit and made her feel less . . . fat. She sighed and pushed the sleeves up to examine the scars on her arms. So much self-hate. So much anger. So much pain. So many life lessons she'd had to learn the hard way.

A knock jerked her out of her musings and she yanked the sleeves down, then pulled the brush through her hair one last time before opening the door. Brady stood there. "Hi."

She blinked. He really was a good-looking man. Even after her admission only seconds ago about liking herself, she still felt like the dumpy ugly duckling standing in front of him. Obviously, she was still working on some issues, so she stuffed those feelings into the corner of her brain that enabled her to compartmentalize—and smiled. "Hi."

"Ready for some breakfast?"

"Sure."

In the large kitchen, she found Linc and Ruthie sitting at the table with another woman and a very large dog resting at her feet. Ruthie looked up and smiled. "Glad you could join us. Meet one of our sisters, Chloe, and her K-9 partner, Hank."

The pretty dark-haired woman nodded. "Good to meet you."

"You too."

Emily slid into the chair Brady held out for her and waited while he settled himself next to her. "We don't usually have time to do meals unless we schedule them weeks in advance," he said. "So this is a treat for us." He passed her the eggs. She took a spoonful and handed them off to Chloe. The discreet, yet very pretty diamond on the woman's left hand sparkled when she took the bowl.

"You're engaged?" Emily asked.

A brilliant smile lit up Chloe's entire face. "I am. The wedding is in four weeks and I can barely stand it."

"Congratulations. Who's the lucky guy?"

"Blake MacCallum. He's a US Marshal."

"That's awesome. How'd you meet?"

Chloe fell silent for a moment. "Well, we knew each other in high school, but we met up again when his daughter was kidnapped by a ring of human traffickers."

Emily gasped.

"And," Chloe said, "the truck she was being transported in was involved in a wreck that was suspected to have drugs on board. Hank and I were called to the scene, found the drugs and the girls, and the rest is history."

"A lot of history," Ruthie murmured.

Chloe shot her sister a grim smile. "What about you and Isaac? You guys had quite an adventure when you decided to go on the run with him."

"Hey, it was either that or let him get killed." She looked at Emily. "He came in with a gunshot wound and I stitched him up. Then someone tried to kill him in his hospital room, so I decided he needed help staying alive." She shrugged as though it were that simple.

Emily knew her jaw was hanging but couldn't seem to snap it shut. When she succeeded, she shook her head. "Sounds like I'm not the only one with some crazy family dynamics."

Brady snorted and Emily thought he might be trying to contain a laugh. Linc simply gave a resigned nod. "You're not."

"I find that oddly comforting."

Laughs surrounded her and she grinned before turning serious and focusing on Linc. "Are my mother and sister still doing okay?" she asked him.

"They are. I checked on them first thing this morning."

"Has she threatened to kill any cop who came within spitting distance?"

The table fell silent. Linc shook his head. "Not yet."

"Wow. That's . . . good. Unexpected, but good." She ignored the questioning looks, but had to admit she was secretly relieved her mother seemed to be behaving herself. "And did you get the subpoena?"

Linc took a large helping of hash browns before meeting her gaze. "I got it last night as well as the phone records. So far there's nothing that stands out. All of Heather's calls matched up to friends, family, coworkers. There were a lot to you, but nothing after Wednesday night."

Emily swallowed and nodded. "I see."

"In the meantime, we can listen to the 911 call if we want to."

"I do. I mean I don't *want* to, but I need to. I have to."

"No. Emily—" Brady said.

She held up a hand. "Don't even try to stop me, please. She's my best friend. I need to go. I can't just sit around here waiting."

Brady and Linc exchanged a look and Linc raised a brow. "I'm fine with her going," Brady said. "It might actually be safer than leaving her here alone since Ruthie has to go in to work. We can let the officers watching the house go and return later when she comes back."

"Okay with me, then," Linc said after a short hesitation.

"Good," Emily said.

Ruthie frowned and clasped her hands in front of her. "I'll say grace."

"And a prayer for protection," Chloe said.

"Indeed."

Once breakfast was over, Emily found herself in the front seat of Brady's truck. Linc said he'd follow since he wanted his vehicle in case he needed it.

The ride to the dispatch office located on Laurel Street took all of eight minutes. "That's convenient for you. Being so close to work and downtown, I mean," Emily said.

"Yeah, comes in handy," Brady said as he parked. "Stay put for a second, will you?"

"Why?"

Brady climbed out and walked around to her side to open her door. She lifted a brow. "Thanks."

"No problem."

Linc slipped up behind her, and while she figured Brady to be the kind of guy who'd hold the doors for the women he dated, this wasn't a date. With Linc hovering close behind her and Brady right in front, she realized they were creating a shield around her. The knowledge humbled her. They didn't even know her and yet these men were willing to risk their lives for her. That fact told her all she needed to know about their character and their commitment to the oath they'd taken.

Once inside the dispatch call center, Brady approached the desk and asked for Director Mason Helms. Emily bit her lip as impatience surged. She wanted to hear that call . . . but didn't. But had to.

Brady's phone rang and he stepped to the side to answer. She couldn't help but wonder who he was talking to and if she needed to know the information that had him frowning. But there was no time to ask. He finished the call as a tall, dark-skinned man with short black hair and friendly eyes approached. "I'm Director Helms, but just call me Mason."

"I'm Emily." She shook the director's hand and followed as he led them into the call center. Multiple stations in organized rows dominated the large room. Each station had three or more monitors. Two dispatchers spoke into their headsets.

Mason stopped at a desk two rows down from the door and touched the shoulder of the woman in the chair. "Dawn, this is Detective St. John and Special Agent St. John. This young woman here is Emily Chastain. She's best friends with the caller."

"Heather," Emily said.

"Yes, Heather," Mason said. Compassion glittered in his gaze, and Emily looked away, not wanting to admit what that communicated about Heather's fate.

The dispatcher was ready for them and handed them all headsets. A wave of nausea washed over Emily even before the woman clicked on the button to play the recording.

Brady kept his gaze on Emily.

"911. Where is your emergency?"

"I'm in the Cannon Street Garage, third floor. My name's Heather Gilstrap. There's a guy following me and I think he's going to kill me."

Emily sucked in a sharp breath, but other than that didn't move.

"The door won't open!" The sound of Heather's harsh breathing reached them. Then a pounding. A harsh grunt. "I can't get out! No, no, no."

Heather fell silent, but he could hear movement in the car and he'd give anything to see what she was doing.

"I can't get out!"

"Heather? I've got officers en route," the dispatcher's voice said.

"My car won't start. My doors are jammed. He did something to my doors." A whimper.

"Heather?" A pause. "Heather? Heather! What's happening?"

"He's almost here. He has a gun. With a suppressor."

"Do you know who he is?"

"No. He has a ski mask on." A sob, sniffles. "Please, God, don't let me die in vain," she whispered. "Please, he's going to kill me—"

"I have someone on the way right now. You have to find a way out of the car and run."

"I can't!"

"Can you break the window?"

Harsh breathing echoed over the line. Emily trembled, her hands shaking. Brady wrapped his fingers around hers and she squeezed. Her gaze met his even as tears streamed down her cheeks.

"What?" Heather's voice.

"Can you break the window?"

"I tried," she whispered. "Tell Em I tried. Emily Chastain, tell her! Warn her she's in danger!"

The sound of breaking glass.

Heather's scream. Then, "Please, don't."

*Click.*

157

## 15

need a bathroom," Emily said. "Now."

"Down that hall, second door on the left," Dawn said. Tears stood in her eyes too.

Emily spun and raced from the call center, hit the hall, then the door to the bathroom. Then the toilet.

She lost her breakfast and a piece of her sanity.

"Emily!"

Brady. "Go away!"

But he was beside her on his knees on the cold tile floor, handing her a bottle of water to rinse her mouth and pushing her hair back away from her wet cheeks. She rinsed and spit and tried unsuccessfully to stem the tears. Finally, he pulled her into his arms. "It's too much," she whispered. "I can't handle this." The grief welled until she wanted to scream. She'd lost too much. A person wasn't supposed to suffer so much—and survive with her sanity intact. "I give up."

"No, you don't. You *can* handle this, Emily. You're strong. You have to be strong."

"I'm not," she cried. "I've been fooling myself for years now. Tricking myself into thinking I'm strong. But I'm not. I'm *not*." Sobs wracked her and her tears soaked his shirt.

He fell silent and just let her cry. It briefly occurred to her that she should care that her ugly crying was covering his white shirt in tears, snot, and black mascara, but she simply didn't. She was beyond caring about anything except the fact that her best friend, the sister of her heart, was dead and there wasn't anything she could do to bring her back.

After she'd cried herself into an exhausted numbness, she sat back, shoulders against the stall wall, and wiped her face with the toilet paper Brady pulled from the roll. "She's gone, isn't she?" Emily said on a hiccup. "She's really gone."

"I don't know, Emily. I would say it's probable that she's dead, but like I said, someone could have taken her just like they did you . . ."

"No. She's dead. He killed her. She screamed at him and begged him not to." The sound still echoed in her mind. She sniffed, then blew her nose. He gave her a fresh batch of paper and she tossed the used into the toilet. "What do I do now?"

"We find who has her—or killed her. We find *her* so we know for sure."

His words resonated. She let them roll around in her mind even as determination solidified. "Yes," she said. "That's what we do. We find her—and them. I want them caught so they can rot in prison."

Brady lifted her chin. "I have to tell you that I think whoever it is, is the same person who's trying to kill you."

She sniffed and swiped the tissue across her cheeks once more. "Probably."

He stood and helped her to her feet and out of the stall. At the sink, she blew her nose, washed her face, and worked to pull herself together. For Heather. She could do this for Heather. *Why, God? I don't understand!*

Brady opened the door for her and she slipped out into the hall while her cry echoed unanswered in her head.

Linc and the director had stepped away from the station, and Dawn was on the phone with someone.

"They're probably in his office," Brady said. He led the way and soon they were sitting across from Director Helms.

Emily cleared her throat. "Thank you for letting me come. I'm sorry I was so emotional, but I needed to be here."

"No apologies necessary," Director Helms said. "I understand. We all do. And we're very sorry you had to hear that."

"Thank you." She stood. "I'll just wait for you guys outside."

"I'm ready," Brady said. He thanked the director once more and they headed for the door. "Are you okay?"

"No."

"Yeah. Dumb question."

"No, it's not. You're concerned. I appreciate that." She drew in a breath. "I'll be more okay if we find Heather's body and her parents are able to give her a proper funeral."

"We'll find her."

He slid a hand under her elbow and reached around her to open the door. "Stand back a little and we'll get you to the truck the same way we got you inside."

With Linc in front of her and Brady behind her, they started down the steps and to Brady's truck parked on the curb. He opened the door and the window shattered.

---

"What the—" Brady shoved her into the passenger seat and slammed the door. "Stay down! Get on the floorboard!"

He dropped to the pavement and rolled under the truck. Linc hollered and dove behind his own truck.

Brady caught sight of the muzzle in the window of the car parked across the street and diagonal to them. He brought his weapon up. Aimed . . .

. . . and a car drove in between him and the shooter.

Three pops sounded from the moving vehicle and it screeched away. Brady rolled out from under the truck and to his feet. He looked inside to find Emily huddled on the floorboard. "You okay?"

"I'm tired of getting shot at!" She glared up at him, eyes spitting fury and fear. But no sign of another wound.

He turned back to see Linc racing to the first shooter's car and took off after him. They came up on the vehicle with guns raised. Brady placed himself to the side so he could see in the window, yet duck if he needed to. "Police! Show your hands! Hands on the wheel! Now!"

No movement. One person in the driver's seat.

And leaning against the headrest, empty eyes open and staring at the roof of the Chevy. Brady didn't need to check the man's pulse to know he was dead. He lowered his weapon and Linc did the same.

"What just happened?" his brother asked.

"Someone tried to take out Emily, but instead got taken out?"

"I'm confused."

"Ditto."

Linc looked over his shoulder. "Help's on the way. I'm going to let one of the officers secure the scene. Why don't you check on Emily?"

"Yeah."

Officers surged onto the scene and Brady knew the deputy coroner or the medical examiner would be there as soon as he could. If it was the ME, he hoped it would be Francisco Zamora. The guy was quirky, but he went the extra mile when it came to helping police solve a case.

Brady jogged back to find Emily climbing out of the truck. He placed his hands on her shoulders. "Are you okay?"

She nodded, face stony, eyes granite. "Fine."

"I think it's time you hid out for a while."

"Hid out?"

"We need to get you someplace safe while we dig into what you and Heather were researching."

"Where?"

"I'm thinking about that."

"Brady?" He turned to see Izzy hurrying toward him. "Are you all right?"

"Yeah, the guy wasn't aiming at me." He introduced Emily. "And this is my sister, Detective Izzy St. John."

"Marshall," she reminded him with an amused glance.

"Right. Marshall." Her being married just didn't compute with him even though he liked and knew her husband as well as his own brothers.

"Glad to meet you, although the circumstances could be better."

"A bit," Emily said.

"Who's going to get this case?"

"Jordan and I caught it." Jordan North, Izzy's partner who was about two years away from retirement and still went after each case like it was his first. "What happened?"

He filled her in while Emily stood silent beside him. It didn't take long. "I'll get the security footage and we'll see if we can get a plate off the second shooter's car," Jordan said.

"I want to watch it," Emily said.

Izzy nodded. "Why don't you two go inside and get comfortable."

"I'll take her statement," Brady said. "And write mine up too."

"Perfect. I'll type them up later and get you to sign them."

"Statement?" Emily asked. "What am I supposed to say? Someone shot at me and I got pushed into the truck. That's about it."

She was approaching the end. The end of her strength, the end of her patience, the end of her endurance. Brady had seen it before. He took her good arm and led her inside to the conference room.

Director Helms brought in soft drinks and bottled water. "Help yourselves. I've got chips and fruit in the break room through that door. Legal pads and pens are in the drawer of the credenza."

"Thanks," Brady said.

"Absolutely. Let me know if you need anything else. I'm so sorry this happened."

He left with the promise to check back later, and Emily lowered her forehead to the table and closed her eyes.

"You're not going to pass out on me, are you?" Brady asked as he grabbed a legal pad and pen.

"No."

"Good." She still didn't lift her head. "Emily?"

She sighed and groaned as she pulled her head up and looked him in the eye. "I have to go see Heather's parents."

He rubbed his chin. "I don't think you should."

"Come on, Brady . . ."

"We haven't found her body."

"Which means what? You think she could be alive?"

With a grimace, he looked away.

"Exactly," she said. "So after the 911 call, the cops went to the garage and found nothing."

"Right. Her car was gone and so was she. The cops then went to her apartment and the manager let them in. It was neat and looked fine, according to the report."

"What happened after that?"

"The officers located her parents and told them about the call and wanted to know if they'd heard from Heather since it had been made. They hadn't, so the cops went back to her apartment to see if they could find anything to indicate where she might be."

"But they found nothing. By then, they probably thought she was dead."

He nodded. "They would have looked for anything that might point them in the direction of her possible killer."

"But again, found nothing."

"Unfortunately. And then the cops went looking for you."

"But I'd already been taken, right?"

"That seems to be the timeline."

Emily groaned and rubbed her eyes. "Okay, what about her office? Did they search that?"

"Yes, and talked to her boss and all of her coworkers who were there the night she disappeared."

She frowned. "And then someone went into her apartment—probably sometime on Thursday after the cops left—and trashed it. And mine as well."

"That seems to be correct."

"This stinks."

"I know." He cleared his throat. "For now, let me get your statement." He grabbed a water bottle, opened it, and took a drink.

She spoke in a monotone and frowned as he wrote. But he took the statement word for word. She read over it, signed it, and passed it back to him. "What's the point?"

"Gotta have it. You never know what might be needed." He finished his statement while she worked on a bottle of water. "I think I know where you'll be safe," he said.

"Where?"

"Another friend with a house on the lake. A different lake."

"I'm not sure I'm up to any more lake house adventures."

He offered her a grim smile. "No more adventures. Just some peace and quiet."

The door opened and Linc stepped inside.

"What's happening out there?" Brady asked.

"I got a picture of the dead guy." Linc took a seat at the table and turned his phone so they could see the screen. Emily leaned in and Brady got a whiff of his sister's shampoo.

"You recognize him?" Linc asked.

She blinked and looked up. "Yes. I do."

Brady and Linc exchanged a hopeful look. "Who?" Brady asked.

"That's the guy who made the late-night, early-morning deposits. The one Heather followed. His name is Martin Burnett."

"Wait a minute," Brady said. "That call I got just before Mason came to get us was from the lab. Officer Schaffer gave them my number to call along with his when they got the DNA back from the lake house. The ski mask specifically."

"That was fast," Linc said. "Impressive for not being a Bureau lab."

"You're a funny guy. Credit goes to updated technology and a technician who owes me a few favors. That helped speed things along."

"And?" Emily asked.

"It matched up to a Martin Burnett."

"Wow," Emily said. "So he and Owen Parker were working together that night."

"Yes. I'm guessing when Parker failed to get rid of you, Burnett took over. Speaking of the *Lady Marie*. They haven't found the boat matching the description you gave and Parker's not saying what he did with it."

"It could be anywhere," Linc said. "Hidden away in a boathouse or someone's garage at this point."

Brady nodded. "I think that's going to be a dead end, but let's search for it anyway. All boats are registered somewhere."

"Do you know how many *Lady Maries* there probably are?" Linc asked. He shrugged. "But, I'll put a call in and get Annie to find out everything she can about Burnett and his known associates. And the boat. As soon as she lets me know, I'll pass the information on to you."

Brady smirked. "This isn't your case, remember? You're on vacation."

"Someone shot at my brother and his friend." He scowled. "I'm going to do what I can to help."

"Right."

Izzy stepped inside and shut the door behind her. "We've got a partial plate on the vehicle that killed our guy in the other car. We'll know who he is soon."

"Well, the dead guy is Martin Burnett," Brady said. "Emily recognized him from something she was investigating with her job at the bank. Linc's offered to use his resources to get more info on him."

Izzy frowned. "No need to bring the Bureau into this. We've got it covered."

"I know, Sis," Linc said. "I'm not stepping on toes, I promise. Just offering to help out during my days off."

She frowned, then shrugged. "Fine. If that's how you want to spend your vacation. As for Martin Burnett, as soon as we find out where he lives, we'll head over there and see what we can dig up on him—and see if he was working with anyone else."

"We know he was working with Parker now. At least the two of them are out of the picture."

Brady turned to Linc. "But Snake Man's not."

"No, he's not."

"What do you think about Emily hiding out for a few days?" Brady said. "She's been so busy being on the defensive and reacting to the things that have happened that she hasn't had a chance to sit down and process. I need to gather information from her and we need to do that in a secure setting. Our house isn't a great place for that."

"What about your office at the police station?" Izzy asked.

"My cubicle, you mean?" he asked. She shrugged. "That would work," he said, "but I'd rather something like a safe house."

"I agree," Linc said.

"Look, I'll be all right," Emily said. "I'll go to a motel or something." She rubbed her eyes and realized it was starting to become a habit. She dropped her hands. "But you're right. I don't want to put anyone in danger. I just need to get my things. My laptop and clothes. But . . ."

"But?" Brady asked.

"I want to go back to Heather's apartment. I keep feeling like I'm missing something. Her apartment was torn to pieces, just like mine. They were looking for something at both places. I want to see if her laptop's there."

"Her place was processed as a crime scene after the 911 call," Brady said softly. "Officers covered it from top to bottom."

"Did they find her laptop?"

"I don't know. Let me call and find out." It didn't take him long to learn no laptop had been found.

"She may have had it with her and they took it when they attacked her in the parking garage," Linc said.

"Maybe."

Brady narrowed his eyes as he rubbed his chin. "Wouldn't it be more likely that she had it at work? After all, that's where she was coming from when she was attacked."

"Sometimes she left it in her desk at work," Emily said. "If it wasn't in her apartment and she didn't have it when she was attacked, then it would be locked in her newsroom desk."

"Well, there's no way to know if she had it with her when she left the office," Linc said.

Emily straightened. "Wait a minute. Yes, there is. We can just ask her boss to check and see if it's there." She grabbed her phone and, with a pang, punched the number in without hesitation. It rang, then went to voicemail. She left a message and hung up. "Maybe we'll hear back from him soon, but in the meantime, while I know the camera in the garage wasn't working—"

"More like tampered with, but go on," Brady said.

"I'm willing to bet the cameras in the newspaper building were working just fine. If we could look at those, see when she left and if she was carrying the laptop, then we'd know. She has a shoulder bag that she uses. If she had it over her shoulder when she left, then we'll know she had the laptop with her."

"It's not a bad idea," Linc said. "The officers who responded to the 911 call would have requested the footage as they tried to retrace her steps. If so, it'll be easy enough for Brady to access."

Brady was nodding. "We'll find a safe place for you and I'll go look."

"Um. No. I'm going too. I know—knew—Heather way better than anyone else on the planet." She pursed her lips. "And I know everyone she worked with. If we need to question them, they'll talk to me."

"The officers investigating have already talked to them, but I'm guessing they didn't ask specifically about her laptop."

Izzy headed for the door. "You guys can figure that out. I'm going back to finding the person who killed Mr. Burnett—and who hired Mr. Burnett to shoot you. Talk to you when we finish processing his place." She eyed Brady. "Keep me updated, will you?"

"Of course, *Detective*," Brady smirked.

She stuck her tongue out at him, then swept out the door. Brady snorted and Linc hid a chuckle behind his hand. "She's going to get you one day, bro, and you're not going to see it coming."

"Oh, I know. But she's so fun to tease."

Emily's gaze bounced between the brothers, fascinated by the exchange.

Brady caught her eye and cleared his throat. "Sorry."

"For what?"

"For joking around when this is serious. We don't mean anything by it."

She tried to offer him a smile but figured it looked more like a grimace. "A little humor is never a bad thing. And you guys took my mind off Heather for a brief moment. It's all good." But just saying her friend's name brought the grief crashing back in on a wave that nearly crushed her.

Brady's hand covered hers and she gripped his fingers, trying to absorb the strength that he offered. Linc patted her shoulder and slipped out of the room. Emily and Brady sat in silence for a moment until he cleared his throat. "Let me see what I can arrange with the security footage. If we didn't get that video yet, we'll get permission from the powers that be at the newspaper office, and David Unger, our department's IT guy, will have it pulled up and ready to play in no time."

He stood and she rose to her feet, her body weighted with the heaviness of her sorrow. But she'd do this. For Heather. If she kept reminding herself that she was doing this for Heather, she could keep going instead of giving up and hiding away from it all. Heather had given her life for this story. The least Emily could do was make sure it wasn't in vain.

## 16

**B**rady led Emily inside the police station and stopped her just beyond the door. "You can take the vest off now if you want."

"Thanks."

He helped her shrug out of the body armor he'd insisted she wear before leaving the 911 call center. "You've been kidnapped, almost blown up, and shot at twice," he'd pointed out. "I think it's time for some precautions."

She hadn't argued with him. A fact he appreciated since he wasn't sure he'd win if it came down to a battle of the wills. But she didn't have a death wish and apparently picked her arguments wisely.

Linc and Derek would stay close by but would take the time to catch up on whatever it was they needed to do while Brady and Emily were in one of the safest places in the city. The basement of the main law enforcement building.

He led her downstairs to the office where David Unger worked day in and day out using his tech skills to help fellow officers catch the bad guys. Brady rapped on the door, and without turning from the monitor, David waved a hand, motioning for them to enter. "Find a seat."

Brady took the chair closest to David, and Emily lowered herself into the one next to him. He set the vest on the floor. "Thanks for doing this, David," he said.

"No problem." David finally spun to face them. "Sounds like some serious stuff going on."

"It's always serious. David, meet Emily. Emily, David."

"Thank you for making this a priority," Emily said.

"Of course. I'm sorry about your friend."

"Thanks." She blinked rapidly, but no tears fell. Her shoulders straightened and her jaw tightened.

David turned back to the computer. "Thanks to the cooperation of the the newspaper people, I've got the footage right here. I'm going to start inside the newsroom and then we'll trail her out into the outer area, to the elevator, and across the street to the parking garage. From what I can tell, she's not carrying a laptop or any other bag except her purse. Unless the laptop's so small it fits in that."

Emily leaned forward. "No, she has one of those cross-body messenger bags that she uses for the laptop."

David clicked the play button and the footage started with a woman sitting at her desk.

"Is that Heather?" Brady asked.

"Yes," Emily said, her voice taut with emotion.

David zoomed in on Heather and kept the footage focused on her as she moved. "So," David said, "it's late. 11:21. She's working. I guess she decides to call it a day, gets up, and grabs her purse."

"But not her messenger bag," Emily said. "She's using her desktop while she's working. I don't see her laptop anywhere."

"And then she exits, goes to the elevator. Waits. Goes down and out of the building. I was able to pull some footage from where she entered the parking garage and got on the elevator." David paused it. "And see this here? I think this guy is following her. He's got a ski mask in his hand, but we get a brief glimpse of him before he steps into the stairwell. Cameras in the stairwell were out too."

He zoomed closer and Emily gasped. "I think that's Martin Burnett!"

Brady leaned back. "And he's dead, so there's no asking him what happened that night."

"That's the last of the footage from this level," David said.

"It's okay. We know Heather didn't have the laptop with her when she left the building," Brady said.

"She could have had it in her car, I suppose."

Brady sighed. "Won't know that until we find it."

Emily swiped a stray tear. "Well, the car wasn't there when the cops got there, right? That means it left the garage. Surely there's footage of it leaving?"

David nodded. "I thought about that too." He clicked a few keys on the keyboard. The outside of the parking garage popped up on the screen. "There," he said. "The car leaves at 11:40."

Brady straightened. "Can we follow it? See where he goes?"

"Only so far. I tracked it to when they got on I-26 East. After that, I lost it. I tried different cameras along the exits but never did pick the car up again. I'm sorry."

"There's a BOLO out on it," Brady said. "Maybe someone will see it and call it in sometime soon." He sighed and rubbed his eyes. "For now, I'm going to take Emily and we're going to grab her stuff from the house and head somewhere safe."

"Where?" she asked.

"One of our safe houses." He looked at her.

"Does it have a secure Wi-Fi connection?" she asked.

"Yes. Why?"

"I want to use my laptop but have been hesitant because as soon as I log in to the bank's software, someone would be able to track me."

He lifted a brow. "I'm glad you thought of that."

"I do think things through occasionally." She smirked, then sighed. "Although, it doesn't seem like it matters. They've been able to catch up with me—us—regardless."

"But we haven't been trying to hide you. Up to this point, it wouldn't take much effort to follow you—or us." But that was about to change. He pulled his phone from the clip on his belt and called his boss, updating him on everything and requesting a specific location for the safe house. He wanted to be on the water.

"She needs to pass on what she knows and our investigators can take over," the sergeant said. "We've got resources that could be a big help in getting those involved."

"I know. And we'll need access to those resources, but we need a little time. Emily's the one who discovered this. She's the one who's been on top of this from the beginning. Give us a safe place to catch our breath and gather the information and we'll share when we've got it so it makes sense to someone just coming into it."

"Our people can read too, you know."

"I know, Sarge. Come on."

A sigh. "Fine, you can use the house on Lake Wateree, but I want regular updates. You know where to find the key."

"Thanks."

"Stay in touch." He hung up.

Next, Brady sent a text to a friend who was a detective and also on the dive team when she was needed. Mary Beth Habishaw. He requested she join them at the safe house and bring a dry suit and equipment. While he and Emily were on the lake, he planned to see if she'd be interested in joining the protection detail he wanted to have in place. And besides, he could see Mary Beth and Emily connecting and becoming friends in the long run.

---

Emily wasn't sure she wanted to head to a safe house, but she had to admit she needed a breather. So much had happened so fast, she hadn't had time to even process most of it. When Brady hung up with his sergeant, he turned to David. "I have one more request."

"What's that?"

"I've got pictures that I need to look at while we're here. If I forward an email to you, will you pull them up?"

"Sure."

Within seconds, they were scrolling through the pictures. While some were more clear than others, Emily still recognized them from the Emergency Department. Unfortunately, none of the faces were familiar, but the guy with the baseball cap caught her attention. "Can you zoom in on him?"

"A little. These aren't the best pictures."

"I know." The frame adjusted, blurred, then cleared. "There, on his neck." She pointed. "See that? Is that a tattoo?"

David zoomed closer and even though the pixels separated more, Emily could clearly make out the head of a snake. "That's one of the snake men," she said. "From the office building. I can't see his face, but I'm sure he was one of them."

"I think you're probably right," Brady said. "Well, at least we know how *they* knew I left the room and when to time their communications with you."

"I agree. But how did they know I was at the hospital?"

Brady rubbed his eyes, then met her gaze.

She held up a finger, signaling him to stay silent. "Never mind. They've been following me. Us. Obviously."

"Yes."

She crossed her arms. "Maybe they were biding their time so they could grab me but realized they couldn't because I was never alone or without protection."

"So, they had to lure you out."

"Exactly."

"Okay, your mother and sister are safe," Brady said. "Is there anyone else they can use that we need to get under protection?"

"No one that I can think of right off. Heather and I were best friends. I mean, I have friends at the bank and friends at church, but no one that I can see them going after. Maybe Heather's parents, but that's a stretch. Although, they haven't called me back and I'm getting worried. I know they've got all kinds of family there, so I'm not really worried they're hurt or in trouble. I just want to know why they won't take my calls or call me back."

"We won't take any chances. I'll request patrols be increased in that area. Where do they live?"

"In Forest Acres." She gave him the address.

"Forest Acres? You said you and Heather had been friends since fourth grade. Is that where you grew up?"

"Yes. Different sides of the track, so to speak, but yes."

He nodded. "All right. We're going to go by the house and get your things. We'll work on finding Heather's laptop or any kind of storage device that she could have backed information up to." His phone buzzed. "Hold on a second. Hello?"

While Brady took the call, Emily watched David work to make the pictures even more clear. "You're very good at that."

"Thanks." He shot her a grim smile. "I'm not a huge people person and I'm too much of a wimp to chase the bad guys in person, but I've always wanted to be in law enforcement in some way. This job suits me."

"Yeah. It does. Perfectly."

Brady hung up and Emily turned her attention to him. "That was Izzy," he said. "She and Jordan are still at Burnett's house but promised to meet us at the safe house to fill us in when they're finished."

"Okay. I'd appreciate that. I need to know what they found."

"She did say she got word that the cab driver appears to be clean. He said he was just sitting outside waiting on a fare when you came out."

Emily narrowed her eyes. "There was another car there. An Uber. He honked at us when we left."

"Yes, Izzy also looked into him and thinks he's clean as well. He said he got a notification for a pickup at the hospital. The person who ordered the ride described you right down to the clothes you were wearing. They checked out his records and it all looks legit."

"That's why they rerouted me. When they got word that I hadn't taken the Uber, they texted me the fake address."

"You did great, Emily," Brady said. He checked his phone. "Someone was beeping in while I was talking to Izzy. Let me check the voice mail." He listened and his eyes cut to her. "It's Nicholas Raimes. He said he can meet if I can be at his office in the next fifteen minutes. Otherwise, he won't be able to meet until next week sometime."

She lifted a brow. "He thinks meeting with you is optional?"

"Apparently."

"Then let's go."

"Not so fast. You're staying here with David, if that's all right with him."

"Sure," the man said. "The company will be nice."

"No offense to David," Emily said, "but I'd really like to go with you." She crossed her arms and lifted her jaw.

Brady sighed. "Look, we were headed for the safe house once we're done here. I think it's best to keep to that. Linc and Derek are already on the way here and can take you out there. I trust them to get you there safe. I'll meet up with you there after I talk to Raimes and fill you in on every detail, I promise."

She bit her lip and looked up at him through her lashes. She supposed he was right. If she insisted, she could be putting him and everyone in the building in danger. "Fine. You promise?"

"Yes. If you'll promise *me* one thing."

"What?"

"That you'll wear the gear the whole time you're riding out to the safe house. I don't want to leave you open to a sniper."

She nodded. "Right. No, I don't want to be picked off by a sniper."

"Good, I'm glad we're in agreement on that."

Definitely. She didn't like the idea of being left out of the interrogation process, but this was what Brady did and she'd have to trust him enough to let him do it.

---

Nicholas Raimes's office dominated the fourth floor of a recently renovated high-rise in the heart of downtown Columbia. Fortunately, the building was only about three blocks from the police station and Brady parked out front in the circular drive. He placed the card in the window that identified him as a police officer.

With an eye on the surrounding buildings, he hurried through the double glass doors and breathed a sigh of relief when no bullets hurled his way. Although, he couldn't think why they would. Emily wasn't with him. Still . . . he'd admit to some paranoia—and wasn't going to apologize for it.

The elevator carried him upward, and when the doors opened, Brady found himself in the plush lobby of Raimes and Associates. He approached the receptionist, flashed his badge, and gave the twentysomething young man his name.

"Just one second, Detective. I'll let him know you're here."

"Thanks."

Brady wondered if the man would keep him waiting, but before he had a chance to choose a seat, the inner door opened and Nicholas Raimes stepped through. "Hello, Detective St. John?"

"Yes." They shook hands. "Nice to meet you," he said.

"You too. Come right this way and we'll talk in my office. I managed to push my next meeting a bit so we wouldn't be too rushed."

"Thanks." Huh. The man wasn't really what he expected. Mid to late forties, trim and tall with linebacker shoulders and a tanned face. Green eyes sparkled with life and he had an easygoing smile that probably resonated well with his clients.

Brady settled himself in one of the comfortable leather seats that had been arranged to face a matching couch. A coffee table and end tables completed the sitting area.

"Could I get you some coffee? Water? Soda?"

"I'll take a water," Brady said.

"Absolutely."

Raimes rounded his desk to put in the order using his phone's intercom system. The same young man who'd greeted him in the lobby brought the chilled water bottles and napkins along with a bowl of fresh fruit and toothpicks. Brady thanked him and snagged a strawberry.

"Now," Raimes said, seating himself on the couch. "What can I do for you?"

"Mr. Raimes," Brady said, "are you aware that your office building on Charter Street was being used by known felons?"

The man sighed. "No. I mean, of course, I got the call from the police telling me what had happened, but that building . . ." He shook his head. "I bought it a few years ago when I thought the area was going to make a comeback. Unfortunately, it didn't. I was losing money on the place, sank some cash into it, and rented it out."

"Who's the tenant?"

He stood and raked a hand down the side of his perfectly combed hair. "A man by the name of Hudson. Grant Hudson. I pulled his file last night." He opened it. "We rented the building to him last year. He requested to do some renovations, and I told him as long as he would return it to the original layout when he left, that was fine."

"Did you ever inspect it?"

"No. He paid his rent on time on the first or second of each month and I've never had an issue with him."

"Sounds like a dream tenant."

"You could say that. He called us when the air-conditioning went out shortly after they moved in, and I sent a crew out to fix it. Since then, it's been quiet."

"Do you have a picture of this guy?"

Raimes shook his head. "Sorry, I've never met him."

"Do you mind if I look him up real quick?"

"Help yourself." Raimes grabbed several toothpicks and downed half a dozen pieces of fruit while Brady opened the software on his phone that would allow him access to the department's driver's license database. "What's the home address?"

"47 Parkside Drive," Raimes read in between bites of fruit.

Brady found him. And recognized him. It was Emily's Snake Man.

Brady stood and handed Raimes a card. "Thanks for your time. If you think of anything else, will you give me a call?"

"Of course."

"Thanks again. I appreciate the information."

"Anytime."

Brady shook the man's hand and headed for the door even as he wondered how things were going with Linc and Derek escorting Emily to the safe house.

# 17

Emily hadn't been expecting the safe house to be so nice. The two-story traditional home boasted a large screened-in porch attached to a wooden deck off the back. The yard sloped down to the covered dock that held a pontoon boat.

After dropping her bag and laptop on the bed in her room, she walked out onto the porch and settled in the swing. She had every intention of getting on the laptop soon, but for now, she needed to breathe—and probably pray—before digging into the mire of a human trafficker's financial dirt. *I don't understand, God. Why did you take her?* She swallowed and closed her eyes. *Help me to not become bitter. I don't want to hate. But I do right now . . . very much. I need you to hold on to me—*

"How are you holding up?" Brady asked.

She looked up from her spot on the porch swing. Brady stood in the doorway leading into the den, leaning against the doorjamb.

"I'm all right," she said.

"Liar."

"I know." She drew in a deep breath and looked out over the lake. "You love the water, don't you?"

"I do. I try to spend as much time on—or in—it as I can. It's good for my mental state."

"I can see why. It's so peaceful here, so calm. And yet, I can't seem to settle my nerves. It's just hard to believe someone killed Heather—and wants to kill me."

He settled into the swing beside her and wrapped an arm around her. "I'm not going to let them get to you. I've called in a few favors. There are only a select few who know we're using this place. I've asked for round-the-clock protection. There are security cameras all over the place that are being monitored 24/7."

"I know you'll do your best to protect me, but eventually, I'm going to have to stick my head up. I can't hide forever and your two-week vacation will end and you'll have to go back to work." Without thinking about it, she let her head rest on his shoulder. When she realized what she'd done, she froze. And forced her muscles to relax. "You smell good." Woodsy with a hint of soap and a little smoky from the fire inside. And uniquely him.

His chuckle rumbled in her ear. "Thank you." A slight pause. "And you *are* my work," he said. "Besides, I've got so much vacation time built up, I could take six weeks without hardly putting a dent in it." He paused again. "Emily?"

"Hmm?" She could easily fall asleep right here.

"Will you tell me about your scars?"

Peace fled. For a moment she didn't say anything as she debated the wisdom of opening that can of worms. The more she let him in, the more it was going to hurt when she had to say goodbye. Because once he knew about everything, he wouldn't ever look at her in the same way. And she wouldn't be able to bear the pity in his eyes. She hated pity. Sympathy, anger for what happened to her, outrage that her nemesis was never punished were all fine. But she couldn't stand pity.

"Em?"

"I don't know if I can."

He fell silent for a moment. "I wish you would trust me, but it's okay if you're not there yet."

Strangely enough, she found herself wishing she would trust him too. Maybe she should just tell him. Telling him now would be like ripping the bandage off fast. It would hurt, but would hurt less than if she continued to allow herself to care about him. Care what he thought about her. "There was an incident in high school that resulted in me getting pregnant."

His swiftly indrawn breath said she might have been a little too blunt. "Rape?" he asked, his voice hoarse.

She drew away from his warmth, immediately missing it, but she couldn't touch him and talk about it at the same time. "No. It was . . . consensual."

"You don't sound so sure."

"It was, but it took him some time to wear me down to agree to it. Needless to say, he finally won the bet."

"Bet?" His soft voice had a lethal edge to it.

She couldn't look at him. "I'll tell you, but it's such a cliché story, you'll wonder if I stole it from the plot of some stupid movie."

"Tell me anyway."

Tears gathered and she blinked them back. "I tell this story all the time to people who've been through lousy stuff," she whispered. "I don't know why it's so hard to tell you."

He lifted her chin and looked into her eyes. She studied him, seeing the concern there. The anger at what had happened to her.

"Is it real? Do you really care?"

He blinked and she realized she'd said the words out loud.

"It's real," he said softly. "I care about you, Emily."

"Why? You don't even know me."

"Because . . . I just do. And I know enough."

"Is it a savior complex? I mean, you've saved my life a few times. Not to offend you, but could it be you just feel responsible in your cop-ly, justice-for-all kind of thing?"

His eyes darkened, but he didn't immediately deny the possibility. Then he looked away. "I'm not offended. The truth is, I thought about that, and I'll admit, you're different than the kind of woman I tend to be interested in."

Wait a minute. Interested in how, exactly? She bit down on those words and instead asked, "Different how? Because I'm not a size 2 and blonde?"

He laughed, but the sound lacked humor. "Partly. I think they're mostly size 6s, though. And I only know that because I have three sisters."

"Yeah, I'm not even close to that one either."

He shrugged. "Doesn't matter."

"Of course it matters. It's always mattered." She glanced down at her hands, wondering if she could really trust him with her deepest hurt.

A hand covered hers. "I'm not talking physical differences. I'm talking about what's inside you. Your heart is different. There's a depth to you that I've . . . avoided with other women."

"Why?"

He cleared his throat. "Because if I don't get too emotionally involved, I won't get hurt . . ."

"I'm familiar with that one," she murmured.

". . . again."

Oh. "Who hurt you?"

"Her name was Krystal. Well, technically, *is* Krystal. She's not dead. She was someone I thought I could help and wound up wrong. Very, very wrong."

"What happened to her?"

"She's in prison."

"For what?"

"Murder."

"Whoa." She stared up at him.

"I know. Tell me about you, please."

He wasn't going to let it go. Tension threaded her shoulders even tighter. "Why?" she cried. "Why do you want to hear about my shame?" She stood. His grip tightened, but not so tight she couldn't pull away.

A heavy sigh left him. "It's not that I want to know about your shame. It's . . ."

"What?"

"Back at the cabin you asked me why I'm mad at God."

She stilled. "Yes."

"And it's because I feel like he failed me. And because I actually believe he's who he says he is, in my mind that means failure is not an option for him. It's obvious you suffered some trauma—even after listening to Heather's 911 call—and yet, you've managed to keep your faith. I want to know how you did that."

"Oh." She took her seat again and he settled her back against him. How did she explain it? "First, let me address pre–Heather's call," she said. "I never had faith until after the . . ." She paused. "Okay, trauma is a good word. Until after that."

"I see."

"My family was really dysfunctional. Abusive father, mother with no backbone who waffled between resenting my very existence and smothering me with rules because she 'loved' me." She shrugged. "You can probably fill in the blanks. I'm an only child. I didn't even have a sibling to love."

"Wait, what about Sophia?"

She hesitated. "I left shortly after she came along." With a shaky hand, she rubbed her eyes and pictured herself back at the center where she volunteered weekly and pulled the words from her soul. "I wasn't exactly the popular girl in school. I was overweight—more so than I am now—and I had extreme self-confidence issues. However, my senior year, I managed to lose a good bit of weight and I was actually starting to feel good about myself. I wasn't a size 2 or even a size 6, but I was eating better and exercising. Jeremy Hightower was one of the guys everyone liked—you know the type, the star athlete who had the eye of the college recruiters, pretty girls stumbling over themselves for his attention. He started paying attention to me, but I brushed him off, certain it was some kind of joke. I kept waiting for the other shoe to fall. And it never did. After two months, he was still being nice, still walking with me in the halls, still coming to my house to study, and still defending me to his friends when they made fun of me." She swallowed. "Slowly, he gained my trust, and when he kissed me, I was lost. That teenager who felt ugly and unloved was being kissed by the guy every girl wanted. It wasn't long after that, that I gave him what he asked for."

"Sex?"

"Hmm." She nodded. "One time in his parents' barn. Literally, a roll in the hay." She swallowed again, the remembered shame washing over her. "And when it was all said and done, he stood up, kicked me in the ribs, and ranted at the time and energy I'd made him waste getting to that point." She watched him. Looking for signs of disgust or pity.

All she saw was an instant blazing rage that looked ready to be unleashed. On her behalf. The sight brought tears. Once again, she forced them back and looked away. "He made sure that I understood just how disgusted he was every time he had to hold my hand or be in my presence." Tears dripped from her chin and a gentle hand swiped them away. She barely noticed. "His best friend stepped out from behind one of the stalls and congratulated him on his win." At his sharply indrawn breath, she shuddered. "Every time I think about it, I remember how gullible and stupid I was." She grimaced. "It's not exactly a great feeling. I . . . uh . . . pretty much hated myself at that point. And that's when I started eating everything in sight—and cutting." She pushed her sleeves up and he ran a finger over the white scars crisscrossing one another. His touch eased something inside of her and the words came easier. "After a few years of therapy, we figured out that I fell in love with food at a young age because food never betrayed me, it made me feel happy and it was always there for me. In the end, it was one of the biggest betrayals of all. It made me fat and vulnerable to the cruelty of others. Although, now I realize I can't blame food, I can only blame my choices."

"I'm so, so sorry, Emily. I can't imagine the strength it took to survive that."

When she finally looked back at him, his red-rimmed eyes stilled her. Was he crying? For her? He looked away before she could decide for sure.

"I wasn't strong. I thought about suicide every day, but in the end decided that was too easy."

"Too easy?"

She nodded. "I deserved to suffer for being such an idiot. Thankfully, that was my senior year and I only had to walk those halls for a couple more months before graduation. Don't get me wrong. Those two months were awful. I thought about quitting, but something inside me wouldn't let him take that from me too. He'd taken everything, including what little self-respect I had. I was going to get my diploma no matter what. And I did."

For a moment he was silent. Then he wrapped her in a hug. "He was a psychopath."

"Maybe." She leaned into his embrace, relishing the comfort, stunned he hadn't run from her in disgust.

"I think you're one of the bravest people I've ever met."

"I'm not brave," she said. "I'm just too stubborn to quit."

"So, what turned you around? It's obvious you're a completely different person than the traumatized teenager you once were." He tilted her chin, and wonder of wonders, there was no pity in his gaze. Her throat spasmed. Could she dare believe it was admiration?

"My aunt Lucy," she said. "She's an amazing woman. She'd been through some hard times herself, and when I called her in desperation to tell her what was going on, that I was pregnant, she stepped in, convinced me I could do this, and that she would be there for me."

"Why didn't you have an abortion?" She gaped and he held up a hand. "I'm not saying that I believe that's what you should have done, I'm just asking why not?"

"Of course I thought about it." She looked away for a moment.

"But I couldn't bring myself to do it. Having that baby was part of my punishment, I suppose, is the way I looked at it. Giving that baby up? Well, that almost killed me."

"What do you mean?"

"Once the baby was born, I went a little crazy. I just couldn't deal with the pain of giving my child away, but I also knew there was no way I could raise her. My father was livid, drinking more than ever, hitting anyone that got too close. He told me to get out, to take the kid and go, that he wasn't raising another brat." Emily drew in a deep breath. Should she go on?

"And?"

"For the first time, my mother stepped in and said she wasn't giving up her grandchild. My father punched her and just started beating her. I was afraid he was going to kill her, so I called 911. There must have been a police car nearby because it was there in less than thirty seconds. By this point, my mother had run out of the house. I was holding the baby and my father was going after Mom. He had a gun and was screaming that he was going to kill everyone."

"Let me guess. The cops shot him."

Emily nodded. "He refused to put the weapon down. He turned the gun on me and they shot him. Three or four times. He died instantly, they said."

"I'm sorry, Emily. I know I keep saying that, but I am."

"I know. And I won't say it's okay, but I've healed a lot from that night. I don't know that I'll ever fully be able to put it out of my mind, but I'm better." She smiled. "So much better." And each time she helped a young girl see that her life wasn't over because of a trauma, it healed another piece in Emily's heart. "My dad made his choices. His death is no one's responsibility but his own. My mother's never forgiven me for that night, though."

"She blames you for your father's death."

"Yes. But, honestly, I'd go back and do it all over again if I had to."

"What happened after that?"

"I remember walking back into the house and looking down at that baby's sweet little face and thinking how she deserved so much more than me." She sighed. "So, when my mom told me to get out, I left. And wound up living on the streets. I was there for a little over a year before Aunt Lucy tracked me down and talked me into coming home with her. She got me back into counseling and convinced me that I could rebuild my life." She paused. "She fought for me. For the first time in my life, someone made me feel like I was worth something. That God had a plan for me and I could walk tall and be proud of who he'd created me to be."

"I love your aunt Lucy."

A laugh escaped her and she marveled at it. "I do too."

"Emily?"

"Yes?"

"Is Sophia really your sister?"

A hiccupping sound that was a cross between a sob and a laugh escaped her. "No."

"I didn't think so."

They fell silent. "God seemed distant," she finally said. "Like someone who only cared about good people but couldn't be bothered with people who didn't measure up. With people who messed up their lives so catastrophically. But Aunt Lucy was able to help me understand that everyone needs him. He's not sitting up there waiting to crack the whip if we mess up, but rather he's waiting for us to run into his arms and be comforted. I never had a dad like that, so it was really hard for me to wrap my head around the idea of it, even as much as I wanted to."

"I can understand that."

"But Aunt Lucy was like that, loving, accepting, and so eager to help me heal. When I finally put two and two together and realized her heart was like God's, it was easier to accept that he truly cared about me and wanted to be the father I never really had."

"She sounds extraordinary."

"She is."

"Where does she live?"

"Not too far from here. She's in Franklin, Georgia. When she's home. Right now, she's on a twenty-eight-day cruise around Europe with some ladies from her church. They've been planning and saving for this for two years."

He gave a low whistle. "Nice."

"Indeed. And she's safe. I don't have to worry about someone trying to get her to get to me."

"So, what do you do to decompress? When the memories crash in and you can't sleep?"

"I work."

He laughed. "We're a lot alike, Emily Chastain."

"Is that what you do? Work?"

"Yes. And dive." He drew in a breath and leaned back, pulling her with him. "It's so peaceful down there. Not exactly quiet, but sometimes you can hear your heartbeat in your ears and you can just be you. No obligations, no worries. Nothing."

"Sounds lovely."

"It is. Especially in the Caribbean. But the lake has its positives too."

She tilted her head up to look at him from beneath her lashes. "I've always wanted to go diving. It looks so exotic."

"It can be."

"So let's go sometime."

---

Brady grinned. "I was hoping you'd feel that way. That was one of the reasons I requested this particular safe house. Fortunately, I have all the equipment in my truck."

"Wait. What? Go diving? Here? Now?"

"Sure."

"Is that safe? What if there's a sniper or something out there?"

"Already thought about that. We'll go down and come up under cover of the dock, the boathouse, or the boat. Inside the boathouse, there's a shallow point near the entrance. It would be perfect for a lesson or two. Then from there we can go under the dock and out into the deeper part of the lake with no one knowing we're under—or when we come up."

She swallowed and frowned. "Uh . . . no . . . never mind. It was a stupid idea."

"No, it's a great idea."

"I . . . I don't have a bathing suit or anything. I can't exactly wear my jeans. I'd freeze. And sink."

"You don't have to worry about that. I came prepared. I had Mary Beth bring a dry suit with her."

"The Mary Beth who's part of the security around here? Uh . . . no. I'll pass, thanks."

Her eyes slid away from his. Tension ran through every part of her body. What was the problem?

She stood. "I think I'm going to get my laptop and see if I can't start gathering the information into some kind of coherent organization so we can share it with the investigative team ready to jump on whatever this is."

He frowned. "Emily—"

She shot him a tight smile. "I'll be in my bedroom. Thanks for not judging me."

"I wouldn't. What happened to you was horrible and . . . and . . . well, there aren't words for it. And it was in no way your fault. But I don't understand why you're running away from me now."

"I'm not running. I'm going to be productive. Sitting here whining about my past isn't going to find Heather's killer and stop a possible human trafficking ring. And that's where I need my focus to be. Where *we* need *our* focus to be."

"It is, I promise."

"Good." She walked away from him without looking back.

Mary Beth stepped out onto the porch, hands in the pockets of the hoodie she hadn't taken off since she'd gotten there. "Everything okay?" she asked.

Brady studied the woman in front of him. Cheerleader pretty, tall, and built like a model. Realization hit him. He closed his eyes. "No, I'm an idiot."

She lifted a brow. "You're a man. That's a given."

"Ouch."

"Aw, I'm just kidding. You're one of the rare ones. You're not an idiot, but I'm guessing you did something dumb. What was it?"

"You know how I told you to bring that dry suit?"

"Yeah."

He grimaced. "Well, Emily shared some stuff with me." No way was he saying what and betraying her confidence. "And she mentioned going diving. I told her I'd take her and said she could use the dry suit you brought. Only I didn't say that it was a larger size than the one you wore. That the one you'd brought was an extra. And I think . . . well . . ." He cleared his throat. "I . . . um . . . guess that she thought I meant she could wear yours, and it embarrassed her because obviously you wear a smaller size than she would and . . ." He waved a hand and covered his eyes. "And I'm an idiot."

"Wow."

"Go ahead," he muttered behind his hand. "Tell me what an insensitive louse I am. I can take it."

"You're not a louse, Brady. But I can see why she'd be offended if she's at all sensitive about her weight. So just go apologize to her and tell her if she wants to dive with you, there's a suit that will fit her. When you described her in your text, I couldn't figure out exactly which size to bring, so I brought three. One will fit."

He stood and hugged her. "You're the best."

"I know." She gave him a light shove toward Emily's door. "Now, go grovel."

Brady mentally rehearsed his apology as he walked back into the house, down the hall, and to Emily's door. He raised a hand to knock just as it swung inward.

Emily gasped and stepped back, placing a hand over her heart. "Oh goodness, you scared me."

"Sorry." He shifted, his mind blank, all of his rehearsing for naught. "I . . . uh . . . I came to apologize."

She frowned. "For what?"

"For not explaining that there's a dry suit that will fit you. Mary Beth brought three and said one of them will work for you." He dipped his head and looked at her through his lashes. "That is, if you'll still consider going."

She swallowed and looked away. "I'm working, but thanks for clarifying that you didn't expect me to squeeze into one of Mary Beth's suits." He sighed and she pinched the bridge of her nose. "I'm sorry I'm so touchy. Talking about my past always brings out the worst in me."

"It's okay. Why don't you bring your computer into the kitchen and we'll sit at the table and see what you've got from Heather?"

Her shoulders relaxed. "Sure, I can do that." She grabbed the laptop off the bed and followed him into the kitchen. "I need a water. You want one?"

"That'd be great."

She snagged two and settled herself at the table. "I was getting ready to work when I decided I needed something to drink—and found you outside my door."

"I'm really sorry I was so thoughtless—in the effort to be thoughtful." He sighed. "I'm not helping, am I?"

"Forget it. It's fine. I need to learn not to be overly sensitive." She opened the laptop and he dropped the subject even though her shoulders had tensed up again. "Okay," she said, "before I was snatched, I was updating the list of deposits made, the branch it was made at, and the times they were—" She gasped.

"What is it?" he asked.

"Text messages from Heather. They just popped up when I opened my iMessages."

# 18

Todd Cavendish threw the phone onto the desk and stood to pace the length of the spacious office. "There's got to be a way to find that boat," he said. "If someone stumbles across it, everything we've worked for is ruined."

The other man in the wingback chair opposite the desk rubbed his chin. "I know, but we've exhausted every option. If you have any other suggestions, I'm ready to act."

"I'm thinking on it. I've got several ideas I'm weighing. We need the Chastain woman, Jeff. She's our only hope."

"We *had* the Chastain woman. My mole got the information for you as to where she'd be, but you jumped into grabbing her way too fast." His friend scowled. "That plan wasn't well thought out at all."

"That was my plan," he said.

"I know that," Jeff said. "I'm just expressing my opinion."

"Well, keep it to yourself," he snapped.

"Since when do I keep what I think to myself? We've been friends since childhood and you've never minded me telling you like it is."

He groaned. Jeff was right. On both counts. It had been a lousy, impromptu plan. And, he grudgingly admitted, he always wanted the man in the chair to speak his mind. "Whatever."

"'Whatever' is right. Anyway, she's got so much protection around her, it'll take an army to get to her. Her mother and sister are in protective custody as well." He paused. "And I don't think Emily knows where the boat is."

"What's ironic is that my brother doesn't know either and he's the one who stole it—or had it stolen. I'm sure he didn't do it himself."

"A fact he probably regrets at the moment," Jeff said. He tapped his chin. "It's possible that he knows what lake."

"Maybe. I'm not sure about that either," Todd said. "Just keep someone following him. Eventually, he'll send someone out there to search for it."

"He knows you've got people watching. He's not going to make any move that would lead you to it."

"True. And he's got people watching me." A pause. "Which is how he knew Reuben passed the flash drive off to me." He shook his head. "I don't care about that. What I care about is, somehow that woman managed to outsmart our guys. Five of our best men." He held up five fingers as though he needed a visual of the number. "Two of whom are dead, two headed for prison, and one in the wind. It's the two in prison who worry me."

"They're so low on the food chain it doesn't matter. They were simply guns for hire and don't know who hired them, so it's not like they have any information to offer. And Hudson will show up when the coast is clear."

"Hudson's okay," Todd said. "He knows how to keep his mouth shut. I'm not worried about him, but I'd feel better if the other two were dead."

Jeff shrugged. "I'd feel better if your brother was dead."

"No. I don't want him dead. I want him to suffer. And the only way to make him do that is to get that flash drive." He traced the scar he wore from temple to chin and scowled. "We have a traitor in our midst. Someone helped my brother steal that boat. I want to know who it was."

"Trust me, I do too," Jeff said. "And I'm working on it, but I've got to tell you, our traitor could be just about anyone on the payroll. You don't exactly hire the squeaky-clean ones known for their loyalty."

Todd rubbed his eyes and swiped a hand down his scar once more. "Fine. Then we're going to have to cut out the middlemen and take care of this ourselves."

"What do you have in mind?"

---

Emily leaned in and watched as the pictures continued to load. "They're of a lake," she said. "And look! A picture of a boat called the *Lady Marie*. That's what they were after."

Brady raked a hand through his hair. "Can you zoom in and get the number off the side? We can figure out who it belongs to with that."

She tapped the picture and zoomed in. "SC-0123-BZ."

"Great. That means it's registered in South Carolina."

"Shouldn't be too hard to find who it belongs to, then, right?"

"One can hope. Can you send me that one with the boat to my phone? I can forward it to David and see if he can pull the owner's name and where the picture was taken. If Heather didn't turn off her geotag option, we'll be able to get GPS coordinates and know exactly where this boat is—or *was* since you said it sank. At least I think that'll work."

"It's worth a try." She clicked a few keys. "There. You should have it now. But I can figure out where the pictures were taken. Maybe." She clicked the keys while Brady sent the picture to David.

Emily continued to scroll through the images.

"It looks like she's a good distance away," Brady said. "It's hard to make out much."

"She probably took them with her phone."

"We can try to run some of these through facial recognition.

How many different people would you say are there?" He leaned forward to squint at the screen.

"All I see are four. Two at the front and two at the back—or at the bow and stern, I suppose I should say. I guess there could be more inside." Emily leaned back and palmed her weary eyes. "They knew about these pictures. That's why they killed her."

"And broke into her apartment. Probably looking for her laptop."

Emily opened the picture in the preview option and worked her way through the short steps to pull up the GPS coordinates. And got . . . nothing. She let out a groan. "She had the geotag option turned off."

"All right. We'll send everything to David. He's got way more advanced equipment and know-how than we do. If there's any information on there, he'll find it, as well as run those four through facial recognition. I think that might be a long shot, but it's worth a try."

She sent all the pictures to Brady and he sent them on to David.

"Which lake is this?" she muttered. "This is what they wanted. This is why they're after me. They knew she sent me these." Her voice rose. "But how? How would they even know to go looking for her? How would they know about the pictures?"

He shook his head. "I don't know unless she showed them to the wrong person. Or someone spotted her taking them."

She frowned. "Heather's phone was password protected. How would they get into it?"

"She was on it during the 911 call, so it was probably open when she was attacked."

"And all her attacker had to do was pick it up and start scrolling. I suppose that's when he realized that I might know something about all this and came after me."

"Yep."

"But they don't know the location of the lake," Emily said. "When Snake Man questioned me, he wanted to know which lake the boat went down on and was furious when I couldn't tell him. Do you know where this is?"

"No, it could be anywhere, but it's probably in South Carolina if the boat decal is anything to go by. David will find it."

Emily studied the area in the background. "It doesn't look familiar. And yet, it's like I've seen it every time I've ever gone to the lake." She paused. "Heather has a professional camera. She's rarely without it and only uses her phone as a backup, but she's a fabulous photographer and the paper often uses her photos to go along with her stories. If she took these with her phone, it's very possible she had her other camera with her and got better pictures. If we could find the camera or at least the SD card, it's also possible the geotag would be on those."

"Okay." Brady raised a brow. "That's good thinking."

"Maybe. Unfortunately, I don't know where the camera is. I mean, she kept it in the bottom left drawer in the desk in her office at her apartment or at work. Or in whatever bag she was carrying."

"I'll ask Derek and Linc to go check out her apartment again."

"Okay. But before you send them, let me call her boss and ask him to check the drawer of her desk."

"Do that." He handed her a phone she hadn't seen before. "Use that one. It's not traceable."

Emily dialed the paper's main number and asked for Trent Caswell.

"Caswell."

"Hi, Mr. Caswell, this is Emily, Heather's friend."

"Emily! Have they found Heather yet?"

She swallowed. "No, sir."

"The police have been by questioning everyone. Several people saw her leave that night, but no one else was in the garage when she was attacked. Do you know what she was working on? She wouldn't say a word, just that I was going to go through the roof when she turned in her story."

"Yes, sir, I know what it was."

He fell silent for a moment. "So, she really was working on something big?"

"Yes."

"And you're not going to tell me."

"No, sir, not right now."

"All right, what can I do to help find her?"

"I just need to know if her good Nikon is in the bottom of her desk drawer. You know where she keeps it."

"Hold on a sec."

Emily bit her lip while he checked, praying it would be there. When he came back on the line, she held her breath.

"Not there, Emily, sorry."

Her lungs released the air. "Ugh. Okay, thanks."

"Can you keep me updated? We're all very concerned."

"Of course."

"And . . . I don't want to sound crass, but . . ."

His hesitancy lifted her brow. "But you want the exclusive when all of this is resolved?"

"Yes."

She tried not to resent the man. This was his job. He had to ask. Heather would have done the same thing. It didn't mean he didn't care or have a heart. "Yes, I'm sure Heather would want it that way."

His sigh of relief was subtle, but she heard it. "Thank you, Emily. I really do want to honor Heather in this."

"So do I." She choked on the words, her emotions high. She cleared her throat. "Thanks, Mr. Caswell." She hung up and turned to Brady. "I guess we need Derek and Linc to go by Heather's apartment after all."

He nodded. "Let me call them."

"Tell them we'll be waiting—and not patiently."

He quirked a sympathetic smile, then stood and stepped out

onto the porch to make the call. Emily looked up to find Mary Beth watching, hands wrapped around a coffee mug, her perfectly proportioned body relaxed as she leaned against the doorjamb. Emily swallowed her immediate surge of jealousy and wondered why she was suddenly battling feelings she thought she'd left in the past. Feelings like insecurity and shame. *I am loved. I am God's. I am made in his image and I will not feel ashamed.* She straightened her shoulders and let the words wash over her. She'd come a long way, and she wasn't going to revisit those issues. Right now, anyway. She forced a smile. "Hi."

"It's chilly out there, but not too bad," the woman said. "Weather's actually perfect for a dive."

"Yes. It's lovely today." She could do small talk with the best of them. "You're on the team?"

"I am."

"What's it like?"

"One big family." She took another sip of the coffee and lowered herself into a chair across from Emily. "Notice I didn't say 'happy family.'"

"You don't like it?"

Mary Beth raised a brow. "Are you kidding? I love it. But out of the twenty-four dive team members, there are four women. I've been out on too many calls to count and have only ended up with another female twice."

"Ah, I get it. Working in a male environment can be intense?"

"To say the least. Especially if the guys try to treat me as anything other than an equal when we're in the water. Out of the water, they'd better treat me with the respect I deserve simply because I'm a woman." She smiled. "Honestly, it's like having a bunch of older brothers. There's no denying, they're mostly great guys, but . . . they're big teases too, so I'm constantly on my guard."

"I don't know what it's like to have big brothers, just a little sister." And she really didn't even know what that was like.

"It's great and awful all rolled into one." She sighed. "But I wouldn't trade it for anything. I know that if I ever needed anything, I could call one of them and they'd be right there to help no matter what."

Emily nodded. "I can see that. Brady didn't even know me and he jumped in to help. Literally jumped in the lake. Then Derek and Linc and you . . ." Tears burned behind her eyes, but she pushed a smile to her lips. "I really appreciate it."

"You're welcome. And you're surrounded by a bunch of cops. You're safe."

"I *feel* safe. Thank you for that."

"Sure." She paused. "I put the dive stuff on your bed. Because it's cold, you'll be using a dry suit. There's a fleece one-piece uni-style layer to go under the suit. Special socks are there too. You can pull on another layer of clothes if you want, but the dry suit is Gortex and should keep you warm enough with the fleece underlayer."

Emily straightened and ran her hands down her thighs. Diving sounded fun. Diving with Brady sounded like an exciting adventure. A way to forget her grief and sorrow, fear and anger if only for a brief moment. "I'll take a look at it. Try it on. But do me a favor?"

"Sure."

"Don't tell Brady. If it doesn't fit . . ." She shrugged and glanced away from the pretty woman.

"Of course. I'll leave all that up to you." She paused. "I don't think I've ever known Brady to take anyone diving with him. You must be pretty special."

Emily flushed and gave a small laugh. "He hasn't known me very long. I can't be that special."

"Hmm." Mary Beth flashed her picture-perfect smile, then tilted her head. "You really have no idea how beautiful you are, do you?"

Emily blinked. "What?"

"Not just physically, but you have a sweetness—a goodness—about you that's magnetic. I hope you're able to see it someday.

Now"—she finished off the coffee—"I've got a perimeter to walk. See you in a bit."

She left and Emily realized her jaw was swinging. Who did Mary Beth think she was? "Of all the nerve . . ." *"You really have no idea how beautiful you are, do you?"* With a huff, Emily stomped back to her room and found the dry suit exactly where Mary Beth had said it would be. *"I hope you're able to see it someday."* "Really?"

She turned to the full-length mirror and studied herself with a critical eye. She had to admit, the short hairstyle flattered her face, making her eyes look large. Expressive. Even without makeup, her lashes were thick and when she smiled, twin dimples appeared. She tried to look beyond that, to her heart. To what made her uniquely her. She genuinely cared about others—especially hurting teens—and was always looking for ways to help. She did her best to do a good job, have integrity, and treat others the way she wanted to be treated. And she wanted more than anything to have a heart like God's.

As she continued to examine her reflection, for just a moment, she thought she could see what Mary Beth was talking about.

Footsteps sounded behind her and she turned to see Brady walking toward her. He stopped in the open door and nodded to the dry suit. "You thinking about it?"

"Thinking. I'll let you know when I've decided."

"That's fine. Izzy and Jordan have asked Linc to step up and help out since he's kind of been unofficially helping anyway."

"Okay."

"Derek's decided he's not going to be left out, so they're all headed to Heather's apartment to see if they can find the camera or her laptop. They promised to call as soon as they know anything."

She nodded and sighed. "So . . . now we wait?"

"Now we wait. And dive?"

"You're persistent, aren't you?"

"Mom calls it the St. John stubborn gene."

Emily drew in a deep breath. She took another look at the dry suit, then let her gaze slide back to the man in the door. The man who'd saved her life. And listened to her story without judging her. Part of it anyway.

Did she really want to do this?

Another glance at the man waiting patiently for her to make up her mind. Yeah. She really did.

---

Inside the boathouse bathroom, Emily changed into the one-piece fleece and pulled the dry suit over it. She refused to look in the mirror of the small changing room. She placed her hand on the knob, took in a deep breath, and as she stepped out she found Brady waiting on her. When he turned his gaze on her, her gut tightened and she waited for the flicker of disgust or disinterest. But his eyes warmed. "You have the most gorgeous eyes I think I've ever seen. What color are they anyway?"

For a moment, Emily could only stand there and gape. Then she snapped her mouth shut. "I . . . um . . . honestly don't know. Purple? Violet?"

"Amethyst."

"Okay, um . . . I guess that works." She offered him a small smile. "Thanks."

"You're welcome."

He continued to stare into her eyes until she wanted to fidget. "So . . . the gear?"

"Oh. Right. Mary Beth is going to act as our tender."

"Our what?"

"Tender. Every diver needs a tender. Only her responsibilities won't be quite as stressful on this dive. Basically, she's just going to make sure all goes well for us in the water."

"Everything going well in the water would be the best way for this to go."

"Exactly. She'll be here in a few minutes to get the boat ready."
His gaze turned clinical. "While we wait on her, let me just check
to make sure the cuffs are tight enough around your wrists. We
don't want water leaking in and freezing you."

His warm hand took hers and he examined the closures at her
wrists, making sure they met with his approval. "We're going to
start here in this nice shelter while I walk you through the basics."

"He liked to scuba dive."

"Who?"

"Jeremy Hightower. He used to go all the time. He told me I'd
sink like a rock if I ever tried."

"I'd really like to punch that guy in the mouth. Obviously he
had some serious issues. But listen to me. You can do this, Emily."
He snagged her gaze and gave her a gentle smile.

Her heart wanted to puddle right into the special socks she wore.
Instead of letting it, she straightened her shoulders and vowed to
have a blast with this man she couldn't seem to help caring about
more and more, minute by minute. Jeremy had no hold over her
anymore. And she was going to prove it. "You're absolutely right.
I can do this. So? Let's do it."

"Whoa, not so fast." He laughed. "First, you have to learn
about your equipment."

"Oh. Right. Teach me."

"This is your BCD vest."

"Uh-huh. My what?"

"Your buoyancy control device."

"I have a good idea what that means, but just clarify it."

"It's exactly what you're thinking. It helps you control how deep
you go. And when you're ready to surface, it helps bring you up."

"Yep, that's pretty much what I was thinking. That's the really
simple version, isn't it?" She slipped her arms into it and fastened it.

"Yes, ma'am, but it's just as accurate as the convoluted one."

Once she had the belt snapped on, he pulled a hood over her

head and helped her tuck her hair under. "Now, you're luckier than most. We're going to be able to talk to each other underwater instead of having to use hand signals."

"How so?"

Emily listened intently as he explained about the special Kirby Morgan helmet, how to defog her lens, and so on. "This is the oral nasal mask," he said. "It holds the microphone."

"Right."

"Ready to try it on?"

"I'm ready."

He helped her get the helmet situated and gave her a thumbs-up. He pulled on a matching helmet. "All good?"

She jumped when his voice came through loud and clear. "Yes. How?"

"You've got earphones in that thing."

Well, duh. "I just didn't notice them."

"They're kind of hidden. So you feel all right?"

"Weird, but okay."

He finished his equipment explanation and held out a hand. "You ready to give it a try?"

"I . . . um . . . yes. Okay."

He grabbed their flippers and led her to the shallow water at the entrance of the boathouse that would allow them to remain protected from any prying eyes or snipers. "We're going to ease in and get you used to the feel, okay?"

"Right."

She pulled the flippers on while he held her steady and then waited for him to do the same. Once she had the tank on her back, she pictured the surrounding area. Officers with weapons discreetly ready if needed. They would be watching for any approaches to the house. Two worked in the yard, their landscaping truck parked off to the side. On the lake, two officers fished while scanning the opposite side of the landscape. Guilt tried to creep in. Using the department's resources like this angered her. Not that she considered the protection a waste or that she wasn't worth protecting, but still . . . they should be out answering other calls, not stuck here because some lunatic wanted to kill her.

He held out a hand. "Put it out of your mind."

"What?"

"Whatever you're thinking. Put it out of your mind."

"I thought I told you to stop doing that." Her voice held no heat and he smiled. "This is a lot of gear," she said. "And heavy. Heavier than I thought it would be."

"This is nothing. You should see what we use when we go out on a call. You'll be fine once we get you in the water. Come on."

She looked at the flippers. "How do you walk in these things?"

"Like a duck or a penguin trying to march. Knee high, heel first."

A duck or a penguin. Just the image she wanted him to have in his head. Lovely. "Seriously, Brady?"

He laughed and led her into the water. Granted, neither one of them was very graceful, but they made it into chest-deep water before he stopped her. "Okay, let's practice going under and breathing. Sometimes people find it weird to be underwater and breathe at the same time. Our first instinct is to hold our breath."

"Okay."

"So don't do that. Just breathe."

"Right. Just breathe. Got it."

Facing her, he held her hands and lowered them beneath the surface. Emily made a point not to hold her breath but found he was right. It took effort to pull in a breath. But she did it. The next thing she noticed was how she immediately felt lighter. Weightless in the water. It was a glorious sensation.

"I know. It's great, isn't it?"

She gasped at the sound of his voice right in her ears again. Then laughed. "Stop doing that!"

"What?"

"Reading my mind. But, yes, it's amazing."

"You like it?"

"Yes!"

"Then let's head into deeper water. Mary Beth, you there?"

"I'm here."

Her words came through Emily's headphones as well. She made a mental note not to say anything she didn't want the woman to hear.

"Mary Beth's going to stay near us in the boat," Brady said. "We'll attach a line to our suits."

"A line?"

"Yep. It can get murky down there if we stir up a lot of sand, and I'm not taking a chance on losing you."

"The line sounds like a fabulous idea."

He gave a low chuckle. "When we're finished, we'll come back to the boathouse."

"Awesome."

With the line hooked to her, she felt safe enough to let go of her initial fears and hesitation. "It's so beautiful . . . and creepy. All at the same time."

His chuckle caressed her ear and she shivered. "I know."

The deeper they went, the more the water cleared. Fish brushed past her.

"Wanna go deeper?" he asked.

"Yes."

"If your ears start hurting, let me know. We'll take it slow." Still holding her hand, he kicked and took them down a few more feet. He glanced at the device on his wrist. "We're about twenty feet down. This isn't the really deep part."

She pointed. "Trees?"

"Yes. Look at the algae draping over them."

"Wow. This is amazing. I can't look at everything fast enough."

"Take your time."

She kicked, the weightless feeling making her bold. Actually, it was probably more the fact that Brady was right beside her that allowed her the freedom to enjoy the dive so much. "Is that a sink? A kitchen sink?"

"Yeah. Don't be surprised at what you see. When we do training exercises, we never know what we're going to come across."

An hour later they surfaced after a safety stop about ten feet from the top, and Mary Beth helped them into the boat under cover of the canopy. With the fabric sides attached, no one could see inside and wouldn't have any idea if they were still under the water or on the boat. She decided not to think about the fact that someone using a machine gun could easily take them all out. With cops patrolling the surrounding area as well as the water, she was going to believe that no one would be able to sneak past the security.

Emily let Brady help her pull off the helmet and drew in a deep breath. "That was fabulous. When can we do it again?"

Brady laughed.

"I think you've created a monster," Mary Beth said.

"We'll do it again soon," Brady said.

"Good." Emily drew in a deep breath. "I really needed that." She paused. "Do you think you could write down some of that stuff about dive times and ND . . . what?"

"NDL," Brady said. "Non-decompression limit. Meaning how long you can stay at what depth without worrying about decompression because of nitrogen build up."

"Right. I understand I should do a safety stop ten to twenty feet from the surface, but all of the facts and figures are running around in my brain."

He grinned. "Sure. I can't believe you've remembered as much as you have. I've had students on their fifth or sixth lesson before they actually understood about NDL and safety stops."

"I guess it's because I'm really interested. And more relaxed.

And I think I'm ready to get back to work on trying to figure out who's behind everything."

"Good," Mary Beth said, "because Derek and Linc are on the way back. Izzy and Jordan are with them as well."

Relaxation fled. "Did they find anything at Heather's?"

"An SD card under the refrigerator and some flash drives in a hidden area. One of the bricks on her fireplace was loose. She had them stuffed behind it."

"That's really cliché," Emily said. "But it sounds like Heather. And they're bringing everything here? Not to the station to David?"

"They talked about it," Mary Beth said, "but Derek decided he wanted to run the contents by you before taking it to David. It's safer for them to come out here than take you to the station."

"Okay. Let me get showered and changed and we'll see what's on the card."

## 19

Brady met his brothers along with Izzy and her partner, Jordan, in the kitchen. Derek held the card up. "Linc insisted on looking everywhere. Even to the point of moving the furniture and appliances. If it was movable, we moved it."

"And there it was," Linc said.

"Well," Izzy said, "we're not sure that it's *the* card, but it's the only one we found."

Jordan and Linc seated themselves at the table. "We also found a couple of flash drives behind a brick in the fireplace," Jordan said.

"We'll go through them all," Brady said.

"No laptop, though," Izzy said. "It wasn't at her place and no one's been able to locate it."

"Chances are, the person who trashed her home has it," Brady said. "Although, I suppose it's possible it could have been in the car with her. I wonder if we could access her cloud."

"If Emily has the password, it sure would make things easier," Linc said.

Mary Beth joined them and headed for the refrigerator. "Emily will be here in a second. She's trying to reach Heather's parents again."

"Before we get started on this," Linc said, "I've got video footage of Emily's kidnapping."

Brady stiffened. "We already saw that."

"It's from a different camera and a different angle."

"All right, let's take a look."

It didn't take Linc long to access it. "It's not a great angle, but it was the only other one we've got. All of the bank cameras that scanned the parking lot were expertly dismantled."

"Just like in the garage where Heather was attacked," Brady muttered.

"Yeah."

"Another indication that whoever killed—or took—Heather is after Emily. They scope their target, find the easiest place for a kidnapping, and then set it up to make it happen. Where did this footage come from?" Brady asked.

"From the toy store across the street," Jordan said. "It's a small camera with a minion cover that faces the area where Emily was parked."

"A what?"

"You know. That Disney movie *Despicable Me*—with the minions? Cute little yellow . . . um . . . *things*?" Jordan shrugged. "I only know about them because of my grandkids."

A smile played around the corner of Linc's lips. "The owner set it up as a display to show customers how it works. Fortunately for us, the two who snatched Emily didn't know about it."

"Fine. Let's see what it got."

Linc clicked the footage forward until Emily walked into the line of sight. "There. She comes out of the bank and down the steps. Heads down the sidewalk to her car." He paused the video and used the mouse to point on the screen. "See that shadow there?"

Brady saw him.

"He falls in behind her and the other one comes out of the

doorway of that restaurant." Linc clicked and the footage resumed playing. "There."

"I see him," Brady said. Unfortunately, facial recognition wouldn't help since the two had on ski masks. They closed in on their prey, and his heart picked up speed even though he knew what was going to happen.

A dark sedan pulled to a stop in the middle of the street. "Is that a Cadillac?" Brady asked.

Linc nodded. "Keep watching."

The two men in ski masks moved fast, grabbing her on either side. She fought them for a brief moment before she went slack. They dumped her in the trunk and sped off. Linc pointed to the time stamp. "Under six seconds from grab to go."

Jaw tight, anger pumping his blood in a rush, Brady sat for a moment. The strength of his reaction stunned him. If her kidnappers were in the room at this moment, he actually wondered if he'd have enough self-control to keep himself from pounding them to a pulp.

"She never saw it coming," Jordan said. Brady detected anger in the other detective's gravelly voice; however, the man's poker face didn't give anything away.

"One good thing," Linc said, "even though we can't see their faces, we do have this." He zoomed in on the license plate of the vehicle that held Emily. "I looked it up. Belongs to Martin Burnett."

"Our dead guy." Brady sat back with a disgusted growl. "We need to find that car."

"Already got a BOLO out on it," Izzy said.

"That's not the vehicle that Burnett was driving when he shot at us at the call center," Brady said.

Izzy nodded. "According to the DMV, he owns three cars. The one he was killed in, the one they used to snatch Emily—which is a very nice Cadillac, by the way—and a 1954 Chevrolet Bel Air convertible."

"That's not cheap," Brady said. "Guess the murder-for-hire business is paying well."

"As well as the trafficking business." Linc shook his head. "You want to wait on Emily or keep going?"

"Let's keep going. I'll fill her in later if I need to."

"All right. Annie couldn't find anything about a boat sinking on a South Carolina lake in the last two weeks, so if it really happened, there's no report of it."

"But I can see that happening," Jordan said. "If the boat was out in the middle of the lake and it sank sometime after dark, then it's quite possible there wouldn't be any witnesses."

Brady nodded to the laptop. "Let's start looking."

Emily stepped into the kitchen. "Not starting without me, are you?"

"Have a seat and we'll fill you in." Brady motioned to the chair next to him even as he noted her fresh appearance. She wore a long-sleeved oversized T-shirt and jeans, and he wondered if she ever wore short sleeves.

He introduced her to Jordan, then told her, in detail, what they'd seen. "You want to watch it?"

"No. Not unless you need me to." She shuddered.

"I don't see any reason you should."

"Good."

"Did you speak to Heather's parents?" he asked.

"Briefly." She took the bottle of water Mary Beth offered from across the table. "Heather's father answered the phone and we spoke for a minute before Mrs. Gilstrap called him away. They had a lot of family over, but he promised to get back to me when they had a minute."

"So, do you feel better?"

"Not really. I got some weird vibes from Mr. Gilstrap."

"Weird how?"

She shook her head. "I'm really not sure how to explain it."

She waved a hand. "I'll figure that out later. Let's see what you found."

Linc turned the computer over to Brady and handed him the SD card. Brady inserted it, then clicked to open it.

Emily settled in the chair next to him, tension radiating from her. He did his best to ignore the scent of her shampoo tickling his nose and focused on scrolling through the pictures.

Emily pointed. "Those are from the last vacation we took together."

"Nice. Which beach?"

"Hilton Head Island."

They went through every picture on the card and found nothing that could lead them to Heather—or the reason someone would attack her in the parking garage.

She sat back. "I can't believe there's nothing there."

"We found that under her refrigerator. She probably dropped it and didn't realize it. Might not have even missed it if she had the pictures on her laptop. Let's move to the flash drives," Brady said.

Linc handed them over.

They repeated the process. "Documents, stories she was working on, a few family pictures," Brady muttered.

"Read through the stories," Emily said. "Anything about human trafficking?"

For the next thirty minutes, they scanned until Brady shook his head. "Nothing." He rubbed his eyes.

Linc blew out a short breath. "All right. You said the boat sank, right?" he asked Emily.

"Yes. At least that's what they said when they were demanding answers from me."

"The date stamp on the pictures is from a week and a half ago," Linc said. "It also looks like the sun is going down, so it's probably around five thirty in the evening. If the boat actually sank, there could have been some casualties. If someone didn't come home that day or the next, there might be a missing person report."

Brady nodded. "And if there was something illegal going on, if there were any survivors, they might be keeping their mouths shut for fear of being implicated in whatever happened to make the boat sink."

"And in any deaths that may have resulted," Linc said. "If it actually sank."

"Right."

Emily rubbed her nose. "We need to find out who those people in the picture are."

"Hopefully, David will get back to us soon," Brady said.

"I'll put a request in on any missing person report during that time period," Izzy said.

"I'm going to get my laptop and see what else I can figure out," Emily said. "This is like a big puzzle. All of the pieces fit somehow, it's just going to take a lot of work to put it all together."

***

Emily sat in the living room with her laptop open and a notepad next to her. Peanut butter crackers and celery eased the gnawing in her stomach, but the food was simply for nourishment. She'd discovered fighting for her life had demoted food a few more steps on the priority list.

More than anything, she wanted to help figure out exactly what was going on and what Heather had been trying to tell her with the messages.

On the notepad, she wrote:

**Jeremy (J) visits Calvin at the bank. Connection?**

**J opens several different accounts (with different names, but trace back to him) with multiple high dollar amounts under ten thousand.**

Multiple withdrawals from the accounts from various ATMs all on J's accounts.

Heather tracked Martin Burnett—making the deposits. Part of a human trafficking ring?

Heather was at the lake and took pictures. Which lake? And what made her so interested in that boat?

Connection between Nicholas Raimes and Martin Burnett?

"What else? What else?" she whispered.

She paused, staring at her notes. She'd always been a list maker, finding great satisfaction in crossing things off as she finished each task. Not only that, she especially made lists when she was confused or needed to think things through.

The last list she'd made regarding her investigation had been on her desktop in her office in a Word document. One she'd simply minimized before leaving. What if someone saw it? But who? No one had access to her computer except her.

And the IT department. Or a really good hacker.

An email popped up from David.

Emily, these are the pictures Heather sent you. I've enhanced and enlarged them as best I can. Take a look and see if you recognize anyone now.

She opened the attachment. One by one, she zoomed in on the faces, wondering how long it would take for the facial recognition software to identify them.

"What are you doing?"

Brady's soft voice made her jump and she looked up. "You sure do walk quietly."

"One of the requirements of the job if you don't want to get shot sometimes."

"True." She turned her attention back to the computer. "I was just making a list, but David sent me the enhanced versions of Heather's pictures, so I've switched my attention to them." She clicked and brought up the first one again, the figure still rather grainy. He looked familiar.

"A list of what?"

"Questions mostly."

"Well, here are a few answers for you. David called and said he traced that boat back to Nicholas Raimes."

"Raimes? That's interesting," she said. Click. Zoom. Next person. "What does he have to say about that?"

"That he sold the boat a couple of weeks ago."

"To whom?"

"He said he's never met the guy. The transaction was done online. He's sending me the bill of sale and we'll track down the buyer and see what he has to say."

"That all just seems like too much of a coincidence, if you ask me."

"I agree, but weirder things have happened. On a positive note, David also managed to identify the four guys on the boat."

She paused and looked up. "Who are they?"

"Three of them are Frank Jarvis, George Hollis, and Lonnie Darlington."

"Who's the fourth?"

"Jeremy Hightower."

She froze. "What?"

"Yep."

"Unbelievable," she said softly, then frowned. "I don't recognize Hollis or Darlington, but Frank Jarvis was good friends with Jeremy in high school. There was a transaction in addition to the others on Jeremy's account that caught my attention. It was a payment to Frank Jarvis in the amount of ten thousand dollars."

"Frank's a big-time charity supporter and active in local politics," Brady said. "Could that payment have gone to one of those things?"

216

"It's possible, but I doubt it."

"I ran all four of them through missing persons and two popped up. Frank Jarvis and Jeremy didn't. Frank's got quite a history. From bar bouncer to county councilman, he's come a long way."

"And there's a long line of greasy palms behind him."

"He bought his way up, huh?"

"As near as I can figure," she said. "In high school, it was his daddy who had the money. He bailed Frank and Jeremy out of more messes than you can count—and paid people off to keep them out of further trouble." She paused. "So, what does this mean?"

Brady frowned. "It's not too much of a stretch to think the two men reported missing went down with the *Lady Marie*."

"Can you talk to Frank?"

"I would definitely like to, but he's in the hospital in a coma."

"Wait, what? Seriously? What happened to him?"

"Car wreck. Broke his neck. He's got machines breathing for him right now."

"Holy wow." She drew in a breath. "All right. Did anyone talk to Calvin Swift? My boss at the bank?"

He nodded. "I asked Derek to go by and find out why he was meeting with Jeremy Hightower."

"And?"

"He said it was just routine. When he has clients who keep a lot of money in his bank, he likes to give them the personal treatment. Make them feel important."

"Okay, that's true. He does that a lot." Could it be that simple? Or was Calvin somehow mixed up in everything?

"Is he a good boss?" Brady asked. "Or is the congeniality just a façade? You know, nice to all the customers, but a pain to his employees?"

She shook her head. "Calvin can be a bit overbearing in the office, but it's only because he's very meticulous about things and hates to fix mistakes—his own or anyone else's. But he's not a *bad* boss overall. Like, I'm not afraid of him or anything. Or worried that he'll fire me over something trivial. He's just very detail oriented and a bit of a perfectionist. As a result, he expects his employees to be the same way. Which isn't always a good thing."

"I know some people like that."

She clicked and studied the next picture. "Once I realized that was just his way of doing things, I was able to relax and do my job. We have a pretty good working relationship, although I'm sure he's wondering what's happened to me by now."

"Derek let him know that you're okay, but that you're helping the police in an investigation. Your job is secure."

A lump formed in her throat. "Really? When did he do all that?"

"This morning, I think."

No doubt Brady was behind the request. "Thank you."

"Sure. And just so you know, no one's been able to find Hightower. He seems to be missing."

"Since when?"

"Since last Tuesday."

"The day before Heather's attack?"

"Yes."

She rubbed her eyes and cleared her throat. "This is all so discombobulating."

"That's a word?"

She laughed. "Yes. Okay, so . . . back to the guys on the boat."

"What are you thinking?"

"They look like guards or something. Like they're keeping a watch. I don't see any weapons, but it's just their stance or something."

He looked over her shoulder and she decided she really liked his nearness. "I see what you mean," he said.

Click. Zoom. Move on to the next person.

Click. Zoom—

She sat straight up, her head bumping his chin. She knew Jeremy was involved but seeing him on her screen made it suddenly real. "Sorry. But David did a really good job zooming in on him." He rubbed his chin while she pointed at Jeremy. "I knew he was connected to all of this, of course. I mean, it all started with him and now this."

"What do you mean, 'started with him'?" Brady asked.

"If I hadn't seen him come into the bank, I might never have discovered the transactions."

"You would have. Eventually."

"Maybe, but not as quickly, for sure. What's he doing there?" She went to the next picture. "And here. He's on the deck, looking like he's going to jump off or something."

"You notice something else?" Brady asked. "The angle of that picture is different."

"What?

"Heather moved. Jeremy's looking right at the camera."

Emily zoomed closer. His eyes locked onto hers and she shuddered. "I see what you're saying. He saw her, didn't he?"

"It sure looks like it."

"Well, I guess that answers how they knew she had the pictures. If Jeremy saw her, he would have recognized her."

"Go back to the first picture for a second."

She did.

"See that?" he said. "In that picture, the dinghy's on the swim platform."

"Okay. So?"

"So, the larger boats sometimes have a smaller one attached. In one of the later pictures, the dinghy's gone."

She clicked between the two pictures. "Where'd it go?"

"In the water, I'm sure."

"But . . ." The light went on for her. "So you think *Jeremy* sank the boat?"

"Looks like it to me."

She gave a slow nod. "That would make sense. Once he sank the larger boat, he'd need to get away pretty fast. The dinghy would allow that." She paused. "But why would the other men be reported missing? Why wouldn't they just be on the dinghy with Jeremy?"

"Could be any number of reasons."

"Originally, you thought they went down with the boat. If they did and Jeremy didn't, then . . . he killed them, didn't he?" she whispered.

"I don't know."

"But you're thinking it."

"I'm thinking it's not such a stretch."

"But why?"

Brady shrugged. "Too many witnesses to what he was doing? A disagreement about something? Could be anything."

"What about Frank?"

"Looks like he and Jeremy made the escape together." His gaze met hers. "I think we need to turn everything over to Linc and let him and the FBI take it from here."

She returned to her list and deleted **Connection between Nicholas Raimes and Martin Burnett?** and typed **Jeremy Hightower** in place of Nicholas Raimes. "If Jeremy saw her watching him and he was doing something illegal on the boat, then he's the one who would've gone after Heather."

"It's a logical theory."

"We need to know if there's a connection between Jeremy and Martin Burnett."

Emily studied her notes and found nothing useful, but . . . "What we *really* need is to find Heather's car—and Heather."

"I agree. Unfortunately, no one's been able to locate the car yet."

"Well, what about this? We know they were going up I-26, right?"

"Yes. East."

"So we only need to check one side of the highway. Most service stations and restaurants have cameras. What if you ask David to examine the cameras of those gas stations and restaurants at each exit where it would make sense for him to get off if he needed to stop for gas and food? If he was driving Heather's car, he was going to need gas. She was always running low. He might not have gotten far before he had to fill up."

Brady nodded. "It's not a bad idea."

"Of course, if she chose that day to fill up, she'll have had a full tank and my idea will be a bust."

"Also possible."

She sighed. "I know it's a long shot, but it might be worth spending the time on."

"I'll call David and ask him to revisit this."

"Thanks." She leaned her head back against the sofa and stared at the ceiling, the 911 call echoing in her memory. Heather. *God, please, let her be alive.*

# SUNDAY,
# OCTOBER 27

# 20

Brady stepped into the den area and ran a hand through his still wet hair. A few hours of sleep and a hot shower had done wonders for his disposition and helped recharge his brain. Just as he was about to grab his laptop and check his email, Mary Beth walked in. "Brady? Izzy's here. She just drove up."

"Did I miss her call saying she was coming?" He checked his phone.

"No, she and I were talking and she said she'd just come on out because she had something she needed to talk to you about."

"Okay. Tell her where we are, will you?"

"Sure."

Mary Beth left, and within seconds, his sister strode into the room and took a seat on the sofa. "Hi."

"Hi." He studied her. She was practically vibrating. "Spill it."

"What makes you think I've got anything to spill?"

He simply raised a brow and she gave a dramatic sigh. "Okay, I've been running around like a chicken with my head cut off. Guess where I just came from?"

"No clue."

"And you don't want to guess."

"Iz . . ."

"Jordan and I discovered Martin Burnett had a second house."

"You're kidding."

"Nope. David found it. It's about ten minutes from here. Around five thousand square feet of super nice with a four-car garage."

"He does like his vehicles, doesn't he? Were any of them actually there?"

Izzy chuckled. "Yep. Found that Cadillac sedan you were looking for. It's being towed to the lab's garage as we speak. They'll be checking for DNA to match Emily and the guys who snatched her."

"What about the classic?"

"Got that one too. And, of course, the car he was in when he was killed."

"Right. What else?"

"They found bank records with some pretty big cash deposits. His neighbors said he worked third shift at a local bar, but if that's the going pay for tips these days, I'm heading down to find me a new job."

"So, where did the deposits come from?" he asked.

"Working on that," Izzy said, "but since they were cash, it's going to be hard to find out."

"Yeah, I know. We need to trace his whereabouts. Any known associates?"

"That bar he's supposed to work at is real enough. While he wasn't an employee, he was a pretty regular customer."

"So, who did he talk to?"

"One of the waitresses said he slipped her a card and told her to call him if she was ever interested in making some extra cash."

"Did she call him?"

"She said she did, but after they talked, she 'got bad vibes' and decided against following through with meeting him."

"Meeting him where?" Brady asked.

"She gave me the address and it's just an apartment building not too far from where Emily and her family were held."

"Can you check it out?"

"Heading that way when I leave here."

"Can you pull his phone records too?"

"Jordan's working on it. I'll let you know if we come up with anything else. And when I hear something on the DNA from the Cadillac, I'll let you know that too."

"Thanks, Sis."

"Yep."

"And one more thing. We found something kind of interesting."

"What's that?" Brady asked.

Izzy pulled a business card from her pocket and handed it to him. "This. Does the name Paul Bailey ring any bells?"

---

Emily stepped into the room just in time to hear the name. She gasped. "Paul Bailey?"

Izzy's eyes narrowed. "I take it you know him?"

"Yes, he's the one who moved into the apartment next to Heather's while his home is being renovated." Emily took a seat on the sofa. "He's living with his cousin Claire."

Brady raked a hand through his hair, then settled onto the couch next to Emily. "I think we need an in-depth background check on Mr. Bailey."

Izzy nodded. "Already sent that request in to David."

"Poor David, he's being overrun lately," Emily said.

"He can handle it. It might take him a little while, but he'll find what we need."

"Paul Bailey. That's too weird." Emily's gaze darted from one person to the next. "The more you guys find out, the more confusing this gets. What does Paul Bailey have to do with Martin Burnett, the man who kil—*attacked* Heather?"

Brady reached for her hand and squeezed. She found herself grateful for his comfort. In fact, she relished it.

"I'm hoping Bailey can help clear up that question," Izzy said.

Emily rubbed her tired eyes. Would life ever return to normal? No. Not without Heather. Nothing would ever be normal again. Grief slammed her and she swallowed.

"When are you going to see him?" Brady asked Izzy.

"Soon. His secretary said he was out showing a property but was finishing up and would be back in his office in about an hour."

"His secretary works on Sunday?"

"Apparently, when Paul works, she works. Real estate is a seven-day-a-week job."

"Kinda like being a cop, huh?"

Izzy smirked. "I told her that we could come to his office or he was welcome to meet us at the station, but we needed to speak to him today."

"If you wind up going to his office, let me know and I'll meet you there," Brady said. "I'd love to see Bailey's face while he's answering your questions."

"Sure."

"And me," Emily said.

Izzy shook her head. "I don't think that's a good idea. You'd be too exposed." Izzy's phone rang before Emily could protest. "Excuse me. That's Bailey's secretary now."

She stepped outside the den with the phone pressed to her ear. Emily didn't let her gaze waver from Brady's. "I can't just sit here and do nothing."

"You're not doing nothing," Brady said. "You're working on finding that financial trail that leads us back to the big boss."

She pursed her lips, then nodded. "Yes, I could do that, but I'm still going."

He scowled. "You're safe here, Emily."

"I know. And I appreciate it, but these people have involved my family and my friends. They didn't ask for that and I feel responsible. If Paul's had a part in any of this craziness, I want to be there to hear firsthand what's said. And, like you, watch his face when he says it."

Izzy stepped back into the room. "That was Bailey's secretary. He's on his way to the station. We'll be in Interrogation Room number 2."

Emily stood. "I'm going."

Izzy and Brady locked eyes. Brady sighed. "Fine, but you're wearing body armor."

"I wouldn't have it any other way."

Emily sat on the other side of the mirror and bit her lip while Izzy and Jordan sat opposite Paul Bailey in the interrogation room. "We appreciate you coming in like this," Izzy said.

"No problem."

"Sorry the accommodations are lacking, but this is all we had available."

Paul smiled, seeming at ease and not at all concerned about being questioned. "Like I said, it's not a problem. What can I do to help?"

"How do you know Martin Burnett?"

"I don't." Paul never hesitated or blinked when he answered, and Emily found herself inclined to believe him.

"Then why did we find your business card in his home?"

He raised a brow. "I really don't know. I'm a realtor. I give my card out to anyone and everyone—probably twenty a day. It's how I do business. I realize that most of those end up in the trash, but every once in a while, it pays off. I guess our paths crossed at some point and I gave him a card."

Emily could see that. Burnett could have come by that card in any number of ways.

Linc sat next to her, his attention focused, head tilted.

"What do you think?" she asked. "Is he telling the truth?"

229

"For some reason my gut's saying no. But I don't have a thing to base that on."

"Hmm."

"What do you think?"

"I have no clue. What he said makes perfect sense."

"I agree."

"So, why is your gut grumbling?"

His lips tilted. "Besides the fact that I'm hungry?"

"Yes."

He rubbed his chin and shook his head, his eyes back on the man in question. "No clue."

"I'd think you've been in this business long enough to have learned to listen to your gut."

Linc turned to look at her. He gave a short nod. "Yeah. You're right."

She shrugged. "So, you just need to keep digging deeper into Mr. Bailey until you figure it out?"

"Exactly." He turned back to the scene on the other side of the glass.

Jordan leaned forward. "I just have a question about your cousin."

"Cousin?" Paul blinked. "Oh yes. Claire."

"Right."

Emily jerked. "Did you see that? He went blank for a split second when Jordan mentioned his cousin."

"I did see that." Linc paused. "Have you seen Claire lately?"

"No." Emily frowned. "Come to think of it, I can't remember the last time I saw her."

"I just have bad feelings all around about this guy."

"So what do we do?"

"Keep an eye on him."

"What do you want to know about Claire?" Paul asked.

"Could we have her number? We'd like to ask her if she saw anything the night Heather disappeared. Or if she saw anyone hanging around Heather's apartment in the days before Heather disappeared."

"Claire's been on a business trip with a coworker, but I can have her call you."

"Could you just give us her number?"

Paul gave a small laugh. "Sure." He rattled off a number and Izzy wrote it down.

"A couple of more questions, if you don't mind."

Paul shrugged.

"Have you seen anyone coming or going from Heather's apartment since she disappeared? Any unusual vehicles or noticed any strange noises?"

"No, nothing like that, I'm sorry."

The door opened behind Emily and she could see Brady's reflection in the glass. He stepped inside the room and shut the door. "Anything interesting?" he asked.

"Not really," Linc said. "He's got a real good excuse as to why a hired assassin has his business card, but there's just something off about him."

"He's looking a little more tense now," Emily said. "Ever since Jordan brought up his cousin. Now I'm wondering if he's even related at all—and where Claire is."

Linc pulled his phone from his pocket. "I'll see if Annie can find out the answers to those questions."

Izzy stood. "Thank you for your time, Mr. Bailey. We appreciate you coming in."

Paul shook her hand, then Jordan's. "I'll be sure to let Claire know you want to talk to her."

"That would be great."

Jordan escorted Paul out of the room and Izzy turned to look at the mirror with a raised brow. "Meet me in the tactical planning room if it's open? My desk space is too small to gather around. Grab some coffee and let's chat."

Linc, Brady, and Emily filed out, down the hall, and into another room. A round table that seated twelve sat in the middle. The coffee station at the back drew Emily, and she helped herself, then took a seat at the table.

Brady settled beside her and Linc on the other side of Brady, who now had his phone out and was tapping the screen.

"Who are you calling?" Emily asked.

"Claire."

She raised a brow and he set the phone on speaker. A cultured, if subdued voice filled the air. "Hi, this is Claire. I'm sorry I can't talk right now. Leave your number and I'll call you back soon."

"Is that her voice?" Brady asked her.

"Yes. Sounds like her."

He frowned and tucked the device into his pocket as Izzy stepped inside the room, her phone pressed to her ear. "Yeah. Okay. Great." A sigh. "Right. I'll tell them." She hung up and dread curled in Emily's stomach.

"What is it?" Emily asked.

"Owen Parker was found dead in the bathroom about an hour ago. Head wound. Looks like he slipped and fell, hitting his head on the wall."

Emily pressed her palms to her eyes. "He said they would kill him." She lowered her hands, wondering why she felt sorry for the man. But she did. He'd tried to kill her, but—

"He was under guard," Brady said. "We told them to watch him. What happened?"

Izzy shook her head. "He slipped away from the guard watching him in the yard. I don't know how."

"We may never know."

Brady pulled his phone from his pocket.

"Who are you calling?" Emily asked.

"Nicholas Raimes. I just thought of something."

"Speakerphone?" Linc insisted.

Brady pressed the button as Raimes answered. "Hello?"

"This is Detective St. John. I thought of one more question I'd like to ask."

"Of course."

He paused. "Have you ever heard of a guy by the name of Paul Bailey?"

"Sure. We run in the same real estate circles. Why do you ask?"

"Just curious as to what kind of person he is?"

"I only know him on a professional basis, but he's always personable when I see him, well-liked by others in the industry." He paused. "What else can I tell you? Uh . . . he's a shrewd businessman, that's for sure. A lot of people envy him and others just want to suck up to him."

"Because of his wealth?"

"Of course."

"And that business with Jenkins?"

"Jenkins? Oh." Raimes blew out a sigh. "I don't know. That was kind of freaky, but I don't think Paul had anything to do with that."

"So, as wealthy as Mr. Bailey is, he's chosen to live with his cousin Claire in a small two-bedroom apartment while his home is being renovated. You don't find that odd?"

"Definitely odd. And did you say his cousin?"

"Yes."

"He doesn't have any relatives in town that I recall. Although it seems like he did mention doing some renos on one of his houses when I ran into him last week, but I couldn't tell you any more than that."

Emily raised a brow. One of his houses?

"Huh. I must have misunderstood about the cousin," Brady said.

"Must have."

"Thanks again."

"Anytime."

Brady hung up and raised a brow. "Well, that's interesting. I think we need to have another chat with Mr. Bailey."

Izzy grabbed her phone. "He's already left, of course. I'll see if I can round him up again."

Brady ran a hand over his lips and sighed. "All right," he said with a glance at Emily, "I guess it's time to get you back to the safe house."

"I guess."

He smiled. "What? You don't like it there?"

"I'm sorry. I don't mean to sound ungrateful. I guess I'm just ready for all of this to be over with."

Preferably with her still breathing.

# TUESDAY, OCTOBER 29

## 21

For the next two days, Brady and Emily had continued the investigation from the safe house, sending everything she found to Linc, who in turn had brought in the Money Laundering and Asset Recovery section of the Bureau. They would work closely with Linc and keep him informed of any updated information.

Each day they worked in the morning and dove in the afternoon.

Today was unseasonably warm, so they switched it up with a shorter dive, first thing in the morning. The afternoon would be busy. Brady and Emily sat on the dock in their dry suits, feet dangling over the edge. "You're a natural," he told her. "I've never seen anyone take to diving like you."

"I love it. I'd stay down there 24/7 if I could."

He laughed. "Yeah, I know the feeling."

"How's your knee?"

"Better. Keeping it elevated and the ice pack on it has helped a lot. I don't think I damaged it nearly as bad as I did last time."

"Good." She sighed. "I can't do this anymore, Brady."

His smile faded and his eyes clouded. "Do what?"

"Hide out. Wait. Live in limbo."

"I know it's hard, but—"

"No buts. It *is* hard. What's even harder is that I've called Heather's mother four times over the past two days and she hasn't called me back. And it's not because whoever has Heather snatched them, because you said officers rode by and saw them working in the yard this morning." She'd been concerned when Heather's mother never called her back after Mr. Gilstrap had assured her that they would do so as soon as they had a moment. Brady had sent officers out to check. "And where is the evidence report from the Cadillac? And why hasn't anyone connected Martin Burnett to someone who can be arrested? And why can't anyone find out where those pictures were taken? And why hasn't David been able to find Heather's car? It's not like this is the seventies. We should know *something* by now!"

He let her vent. She'd been winding tighter and tighter over the last twenty-four hours, and he'd hoped the dive would help. And it had. Just not for long.

When she finally snapped her lips shut, he placed a hand on her shoulder. "Look, I get it. I do. Unfortunately, everything takes time."

"Time Heather might not have."

Brady winced. He knew she wanted to believe Heather was alive somewhere. He just didn't hold out that same hope.

---

Emily took a deep breath to calm down and rubbed a hand over her eyes. "I'm sorry. I'm probably not even making any sense. I know you don't think she's still alive."

"You're making sense." He scooted closer to her and wrapped an arm around her shoulders. "And you don't know how much I hope I'm wrong."

For a moment she was tempted to lay her head on his chest and do her best to forget her problems. Instead she pulled away from him. His closeness just made her long for more and that wasn't going to happen. "I'm going inside to try Heather's mom one more time, and if she doesn't answer, I'm going over there." She stood and grabbed the flippers she'd taken off to climb up on the dock. Only now her feet were freezing and she stumbled on her first step.

Brady hopped up to grab her arm. "Are you okay?"

"Cold feet." She smirked. "Literally."

He laughed and leaned over to cover her mouth with his.

For a moment, she froze, her pulse picked up speed, blood pounding through her veins. Indecision warred with surprise and disbelief. And then it was over.

His hand cupped the back of her head and his eyes smiled down at her. "I wish you could see your eyes."

She blinked. And frowned. "Why?"

"Because they're—"

"No. Why did you do that? Why did you kiss me?"

"Because I've been wanting to do it for a while now, and it seemed like the right time." He looked away. "I guess I should apologize for not asking if it was okay."

"No, don't apologize. It just surprised me."

"In a bad way? I couldn't tell. I didn't set off any bad memories or anything, did I?" He dropped his head and peered at her through his lashes.

Her heart flipped. "No. No bad memories. I don't have PTSD or anything like that when it comes to Jeremy. I'm not scared or upset that you kissed me." She smiled. "I actually enjoyed it once the surprise started to fade." And then it was over. Much too fast.

He let out a slow breath. "Oh, thank goodness. I thought I'd pushed you away for good."

"No . . ."

His eyes snapped to hers. "No, but?"

"But I don't understand what you see in me."

Brady pursed his lips and studied. "Okay, I can see we've got some work to do."

"Work?"

"On getting you to see yourself like I do." Her jaw dropped. He tapped it. "Come on, let's go see if we can get Heather's mother to answer."

Joy fled as they walked back up the hill to the house. Kissing Brady had been spectacular. Well, him kissing her had been. She hadn't been much of a participant, thanks to her utter shock. And she'd admit feeling safe had been amazing and restorative, but Heather was still missing. Whether alive or dead, her friend still needed to be found.

Emily noted that Brady altered his gait to match hers, just like he always did when they walked side by side. Soon, she'd have to ask him exactly how he saw her, but she didn't think she could handle the answer right now.

But soon. Because she needed to know exactly how he saw her if she was going to work on seeing herself the same way.

Whatever that wound up being.

However, two people had said essentially the same thing in a short span of time, so apparently she was missing something.

She desperately wanted to know what that was.

---

The man on the hill lowered the binoculars and pondered his next move. They had to be diving. All of the equipment that was hauled down ahead of them indicated it. They were playing it safe in case of a sniper. Smart. But if Emily could dive, he could use that to his advantage and lose the albatross around his neck. And the fact that she and the detective seemed to be developing feelings for one another was good information to have.

The albatross approached and the man on the hill was almost surprised he'd shown up.

Jeremy Hightower shoved his hands into his pockets. "How'd you find them?"

"Been tracking Heather's parents' phones. There was one number that I couldn't identify as belonging to family or relatives. I took a chance it might be Emily's. It was."

"Good for you." Jeremy cleared his throat. "You said he'd pay."

"I thought he would. I still think he will, but you didn't have to sink the boat." He kept his tone mild. In truth, he didn't care about the boat, he cared about the inconvenience of all the extra work it was causing him by being on the bottom of a lake somewhere. A location that the man on his left refused to divulge. "You hired Martin Burnett to kill Heather Gilstrap, didn't you?"

Jeremy shrugged. "Martin was one of your boss's lackeys who was always eager to pad his bank account. It didn't take too much convincing for him to kill her. She's been a pain in my side ever since high school. Good riddance." He paused. "You seem to want to know the location of the boat almost as much as your boss."

"I do."

"Why?"

"It's in my best interest to know the location. Which you could give me."

"You don't have enough money to convince me to give it up."

The man kept his emotions out of the conversation. "If you would give it up, I would have the money."

"Tell me the combination to the safe."

"Tell me the location of the boat."

"And so it goes." A pause. "I could just dive down there and haul the safe up, you know."

The broker's friend chuckled at Jeremy's delusion. "You and I both know you can't make a move without someone watching you."

"And yet, here I am."

"You were followed."

The albatross scowled. "By whom?"

"The guy who just rolled up on the motorcycle." He pointed.

Jeremy cursed. "Who's he?"

"Just one of my faithful employees."

"I'm done. Don't contact me again until you have the money transferred to the account number I gave you."

He stomped off, climbed into his little red sports car, and raced away. The man on the hill saluted the motorcycle rider, who nodded and roared away.

With the binoculars back against his eyes, the man continued to watch his targets—or at least their vicinity. Brady St. John and Emily Chastain. Brady would be the obvious choice to make the dive once he found the boat, but it looked like Emily could do the job just as well and she would be easier to control. He snapped a few pictures with the long-range lens and tucked away what he'd learned with his little spying mission.

He climbed into his car. It was time to take care of Jeremy Hightower once and for all.

---

Brady couldn't help shaking a mental finger at himself. While he'd enjoyed kissing Emily, she hadn't been ready for it. Then again, she hadn't pushed him away either. She'd just been surprised. He couldn't help glancing at her as they rode down the highway toward the exit that would take them to the Gilstraps' home. He wanted to protect her, to wrap her in a combination of bubble wrap and Kevlar to make sure no one ever hurt her again.

But since that wasn't possible, the best thing he could do was hover. And keep his gun close by. His phone rang. "Excuse me."

"Sure."

He activated the truck's Bluetooth. "Luis? What's up, man?"

"I need you out at Lake Murray," the dive team leader said. "We've got a body."

"Already recovered?"

"Part of it."

"Ah. The others on the way?"

"Yep."

"I'll be there as soon as I can." He hung up. "I've got to head to the lake."

"You go there. I'll catch a cab to Heather's parents' house."

He laughed, a short sound that ended in a snort. "I don't think so."

"Well, I'm not too keen about diving and looking for body parts, so do you have a better suggestion?"

"Wait in the car?"

"Too unproductive."

He nodded. "I'll get Linc to go with you."

"Linc doesn't have time to babysit me."

"Someone's going with you. It's nonnegotiable."

She huffed a sigh. He was right and she just needed to accept her limitations for now. "Fine."

Thirty minutes later, after Linc agreed to come get Emily, Brady pulled to a stop in front of the yellow crime scene tape and climbed out. He leaned back into the open door. "I'm going to get geared up. Linc will be here shortly."

The wind blew hard enough to cause the tape to snap, then relax. Snap, relax. He hated that sound. It was like someone snapping their fingers, rushing him, telling him to hurry up and find the killer. A body had been dumped in Lake Murray. Unfortunately, they couldn't find the head. Other team members were already waiting and ready to go. Mary Beth, Danny, Vic, Gavin, and Luis. Brady shot Mary Beth a questioning look. "How'd you beat me here?"

She shrugged. "I knew a shortcut."

"You'll have to let me in on that one. Hey, Francisco, thought you would still be at the shooting."

Francisco Zamora, the medical examiner, looked up. The man could have been a model with his dark good looks, compliments of his Spanish ancestors, but he'd chosen to use the brains that came with his good looks. "Brady, how considerate of you to finally join your teammates."

"Thanks. Good to see you too. Again."

"Herrera took over the other case. I wanted this one." One of the deputy coroners. Francisco didn't have to go out to the scenes. In fact, in their city, it wasn't even protocol, but everyone indulged Francisco's uniqueness since he claimed it made him a better examiner. Brady didn't care, he just wanted answers.

"What do you have?"

"A dead guy."

Brady did his best to refrain from rolling his eyes. "No kidding. And you went to med school for that?"

Francisco smirked at him, then returned to his study of the bloated, headless man. "Our poor victim here washed up a short while ago. The unfortunate witnesses were removed from the area."

Brady nodded. "How long has he been in the water?"

"You know I can't answer that with any guarantee of accuracy yet."

"I know, but I'll take your best educated guess." Because Francisco was rarely wrong even with his educated guesses.

"Probably about a week, give or take a couple of days on either side of that."

"Any ID on him?"

"Actually, yes. Had his wallet still in his pocket. It's kinda messed up, but I could make out the name on the license." He handed it to Brady, who took it in his gloved hand. "Reuben Kingman?"

A gasp sounded behind him and he spun. Emily stood watching, her hand over her mouth. "Reuben?" she said.

Brady shoved the wallet back in Francisco's hand and strode over to Emily, noting that his knee only gave a light protest at the sudden movement. "Don't look." But it was too late. Her pale face and constant swallowing said she'd always have to live with the image of the corpse. "You know him?"

"He worked at my bank." She ran a shaky hand over her hair. "Why would someone kill Reuben? Why would someone *do that* to him?"

"What'd he do at the bank?" Brady asked.

"He was our Information Security Operations Center Manager. Which is a fancy title for making sure all of the bank's operations were secure and running smoothly. He was a genius. Especially when it came to computers. IT even sometimes called him for help." Emily shook her head. "I don't believe this. First Heather and now Reuben." Tears hovered on her lashes, but didn't fall. She blinked. "He was supposed to be on a two-week vacation-slash-leave, visiting family. His father had just had bypass surgery and his mom needed his help. I'm sorry, I don't know all the details."

"We'll see if there's a missing person report filed on him. If he didn't show up at his parents', surely they would have called someone."

"I'm sure." She raked a hand through her hair.

"Were you especially close to him?" Brady asked. He wasn't sure if he was asking for the investigation or for himself.

"No, not really. I mean, we were friends. We talked on a daily basis, had lunch together occasionally, commiserated about our failed efforts to reach our goal weight, but we weren't especially *close*. Like we didn't socialize outside of work."

"Any other relatives or close friends?"

"He has a sister in Columbia who's married with four children. He was crazy about his nieces and nephews. His parents live in Raleigh, North Carolina."

Linc walked up and Brady filled him in.

"Hey, St. John, you coming?" Mary Beth stood, hands on her hips, brow raised.

Brady's eyes connected with Luis, who was getting the gear ready, but had looked up at Mary Beth's call. "Stay here a sec," he told Emily.

"What's up?" Linc asked.

"I'll be right back." Brady jogged over to the dive team leader. "Could I sit this one out?"

"Why?"

"Emily knows the victim."

Luis sighed and looked around. "Yeah. I think we can handle it. I can always call in one of the others if I find we need more help."

"Thanks, Luis."

"Sure." He flicked a glance at Emily. "She's special to you?"

Brady ignored the heat climbing into his face and nodded. "Yeah, she's special."

"All right. Go." They shared a fist bump and Brady jogged back to Emily.

"Come on."

"What?"

"I'm going with you."

"What happened to the dive?"

He shot her a tight smile. "I got permission to sit this one out. Sorry to call you out here for nothing, Linc."

Linc slapped him on the back. "Not for nothing. I'll follow you to the Gilstraps' home just in case you need some backup."

# 22

"Where is she?" The broker slammed a fist on the table and raked a hand through his hair. His eyes rested on his friend who'd walked in thirty seconds ago.

"We spotted her out at Lake Wateree with her boyfriend cop. They've been out there for a few days now."

"Then why not grab her? I want her dead! She's the only one alive that can ruin me. The boat and the flash drive are at the bottom of the lake. As long as it stays there, I'm safe. In the meantime, she's my loose end and I need it tied up ASAP."

"We couldn't get close enough. They had lookouts all around the place. She's got so much coverage, you'd think she was a celebrity or something."

"No, she's just a woman with the power to put me in prison the rest of my life." He wanted to hit something. Something other than his desk. Something like his brother's scarred face. He took a deep breath.

"Frankly, I don't think she knows anything," his friend said.

"Burnett said Gilstrap was in the process of sending those texts before he stopped her," he said. "She knows."

"Then why haven't the cops arrested you?"

He frowned. "Because they can't find me. This house is in my grandmother's name, not mine."

His friend leaned forward and clasped his hands between his knees. "Here's what I think. I think Gilstrap sent those lake pictures to Emily, but Emily doesn't know which lake."

"Even if she doesn't, it won't take her long to figure it out. That Gilstrap woman wouldn't have sent her those texts if she didn't think Emily couldn't figure out what she meant."

"Maybe."

"No maybe about it. She—and Hightower—are the last dangling threads and I want them snipped." He walked to the window and looked out. This home sat gracefully on the gently sloping hill of one of the most prestigious neighborhoods in Columbia. The rock wall surrounding it gave him a measure of security. As did the multiple security cameras and the crew who monitored those cameras 24/7. "Things were never the same after my parents divorced. All of this is their fault, you know." He turned back to the window and shoved his hands in his pockets.

"So you've said. Many times." A sigh filtered from the man. "But come on, man, we're big boys. We made the decision to live this kind of life because we love money and will do whatever it takes to have a lot of it."

The broker laughed. "You never were one to blame others, were you?"

"Why blame others when I'm the one in control?"

"Good point." His gaze went back to the window. Two illegals worked in his garden. "He changed his name, you know. After the divorce. Dad took me and Mother took him. They hated each other."

"I know. I was there, remember?"

"We were pitted against one another from birth. I suppose a showdown is inevitable."

"Dude, you're wallowing. You need to get out of this house and take your mind off things. Business is going well, you're making more money than ever. The cops can't find you. What's to worry about?"

"Blackmail," he snapped. "Blackmail is a big worry for me."

"Yeah, I guess there's that, but as long as those pictures are at the bottom of a lake, what's the problem?"

"The problem is, he's looking for those pictures too. And if he finds them, I'll be right back where we started with Kingman."

"Kingman must have been telling you the truth. If your brother had more pictures, you would know it by now."

"Exactly. Which means I have to get to them first."

"It'll happen. We just have to bide our time and wait for the right moment."

"Biding our time is costing me money."

"You've got plenty of it."

An annoyed snort escaped the broker. "That's beside the point. I shouldn't be spending it on this." He rubbed his chin. "No, as much as I want him to suffer, I think it's time for him to die."

His friend stood and placed his bourbon glass on the coaster next to the wingback chair where he'd been lounging. "Then I'd better get busy. We've got some work to do in coming up with a plan to rid you of your brother. I'll keep you informed."

The door shut and the broker swigged the last of his own drink while his mind dismissed any plan his friend might be working on. It was time to form one of his own.

---

When Brady pulled the car in front of the Gilstrap home, Emily's fingers tightened around the door handle. Their white Honda was in the drive along with several other vehicles. Maybe Mrs. Gilstrap really hadn't had time to call her back. Frowning, she climbed out of the vehicle. Linc pulled up and parked behind them, where he'd stay as an extra set of eyes for protection.

The curtain in the dining room moved and she caught a glimpse of Heather's mother. The drape snapped back into place and the front door opened. "How dare you! How dare you come here?"

Emily froze. Brady's hand gripped her bicep. She blinked. "Mrs. Gilstrap?"

"Heather's dead and it's your fault." She jabbed a finger at Emily as tears streaked her cheeks.

"What?" Emily gaped.

"Ellen!" The sharp command from the man behind her had no effect on Heather's mother as she continued her charge toward them. Brady pulled Emily back.

"Ellen, stop it right now!"

A former Marine, Eric Gilstrap's drill sergeant snap halted the woman in her tracks. He reached her in four strides. "We talked about this." His voice softened.

Tears tracked Mrs. Gilstrap's cheeks as she glared at Emily. Never had Emily ever seen such a look on Heather's mother's face and it devastated her. "Please, Mrs. Gilstrap. What do you mean? Why is it my fault? You called me and left me those messages concerned about my safety. What's changed since then?"

Heaving with her emotion, Mrs. Gilstrap couldn't speak. Emily turned pleading eyes to Mr. Gilstrap.

He sighed. "Come inside. No sense in standing out here in the cold."

It hit Emily at that moment just how cold she really was. Probably more so from the shock of Ellen Gilstrap's accusation than from the weather.

Emily shot a glance at Brady, who squeezed her shoulder and stayed close as they stepped inside the Gilstrap home. Mr. Gilstrap whispered something in his wife's ear and she nodded, shot another look over her shoulder at Emily and Brady, and headed for the kitchen. A woman Emily thought might be Heather's aunt from the West Coast slipped an arm around her sister's shoulders.

"Let's go in the den," Mr. Gilstrap said. "Mark is on the way from Virginia. He should be here in the next hour or so." Mark, Heather's brother.

"What about Shelly?" Emily asked. Heather's sister lived in Tennessee, working as an accountant for a prestigious law firm.

"She'll come this weekend." He shook his head. "I sure thought Heather would have shown up by now." He cleared his throat.

Brady held out a hand. "Sir, I'm Detective Brady St. John."

"Detective St. John? I asked Detective Carlisle to keep me updated." Fear flickered in his eyes and he shot a glance into the kitchen, where his wife pulled water bottles out of the refrigerator. "What's going on? Have you heard something about Heather?"

"No sir. Unfortunately, that's not why we're here."

"I see."

Emily frowned. "Please, tell me why Mrs. Gilstrap thinks Heather's disappearance is my fault?"

He turned kind eyes on her. "It's not your fault, Emily. Heather came by the house the day she disappeared and was bent out of shape about something. She wouldn't say what exactly, just that she was working on a story that you'd come across and promised her the exclusive. At first Ellen thought you both had disappeared, then when she got your call and learned you were safe, but Heather possibly wasn't, well, she started stewing on it and got it in her head that you shouldn't have given Heather such a dangerous assignment."

"But I didn't. I mean, it wasn't an assignment. I don't give Heather assignments anyway, her boss does. I just told her a few things about something I'd found at work and simply asked her opinion about it. I knew she'd done a story on human trafficking not too long ago and I needed her feedback on some things from the financial perspective. She took it upon herself to do some digging and confirmed some of our suspicions—including the identity of one of the men involved. And then she disappeared. And I was taken too."

Mr. Gilstrap's eyes widened. "You said something about that in your initial message, but we didn't have time to discuss it Saturday night. What happened?" She explained, and he blew out a low breath. "Emily, honey, I'm so sorry. And I'm glad you're okay."

"Thank you. But I'm so worried about Heather." Her voice cracked on her friend's name. "Everyone's trying to find her."

He nodded and his throat worked a moment before he cleared it. "Don't worry about Ellen. She'll come around. Deep down she knows none of this is your fault, she just needs someone to be angry at right now."

"I guess I can understand that." And she could. At least the needing to be angry part. She'd love to express her anger, her outrage, her pure fury at the people who were doing this. "Can you think of anything that would help us?"

"No, nothing."

"What about her camera?" Brady asked. His phone rang and he glanced at the screen before sending the call to voice mail. "Or her laptop?" Emily was glad he didn't stop to take the call. "We found some pictures that she took," Brady said, "but she had her geotag option turned off when she sent them."

"I know she probably had her good camera with her at the time," Emily said. "Do you know where it could be?"

"You two need to leave now." Ellen Gilstrap stood at the entrance to the den.

"Honey—"

"No, Eric, I'm not staying quiet this time." She turned a cold gaze back to Emily. "Get out of my house and don't come back unless you have Heather with you."

Tears clogged her throat and Emily couldn't respond. She ran from the room, through the foyer, and stopped at the front door. Brady's shout echoed behind her. He caught up with her at the door.

Even though she was upset, she had more sense than to go barreling outside and give someone a clear shot at her. But she wouldn't stay in Mrs. Gilstrap's home one minute longer than she had to. Not because she was angry at the woman, but because it was obvious her presence caused Heather's mother extreme grief.

Emily leaned her head against the wall and closed her eyes. "What do I do about that?" she whispered, more to herself than him.

"Exactly what Heather's father said. Don't blame yourself." He took Emily by the hand and went out the door, keeping her behind him. Linc nodded at them from his truck.

Brady's phone rang again and he ignored it until he got Emily into the truck, then with another glance at his demanding phone, he grimaced. "Sorry, but I've got to take this call before we leave."

"Sure."

He answered as he hurried to the driver's side and hopped in. She only halfway listened as she pondered Mrs. Gilstrap's reaction. How could she believe that Emily would deliberately put Heather in danger?

"Toyota Camry?"

Emily sucked in a harsh breath and laser focused on Brady. "What color? Silver?"

He nodded, his eyes darkening with an emotion she couldn't put her finger on.

"Where?" she demanded.

He shook his head.

"Where?" Emily insisted.

Brady closed his eyes for a moment. "All right. I'm on the way. I'm going to suit up. See you in a few minutes."

Emily gripped his forearm. "Tell me."

"We can tell David he can quit searching for Heather's car." He sighed. "Two scuba divers found it."

"Scuba . . ." She swallowed, unable to finish repeating his words. "Where!"

"At the bottom of Lake Murray."

---

Brady twisted the key and the engine purred to life. "We don't know that Heather's with the car, so let's not panic yet." He caught

Emily's hand in his. "I'm going to drop you off at the station where you'll be safe and head to the site."

"No. I'll ride with you."

He hesitated, then shrugged. "I won't argue with you. I know you'll insist, but I don't think it's a very wise idea."

"Probably not, but I'm still going. I need to know."

"Yeah," he said softly. "I know." He wouldn't be able to talk her out of it. "You'll have to stay in the truck." He placed his hand back on the wheel.

"That's fine. As long as I'm there." She paused. "How do they know it's hers?"

"One of the divers got the plate number and looked it up on his phone. When he realized the police were searching for that car, he called it in."

"Right." She shuddered. "What if she's with the car, Brady?"

"Just pray she isn't."

"I've been praying."

He pulled into the entrance to the park, followed the directions he'd been given to the dive site, and found he was the first to arrive. With a flash of his badge, Brady was allowed onto the scene. He parked, spotting the boat out past the long dock. If the car was in the deep area past the dock, someone had driven it off the end.

Brady turned to Emily. "I'm going to meet up with the team. Stay in the truck, please?"

She nodded, but he easily read the turmoil she was trying to control. He squeezed her hand and climbed out of the truck. Conflicted between wanting to dive and wanting to stay with Emily, he headed toward his team members who were already were gearing up. The others would be rolling in any second.

Luis walked toward him, already dressed in his dry suit. "Ready?" Because Luis was one of the deputies who worked with the coroner, he'd be the one to assist with recovering any bodies. Should there be any in the car. He was praying for an empty car.

Brady nodded. "Ready."

"You sure you're going down then."

"I have to. If Heather's down there, I want to be the one to break it to Emily."

"Mary Beth's got your rope."

"Got it."

He glanced back to the truck. Emily sat staring at the boat and he didn't even want to imagine what was going through her head. Actually, he didn't have to imagine it. He went to her and she rolled the window down. "Are you going to be all right?"

"It depends on if Heather's in that water or not."

"Yeah." His throat tightened at the rampant fear in her eyes. "Keep praying."

"I haven't stopped."

He kissed her. A quick press of his lips against hers that he hoped conveyed comfort and a silent promise to be there for her no matter what they found.

Her eyes filled with tears and she sniffed and nodded. "Go."

He grabbed his gear and went, but not without a look back over his shoulder. She sat, shoulders straight, eyes on the water, jaw set. He could only hope God listened to her prayers better than he'd listened to Brady's.

The other divers were there looking at the sonar pictures and discussing the best strategy for raising the car. Once Brady and Luis examined the vehicle for evidence, they would hook it up to the cables that would pull it from its watery grave.

Brady finished donning his gear for his dive, made his final check, then gave Mary Beth the okay sign and lowered himself feet first off the end of the dock. Luis followed him. Normally they'd let the boat take them to the dive site, but the car was just a few feet away from the dock. It made sense not to stir the murky lake water any more than necessary.

Once in the water, they dove down, allowing time for their bodies to adjust to the change in pressure. The water was surprisingly clear for lake water. The fish swam around him, curious, but not venturing too close.

Their descent continued, stopping every so often to adjust. Finally, he could see the vehicle resting on its hood. "Based on the depth and location of the car, I'd say it was pushed off the end of the dock," he told Luis. "Engine pulled it down, it flipped, and there she rests."

So many variables factored into how far a car would travel once it hit the water. The fact that this one wasn't too far away from the end of the dock indicated it wasn't running when it went off the end. The slight slope of the dock would allow gravity to help send it over.

"We'll know if it's in neutral," Luis said.

Being able to communicate on dives as complicated as these made Brady all the more grateful for the voice technology they now had. Interpreting hand signals could be time consuming and frustrating.

Brady gave a kick and drew next to the rear passenger window. A quick glance inside showed it empty. While he wanted to be relieved, he wouldn't be until they examined the trunk and found it empty as well. He checked the gearshift. "Neutral."

"Pushed then."

"Yep."

Brady kicked to the back of the vehicle and checked the trunk. A piece of cloth stuck out of one side. "Look."

"What's that?"

"Don't know. Could be the sleeve of a jacket?"

"Aw, man."

"Yeah."

For the next fifteen minutes, they communicated with those at the surface as they scoured the area for anything else that could be evidence. Finally, Brady decided they were finished. "What do you think? We done?" he asked Luis.

"I'd say so. Let's get it hooked up and hauled to the top so forensics can have a go."

# 23

Emily couldn't pull her gaze from the water. Brady and Luis had gone down about fifteen minutes ago and all she could do was sit there and pray. And watch. Her phone buzzed and she picked it up without taking her eyes from the boat. "Hello?"

"Emily?"

She blinked. "Mr. Gilstrap?"

"Yes. I . . . uh . . . I'm here. My friend at the station called me to let me know what was going on."

Emily looked back toward a gathering crowd, trying to find the Gilstraps. "I figured you would be here somewhere."

"I have the SD card from Heather's camera."

"What?"

"When Heather came by on Wednesday, she was nervous, jumpy, and, now that I think about it, scared. She left her camera on her dresser in her old room. After you and Detective St. John left, I got Ellen calmed down, then went and got the SD card. I was going to call you and tell you to come back and get it when I got the call about Heather's car being found."

Emily opened the truck door and stepped outside. "Where are you now?"

"On the other side of the crime scene tape. They won't let me past it."

257

"The only reason I'm on this side is because I was with Brady. I'll come get the card."

"First, if it's not too much trouble, can you tell me what's happening?"

With her eyes glued to the action now playing out before her, she spoke softly. "It looks like they're bringing the car up." The cables pulled, moving in what she considered slow motion.

"Tell me when it's out of the water, please." His voice had roughened and she knew he was holding back tears.

She could relate.

The car finally appeared and within a few more minutes the cables pulled it toward the tow truck waiting at the edge of the stretch of beach next to the dock. "It's out and they're going to put it on the tow truck," she said.

"Thank you," he whispered.

"Do you want me to keep watching or come get the card?"

"Keep watching. I need to know. I'm assuming the forensics people will take over once the car is on the truck."

"Yes." She cleared her throat. "I think that's how it works."

"But they'll know soon if she's in there, right?"

Why did he insist on asking her questions she didn't have the answers to? "I'm not sure, but I would think they'd know something soon."

*Please, God, don't let her be in there. Or if she is, don't let her have drowned. She hated the water. But it would be better if she didn't drown. Please.*

Emily stood in the cold with the wind whipping her hair around her face and into her eyes. As soon as she knew one way or the other, she'd find Mr. and Mrs. Gilstrap and tell them herself. Mrs. Gilstrap may not want to hear it from her, but she felt she owed them.

Inch by agonizing inch, the cables continued to pull the vehicle back until it was resting on the back of the tow truck. The forensics team gathered around the truck.

"What do you see?"

She jumped at Mr. Gilstrap's voice in her ear. "Nothing at the moment. It's going to take them a few minutes, I think."

"Stay on the phone with me?"

The heartbreak in his voice brought the hovering tears to the surface. "Sure."

Brady and Luis surfaced and hauled themselves onto the dock. And while Brady was too far away for her to see his features clearly, she thought he looked her way. She wished he would somehow signal whether Heather was in there. But he didn't.

Dressed in their hazmat suits and looking like they belonged in an alien movie, a forensics team approached. Once law enforcement had the car settled where they wanted it, one of the forensics team members climbed on the bed of the truck and pulled a tarp over most of the vehicle.

For the first time, Emily noted the helicopter hovering above and the news vans gathered behind the crime scene tape. And she noticed the medical examiner's vehicle. Her stomach twisted. He shouldn't be here. They hadn't found a body yet.

After several long and agonizing minutes, the trunk popped open. For a moment, no one moved. They simply stared. Then someone waved to a man in the crowd.

When Francisco Zamora stepped from behind the yellow tape, she drew in a sharp gasp. "Francisco!"

He paused and detoured over to her. "Emily, right?"

Tears hovered on her lashes and she set the phone on mute. "You tell me if it's her. If it's Heather, okay?" she whispered. "All you have to do is meet my eyes and shake your head and I'll know. If it's not her, just give me a thumbs-up. Please?"

"Emily—" The compassion in the man's voice stiffened her resolve.

"Here's a picture of her." She held her phone out to him. He studied it. "She also has a birthmark on her left thigh in the shape of a crescent moon." She bit her lip on the sobs that wanted to break through. "I need to know. You know I do. It's better now than to keep wondering, I promise."

He gave a slight nod. "Okay."

Brady was packing his gear by the time Francisco reached the vehicle. The ME climbed onto the bed of the truck and disappeared behind the makeshift privacy screen. It had gone up in record time and she could no longer see Francisco or anyone else on the forensics team. She waited. And waited. Just when her heart started to lift, Francisco appeared, his gaze met hers, and he shook his head.

Emily's legs gave out and she dropped to the hard ground. Her phone landed beside her. "No!"

---

Brady unhooked three evidence bags from his belt and handed them to Luis. "Can you pass the evidence on to where it needs to go?"

"Sure, but what's up?"

"I have a friend who needs me."

"Gotcha."

Anxious to get to Emily, he slipped off his heavy gear and grabbed it. He looked toward his truck to see Emily crumple, and his heart pounded a painful rhythm. He could only conclude they'd found Heather in the trunk. Or someone she thought was Heather. And someone had beaten him to telling her.

"Was that Francisco?" he asked.

"Yeah," Luis said. "Someone must have had him on standby just in case."

"Oh man. She's met Francisco and knows exactly who he is and what he does. He sure is making the rounds lately." Brady shut his eyes and wished he could pray for her. But what was the point in wishing? He needed to just do it. *God? I don't know why you'd listen to me after I've shut you out for the past eight months, but*

*Emily needs you and since I can't be with her right this minute, could you hold her? Let her know she's not alone? Please?*

He didn't know if the prayer was heard or not, he just knew he felt better for trying on behalf of Emily. He hurried down the dock toward his truck, stopping near the recovered car only long enough to speak to Francisco. "Is it Heather?"

The man looked up, his jovial eyes sad, laced with a weary heaviness that always came with a dead body. "Female, late twenties, single gunshot to the head. Wearing the clothes you identified her as having on the night she disappeared." He shrugged, but it wasn't a nonchalant, dismissive lifting of his shoulders. It was just his way of expressing his sorrow. "According to Emily's picture, it's her. The water is frigid, so even after being under for several days, she's discolored, but recognizable. And she has a birthmark on her left thigh in the shape of a moon." He sighed, his eyes even more hooded. "It's her."

Grief crashed over Brady. He hadn't known Heather, but he knew Emily and the woman's parents would be devastated. "Thanks, Francisco. You told her, didn't you?"

"She asked me to let her know by shaking my head or sending a thumbs-up."

"Great."

"I'm sorry. Should I have refused to tell her?"

"No, no." Yes. "I'll take care of her." He cleared his throat as he hurried to his truck.

Only to reach it and find Emily gone.

He frowned and stowed his gear while looking around for her. He spotted Linc talking to Sheriff Kirk Johnson and hurried over to them. "When did you get here?" he asked his brother.

"Just now."

"Did you see Emily?"

"No, why?"

"Just need to find her. She was by the truck just a few minutes ago." He spotted a group of officers not too far away and jogged toward them. "Hey, any of you guys see the woman who was waiting in the truck?"

"Yeah, saw her duck under the crime scene tape just a couple of minutes ago."

"Duck under—" What did she think she was doing? "Thanks." He took off in the direction the officer pointed.

---

It was Heather in that trunk. It had really been her. Emily hated that she'd been hoping it would be someone else, but she had. Of course, she wouldn't wish the grief of losing a loved one on another family, but . . . she just hadn't wanted it to be Heather. The grief clamped hard. No, now wasn't the time to break down. Now was the time to find that boat and stop the people who'd killed Heather. It might be the last thing she ever did, but if it brought the killers to justice, she was willing to risk it.

She shoved through the crowd of people who'd gathered to gawk and she wanted to yell at them to go away and mind their own business. Instead, she focused on reaching Mr. Gilstrap, who'd demanded to know what was going on. It had taken her several minutes to gather her composure after realizing that Heather was dead. She'd picked up her phone and held it to her ear to hear him yelling at her. "Tell me!"

Emily nodded, unable to speak past the lump in her throat. Finally, she'd gasped. "It was her, Mr. Gilstrap. It was Heather. I'm so sorry."

His hoarse cry still echoed through her mind as she made her way to his car. Just behind the crowd that had gathered, he and Mrs. Gilstrap clutched one another and tears freely flowed.

Emily had forced herself to go numb—something she'd learned while battling to survive on the streets. She couldn't do what she needed to do if she had to wrestle with emotions. So she stuffed them. Deep down inside where nothing and no one could touch them. She stood frozen, unwilling to interrupt the grief, knowing she wasn't welcome to share in it. Not with Mrs. Gilstrap anyway. Finally, Heather's father lifted his head and his gaze snagged on hers. He turned his wife so her back was to Emily, then reached into his pocket and held out his hand.

Emily approached, tears threatening to burst through the numb—and fragile—façade she'd managed to pull around herself. With his wife's face still buried in his shoulder, Mr. Gilstrap opened his hand, palm up. Emily took the card from him and slid it into her pocket. "Thank you," she mouthed.

He nodded and she spun to return to the truck only to have something hard jam into her rib cage. "Ouch! What—"

"Shut up and keep walking," the voice commanded in her ear. Emily wanted to freeze, but he wouldn't let her. With a hard shove, he spun her away from the crowd and propelled her toward a dark blue cargo van. The side doors stood open. "Get in."

She knew that voice. Snake Man. Terror-induced adrenaline pumped hard through her veins. If she got in that van, she was dead. Emily screamed and jerked on her captor's hand. "No! Let me go!"

People turned to look and point. Emily yanked violently and let out another piercing scream.

"Hey! What are you doing? Let her go!" a man from the crowd hollered.

The weapon fell away from her back long enough to fire a shot into the crowd. Then it was back and Emily's knees weakened to the point she wondered if they would hold her. And still she struggled.

Screams echoed around her and he slammed his weapon against her head. Pain shafted through her and she stumbled. His grip kept her from going to the ground. "Keep fighting and next time the bullet hits someone. Get in the van and I don't shoot at anyone else."

"Emily!"

Brady's yell gave her hope.

"Why are you doing this?" she cried.

"Get in!"

"Brady!"

Her captor fired into the crowd once more and Emily clamped her lips together as more screams answered his shot. *Oh please, don't let anyone be hurt.* Emily gave one more desperate pull, but her strength was no match for his. He shoved her into the van. She hit the floor hard, and lightning quick, he was in the back beside her. "Drive!"

The van screeched away. Emily scooted toward the double doors in the back and eyed her captor, who still sat on the floor. Definitely Snake Man. Then her gaze turned to the man in the driver's seat and she blinked. "Paul?" But no, it couldn't be him. This man had a long scar going down the side of his face.

"Afraid not. This time Paul loses." He yanked the van to the right and Emily braced herself to keep upright. "Get up here and drive," Todd said to Snake Man. Snake Man moved to stand beside Todd and held the wheel while Todd slid out of the seat and Snake Man took over. The two men made the exchange so smoothly that Emily gaped. Todd slipped into the captain's chair behind the passenger seat and motioned for Emily to take the one next to him.

She did. "Who are you? Why are you doing this?"

"I'm Todd Cavendish. Paul Bailey is my brother. Twin brother actually. As to why I'm doing this? Let's just say it's a personal vendetta." His eyes narrowed. Emily gaped. She couldn't help it. Todd ran a finger down his scar. "If it wasn't for this, you wouldn't be able to tell us apart."

She clasped her hands to control the trembling. "How do I fit in all of this?"

The van lumbered up a hill and she fought to hang on to her breakfast.

"You're going to get me a flash drive that's going to make me rich."

"Flash drive? I thought everyone was looking for the boat that sank."

"They are. The flash drive is in the safe on the boat that's resting on the bottom of a lake. Although which lake is the big question. But I understand you've recently come into the possession of the SD card that has that location on it."

He knew about the SD card in her pocket. "You've been watching me."

"I've been watching a lot of people."

"Including Heather's parents?"

"Nice people. Pretty boring, but listening in to their conversations finally paid off."

"You bugged their house?"

"Of course. And now that you have the SD card with the pictures, it's going to tell me the location of the boat."

"Pretty clever. Why would I help you?"

"Because the minute you're no longer useful to me, you die."

"Of course," she whispered. And as long as she was alive, the opportunity for escape might happen. "Why did you kill Heather?"

"I didn't."

"Okay, maybe not you, but Martin Burnett did."

"I don't know who Burnett is."

She frowned. "He killed Heather. His face was caught on a security camera, and then Paul's card was found in his house."

"Who found it?"

"The police. They believe he's somehow involved in Heather's murder. I thought you might be working with him, but I guess not."

"No, I'm definitely not working with Paul." He rubbed his chin for a moment. "Heather knew where the boat sank and he doesn't want me to find it. He doesn't want anyone to find it, is my guess."

"Why not?"

"Because of the pictures on the flash drive."

"Of . . . ?"

"Pictures that will send him to prison and probably death by lethal injection. The prison part sounds good. Lethal injection is too fast and easy for what I'd like."

"Why do you hate him so much?" she whispered.

He frowned. Hesitated. Then shrugged. "Because I was taught to."

# 24

**B**rady sagged against the passenger seat of Linc's blue truck even while his mind raced. "Who took her? Did anyone get the plate? Someone tell the news chopper to follow that van! Patch me in to the chopper!"

Was anyone listening? Linc had handed him COMMS just before jumping in the driver's seat, and Brady had shoved the piece into his ear.

"This is Chopper Ten. Who's this?"

"I'm Detective St. John. I need you to follow that van!"

"We got the kidnapping on video. My camera guy zoomed right in to the plate on the van." He gave it to Brady, who shot it to David with "911" after the text.

David texted back immediately.

On it.

Brady caught a glimpse of the van as it careened around the next corner. "Go, go, go."

"I'm going, I'm going. Where's the news chopper?"

"Still there."

"Backup?"

"Coming fast from behind and in front."

The text from David pinged. Brady opened it and read,

Van was reported stolen early this morning.
Plates were stolen, too, as they match up to a
similar van, but not the one you're chasing.

The van spun around the next curve and headed for the trees lining the road. It bounced and landed with a jarring thud, but kept going. Around the next curve and then . . .

"Where'd he go?" Brady yelled.

"He cut off," Linc muttered as he slammed on the brakes. "That side road back there. He shot around the curve and immediately took the left." Linc shoved the gear into reverse. The tires spun for a moment on the dirt road before catching traction and shooting the truck backward.

When Linc was on the back road, Brady kept in touch with the chopper. "We lost them," the pilot reported. "They're off the main road and into the trees, we can't see them."

"They did that on purpose," Brady growled. "Stay up there and see if they surface." *Please surface.*

When the department chopper arrived, the news chopper banked and got out of the way. For the next ten minutes, Linc drove while Brady kept an eye out for the van, desperately searching, heart pounding. "Where'd they go? Come on, someone, find them!"

"No visual. Flying in a grid. They're staying under the trees." The radio went silent. Then crackled to life. "Spotted the van. It's stopped on the side of the road."

"Anyone in it?" Brady asked.

"Can't tell."

"Route me there."

Linc drove. Brady glanced at the rearview mirror and noted the backup behind them. They broke into a clearing and there was the van. Linc slammed on the brakes and Brady threw open the door, weapon in hand. Together, he and Linc approached, guns held ready. "Hands up! Hands on the dash! Linc? You see anyone?"

"No. Could be hiding in the back."

Other officers approached the rear of the van. "Open the door! Out of the van!"

Brady reached the side door and yanked it open with one hand, gun aimed with the other. "Empty on the side!"

"Front is clear!" Linc called.

"Back is clear!"

Brady raced back toward Linc's truck. A crime scene unit would be called, but he wasn't waiting for them. "Let's keep searching," he said as he climbed in.

Linc sat in the driver's seat. Still.

"What are you doing? Let's go!"

"No. We're not going to find her this way. We need to think."

"But—"

"Think. We don't know who has her. We don't know where they're headed."

Brady fell silent but pounded a fist into his open palm while he thought. "This is all about finding that boat," he said. "We haven't talked to the one other person who might know where it is."

"He's in the hospital, still unconscious. He's not going to be able to tell us anything."

"Who brought him to the hospital?" Brady asked.

"I don't know. The wreck happened in North Carolina. I was only able to track him down because I called his wife and she told me where he was."

"North Carolina, huh?"

"Yeah."

"I wonder exactly where that wreck happened in North Carolina," Brady said.

"Let's find out."

*I'm coming, Emily. I'm going to find you.*

The question was, would he be too late?

269

Emily's wrists hurt.

Her arm throbbed.

Her foot ached.

Her head pounded and her fear was off the charts.

She clenched and unclenched her fists, keeping the blood flowing. When they'd stopped the van, she'd had hope. Only to have it fizzle when they'd hauled her out and into a waiting sedan. They drove for about thirty minutes until Snake Man had pulled into the U-shaped drive of the large home. He then escorted her to a chair in the kitchen and held out his hand. She gave him the SD card without a fuss. He would just search her for it and she refused to be subjected to that.

Then he'd tied her up and disappeared.

According to the clock on the microwave, an hour had passed. With each passing minute, her anger rose.

Tears broke the surface and slid down her cheeks.

The door burst inward and she sniffed, stiffened her shoulders, and glared at Paul's scarred look-alike. "You're up." He moved behind her and released her hands.

"What do you mean?"

"I mean, we know what lake we're headed to."

Which meant they didn't need her anymore.

"Come on," he said, and gave her a shove toward the kitchen door.

"Where?"

"The car."

"So you can dump my body somewhere?"

He gave a low chuckle. "Emily, I don't want to kill you."

"For some reason, I heard a silent 'yet' on the end of that." She hated the shakiness in her voice.

His smile faded, leaving a jaw of granite and eyes of ice. "Just do what I ask and we'll see about you walking away." She wasn't that stupid, but she'd let him think she believed him. For now.

"You don't believe me." At her flinch, he shrugged. "Your eyes give you away."

Emily ignored that. "But you have the lake where the boat is. What do you need me for?"

"For something special. You've been kept alive for a reason, you know. Now walk."

His tone refused to be argued with.

She walked. "You've been watching me," she said. "Just like you've been watching Heather's parents."

"Not me personally, but yes, I've had people watching you."

She shuddered.

"Did you know Paul was the one who was trying to have you killed?" he asked.

"Um . . . yes. Well, we sort of figured out that he had Heather killed."

"Stupid," Todd muttered. "Paul gave a business card to the man he hired to kill someone?" He laughed. "That's priceless." His laugh turned into a frown. "That actually doesn't sound like him. He's usually more careful than that." He continued to frown as he pondered that information and Emily bit her lip. He finally shook his head. "He wanted you dead because he was afraid you'd figure out which lake the boat was in."

"Didn't he know that?"

"No. He hired someone to steal the craft from me. Can you believe it? But here's some irony. From what I understand, that person tried to blackmail him into paying him more before he'd release the location of the boat." Todd laughed and shook his head.

"Jeremy Hightower," she said flatly.

Todd shot her a surprised look. "Yes."

"He was in the pictures Heather sent me."

"The same pictures on the SD card."

"I wouldn't know. I haven't seen those, but I would assume."

He smirked. At least his lips did. His eyes never changed. He sounded so congenial when he talked, so laid-back and easygoing, but he was a cold one. And that scared her more than just about anything at the moment. She couldn't let herself believe he planned to let her go. No matter how reasonable he sounded. He was a cold-blooded killer, and she needed to find a way to escape.

A long blast from the horn nearly sent her into cardiac arrest. Snake Man sat behind the wheel of the sedan with a scowl on his face.

"Get in," Todd told her.

"I don't understand. Where are we going?"

"To the bottom of Lake Porter in Carrington, North Carolina."

She buckled up and sat for a moment while that information processed, absently noting that they'd not tied her up. Nor were they trying to hide where they were going. Instead of letting the fear take over, she'd do her best to get as much information as she could from them. On the off chance she managed to escape, she wanted to be able to use whatever she learned. Because if she didn't escape, she knew she'd be dead. "Jeremy took the boat to Lake Porter? How?"

Todd sat next to her while Snake Man drove. He shot her a look as though weighing whether or not he wanted to talk, then gave a minuscule shrug. "The boat was in the water. I'd just pulled in to the dock and left the key in the ignition. One of the marina workers usually takes it to the fuel dock and fills it up so it's ready for the next time I decide to take it out."

"Wait a minute. The *Lady Marie* belonged to a man by the name of Nicholas Raimes."

"So, you figured that out, eh?"

"The boat decal was visible in one of the pictures. But he said he sold it."

Todd scoffed. "He didn't sell it."

Brady never had mentioned getting the bill of sale from the man. "What's your connection to Raimes?"

"He lets me use the boat every once in a while. Actually, he lets me use it whenever I want." He chuckled. "It's more my boat than his. I think he's been on it maybe twice since he bought it a few months ago."

Emily's mind reeled. Okay. Todd, Paul, Raimes. The question was, what was Raimes's role in everything?

Nicholas knew Paul and Todd, but that didn't necessarily mean anything. Just because Todd used the man's boat didn't make Raimes complicit in Todd's crimes. Although, why say he sold the boat when he hadn't?

She shut off her many questions about that and focused on the man beside her. "What is my role in this? We're going to the lake that you now know about. I thought you were keeping me alive for that reason. What else is going on here?"

"You, my dear, are going to dive down, open the safe, and retrieve the contents."

---

The more time that passed, the more Brady's nerves twitched and his adrenaline flowed. It had been almost two hours since Emily had been snatched, and he was ready to climb the walls. Or knock some down. Instead, he found himself tracking down the man who'd survived—barely—the sinking of the *Lady Marie*.

All hospitals smelled the same, and the one that held Frank Jarvis was no different. The man's wife, Jenna, paced in front of his room while they talked. "I just don't understand," she said. "He was on a boat?"

"Yes." Brady showed her the enlarged picture of her husband's face. "We're not sure we have the entire story either, but we need to know where the wreck happened."

She smoothed her hand down the back of her head. A gesture that looked more like habit than the need to straighten her hair. "Um . . . not too far from here. He called and said he'd been stabbed and was driving to the hospital. Then I heard a loud crash. His OnStar system kicked in and that's how the police and paramedics got to him so fast."

Brady straightened and exchanged a glance with Linc. "Wait a minute. Stabbed? Before the wreck happened?"

"Yes."

"Did he say who stabbed him?"

"No."

Brady tapped the maps app on his phone. "Where exactly was the wreck?"

She gave him the location and Brady looked it up. Then a slow smile spread across his lips. "Lake Porter. I guarantee you, he was with Jeremy and somehow managed to get to shore after Jeremy sank the boat. Or they sank it together and Jeremy turned on him."

"Frank wouldn't do that. And neither would Jeremy. They were friends."

Brady wanted to open her eyes to her husband's friend but didn't figure that would help the situation any. "All right, let's get a chopper in the air over Lake Porter and see if we can spot any activity going on out there. It's a huge lake. Lot of square miles to cover. The good news is, not many people are going to be on the water this time of year, so if there's anything going on, it should be easy to spot."

"A chopper's going to alert whoever's got Emily," Linc said. "Might not be the wisest course of action."

"And it might be the only thing that saves her life." He paused. "I've got friends on the Carrington dive team. I'll give Gabe Chavez a call and see if they're available for backup. He'll have to clear it with the team captain, Anissa Bell, but hopefully, that won't be an issue. If whoever has Emily has divers going after whatever's on that boat, then we're going to need some experienced people in the water."

Linc blew out a breath and nodded. "All right. Let's get to work."

# 25

He lowered the binoculars from his spot on the small hill overlooking Lake Porter.

Soon. That's what he kept telling himself. Soon. If he could just be a little more patient, the craziness would die down and he could retrieve what was always meant to be his. All of his careful planning and skillful maneuvering were so close to paying off. Juggling everything had taken its toll, but the showdown was near and the stress was coming to an end. Now, he just needed to kick back and watch it all unfold.

He let the binoculars rest against his chest, then shoved his hands into the front pockets of his five-hundred-dollar pair of perfectly pleated pants. The material soothed. He loved the way it flowed against his skin and fit around his trim waist. Five hundred dollars for a pair of pants. It was absolutely ludicrous.

When he got his hands on that flash drive, he was going to buy ten more just like them. He pulled his phone from his pocket and tapped the app on the screen that would allow him access to the surveillance equipment he'd installed weeks ago when he'd come up with his plan. A plan that had taken some serious detours along the way, but seemed to be back on track.

Excitement built. He'd honestly thought the Gilstrap woman

was going to bring everything crashing down, but Martin Burnett had taken care of her. And then the Chastain woman and her law enforcement friends. But now, it looked like everything was going to work out. As long as Todd didn't mess up.

---

Emily stared at the dry suit the man held out to her. "Are you kidding?"

"Do I look like I'm kidding? I know you dive. My men were watching you and your boyfriend out at the lake. You seemed to enjoy it."

"I did. Very much. But I only started diving that week." She swallowed and held up a hand. "I can't dive by myself."

Todd scowled. "Well, let's put it this way. I have no other options. You have more experience than Hudson or I do, so you're it. Get into the suit and let's get this done." He picked up the helmet. "I even got you the same kind of helmet so there wouldn't be any kind of excuses that you didn't know how to use the equipment."

"But I—"

"Go!" Snake Man stepped forward, his weapon aimed at her head.

She knew as well as they did that her arguing was only prolonging the inevitable. "Seriously, I've only done this a few times," she said, unable to help herself from trying one more time. "And that was with an experienced diver who walked me through everything step by step." Except the last couple of times. He'd made her take over the role of teacher, gently correcting her if she made a mistake. She hadn't made many. And that might be the only reason she would survive this. That, and God. She sent up silent, pleading prayers.

Todd let out a growl of frustration and looked at Snake Man. "Can you do it?"

The man laughed. "Me? I don't even wade in the ocean, man. No, I can't do it."

"You need someone experienced in diving," Emily said. "Didn't you think about this when you were concocting your plan?" Was she really taking him to task for not planning her kidnapping better? But still . . .

"I planned it perfectly," Todd said through gritted teeth. "How was I supposed to know that you weren't experienced? You sure looked experienced." He leaned closer, eyes narrowed, nostrils flaring. "If you've had a few lessons, then you'd better pull out every scrap of knowledge your boyfriend ingrained in you and get this done." He drew in a breath and stepped back while keeping his gaze locked on hers. "Let me put it this way. Your mother and sister can't stay hidden forever. If you don't do this, I'll track them down and kill them both."

She didn't doubt it. With a shaking hand, she pointed. "Hand me the suit. You'll have to fasten the back." She compared this time to the first time she'd decided to pull on a dry suit. When she'd been going with Brady, she'd been so worried about the suit not fitting for a variety of reasons. This time? What if the suit didn't fit? Would he make her go shopping for a new one? Why did the thought make her want to giggle?

She was losing it. Emily slipped off her pink tennis shoes, and the cold from the dock bit into her feet, but she pulled the suit over her clothes and made sure the elastic was secure around her wrists just like Brady had taught her. And wonder of wonders, it fit. That very fact alone sent chills through her. Chills that had nothing to do with the blustery weather. That it was the exact size she needed meant they'd been watching her very closely.

"You have to attach the line to my belt, and when I pull on it four times, it means I have the flash drive," she said. "Then you bring me to the surface. Okay?"

"You be sure to have the contents with you."

"I will. Two sharp tugs means I'm in trouble or I can't get the safe open or something's wrong. Got it?"

"Yeah, but that better not happen." He handed her a device almost identical to the one she and Brady had used. It was a small underwater computer that would tell her exactly how deep she was, how much air she had, and how much time she had before she reached her NDL. Meaning, she could safely surface without stopping to decompress.

She drew in a deep breath and blew it out slowly. "Are you going to kill me after I get you the flash drive?"

"No. Your job's only getting started."

Emily frowned. "What are you talking about?"

"There's information on that flash drive that I need you to handle. You can still access your bank's software, right?"

"Yes," she said, wary where he was going with this.

"Then that's all that matters."

She wanted to press him for more details, but a flash of light behind Todd caught her attention. Could that be help on the way? Hope sparked. Then fizzled. No one knew she was here. It was probably someone just out for a boat ride. And if she alerted them to the fact that she needed help, they would die.

Nausea curled within her.

"You've got the ROV, right?" Todd said to Snake Man.

Emily frowned. "ROV?"

"Remote Operated Vehicle," Todd said.

"I've got it," Snake Man said.

"Good. Get in the boat. We've got a sunken vessel to find and plunder." Todd grinned. "I feel a bit like a pirate. How about you, Hudson?"

Todd's companion didn't seem to be the least bit amused and, without responding, climbed into the boat with the piece of equipment Emily assumed would tell them the location of the *Lady Marie*. She grabbed the flippers and raised a brow when Snake Man held out a hand to help her in. "So you have manners? Who taught you those?"

"My mother."

"I'm sure she's very proud of you."

His grip on her wrist tightened and she refused to flinch. "Don't want you falling on your way in."

Of course not. That would really mess up the plan, wouldn't it?

When she was in the boat, she made her way to the back and sat in the seat farthest away from the driver's. She set her tennis shoes on the seat next to her and vaguely wondered if, once she was at the bottom of the lake, she could simply unhook the rope and swim away. The thought quickened her heartbeat a tad and she could only pray she'd be brave enough to do it when the opportunity presented itself.

It didn't take long for the little boat to make its way out of the cove and into the deeper part of the lake. Emily recognized the hills at the far side of the water as being the ones from Heather's pictures. The wind whipped the hair around her face and she shivered in spite of the dry suit.

Once they came to the area Todd deemed the right place, Snake Man cut the motor. And wonder of wonders, the shore wasn't too far away. Maybe half a mile? She could easily swim that in her suit.

Snake Man sent the ROV into the water. He moved it in a slow back-and-forth pattern and Todd became more agitated by the minute when nothing showed up.

"What's wrong with that thing? Are you sure it's working?"

Snake Man shot Todd an irritated glare. "It's working. It just takes time. This could take a while."

"We don't have a while. I don't know who followed us out here."

"No one followed us. I made sure of that."

Todd relaxed a bit at Snake Man's reassurances, but Emily wasn't so sure. She'd been watching the shore for anyone who might be a potential source of rescue, and the only thing that caught her attention was the occasional flash of light from a vessel that was keeping its distance. Was someone watching?

"There," Snake Man said. "I've got it."

A huge breath whooshed from Todd. "Great." He nodded to Emily. "Get the helmet on. You're going down."

She didn't bother to argue. Desperately, she tried to remember everything Brady had taught her as she pulled on the tank and the helmet. It was just like the one she'd used with Brady. Wow.

Within seconds, she was ready. "How far down is it?" she asked.

Todd glanced at Snake Man, who consulted his ROV. "Around fifty feet."

That helped a little. She and Brady had gone a little deeper than that.

"The code to the safe is 5-4-30," Todd said. "Simple enough. You can remember that, right?"

She nodded and looked off in the distance once more to see the light moving closer. A helicopter passed by overhead, high enough that the two men spared it only a glance, but Emily took heart.

"You got the light?" Todd asked her.

"It's attached to the BCD vest." She glanced at the clear, cloudless sky. The sun shone brightly overhead. "I might not need it." Then again, she might, depending on how stirred up the water was.

The thought chilled her again.

"You'll need a crowbar to get the door to the safe open." He pressed one into her gloved hands. "Take this too. There's no way you'll be able to turn the dial on the safe with those gloves."

She shoved the tool that looked like a curved wrench into one of the slots on her belt. *Oh, God, what am I doing? Please be with me!*

He clipped the rope to her belt, then zip-tied it through the buckle. Dread curled in the pit of her stomach. So much for swimming away. She settled herself on the dive platform just like she'd done when diving with Brady and slid feet first into the cold water.

---

Brady waited impatiently at the stern of the boat while Gabe Chavez and three of the other Carrington dive team members talked softly amongst themselves. Adam Campbell, Ryan Parker, and Anissa Bell. He knew that beneath their relaxed demeanor there was a tension that was ready to spring as soon as they got the location and the green light to go.

Brady and the four had attended various training camps and continuing ed classes together, and he'd gotten to know and respect each of them on a professional level as well as personal. The fact that they'd responded to his request for help, dropping everything to suit up and go out, meant more than he'd ever be able to convey.

So far, the helicopter had made several passes of various areas of the lake and had reported nothing.

Gabe stood next to Brady, watching the water lap the dock. "She means a lot to you?"

"Emily? Yeah."

"Glad to see you've moved past whatever was haunting you about six months ago."

"Krystal," Brady said.

"Didn't know her name or the details, but I could tell you were distracted. And angry."

"I was." He let out a sigh and shook his head. "Krystal put on a great show for most of the world, but she had an addiction to painkillers that was her downfall—and almost mine."

While Brady relayed the information, his mind was only halfway on the telling of the story. The other half was frantic with worry over Emily. Was she okay? Scared? Hurt?

"We'll find her."

Brady blinked. "Sorry. I zoned for a minute, didn't I?"

"No apologies necessary."

"We've got some activity on the lake." The pilot's voice came through Brady's COMMS earpiece. "Repeat. Activity on the lake." Next came the coordinates. "One diver in the water. Two men on the boat."

"Any sign of Emily Chastain?" He'd sent pictures to those hovering over the water.

"That's a negative. But it's possible she's the one in the water. Looks like there's a pair of women's shoes on the back seat."

"Color?"

"Pink running shoes."

Horror hit him. *No. She wouldn't go down alone, would she?* Of course she would if she had a reason to. A threat to kill her would do it. Or a threat against her mother and sister. "That's a few miles away from here," he said. "It'll take us a good ten minutes to get there. Let's go."

The engine roared to life and the team chatter ceased as they focused on the job. Rescuing Emily and catching a possible killer.

---

Emily kicked deeper, realized she was going too fast, and quickly inflated the BCD. As it filled with air, her descent slowed. And just like with Brady, she stopped every so often to let her ears and body adjust. She guessed she'd gone about fifty feet when the hull of the boat snagged her light and she gasped, trying to backpedal while her heartbeat thundered in her ears.

*It's just a boat. It's just . . . a boat. There's more above the water that will hurt you than what's on the bottom of the lake.*

The reminder helped. Some. Okay, not much. This was crazy. She didn't know what she was doing and she was probably going to die, but giving up wasn't an option.

Trying to keep her breathing even, she swam closer to the vessel, her light skimming across the surface.

The safe was inside the master bedroom toward the rear of the boat—the stern. Todd had given her directions to it and made her repeat them back to him. And now all she could think about was that there was no way she wanted to go inside it. But she had to. She kicked her way over the bow and found the sliding glass doors that would allow her entrance into the living area.

Reminding herself to breathe normally, she noted the door was open and glided through, stopping just inside to take in the surroundings. Bolted to the floor, the furniture was eerily in place— exactly like it would have been the day it went down.

She checked her pressure gauge and noted she had plenty of air. Which meant she could take at least one deep breath she desperately needed.

Once her lungs were satisfied, she tried to see if there was another way out of the vessel, should something happen to the way she came in. It seemed logical to have more than one way in and out. She noted a side door in the living area to her right that stood open. Okay, that was good. Next she tried to pinpoint anything her rope could snag on or get tangled around. There were a lot of options that left her feeling a bit sick. But again, she had no choice but to pray God got her through this.

She started for the bedroom.

A flash of light followed by a dark shadow passed by the window to her right and she froze for a second while her heart sped up. She kicked over to the window and looked out. No light, just fish. When nothing else appeared, she propelled herself toward the bedroom once again.

The spooky murkiness sent her adrenaline flowing faster, and she just wanted out, but thoughts of her mother and sister kept her going. Along with the knowledge that the sooner she got this done, the sooner she could surface. While she liked being underwater with Brady, she didn't like this *at all*.

Bypassing the instrument panel, she stopped in the galley that looked like it could be used to cook up a scrumptious meal at any moment. A knife. She could cut the rope and swim to shore. Heart thudding, she made her way to the set of drawers and opened the top one. No knives. She continued until she reached the bottom and found a full block of knives. Emily pulled the largest and reached for the rope. And stopped. Floating, she slowly kicked her flippers to hold herself in place.

She needed to get that flash drive. The police would need whatever was on it. Emily slipped the knife into the side of her belt, careful not to slice her dry suit, and decided to get this done. She continued her journey to the back of the boat, passing the table that seated six. She made her way down the hall and past the bathroom. The door hung open and she glanced inside.

And stopped.

Realized what she was looking at and shrieked. Heart pounding, nausea swirling, she turned away and swallowed. Once. Twice. *Don't puke, don't puke. You can't throw up or you'll drown.*

When she had her gag reflex under control, she shuddered and looked again. Two dead bodies had been shoved into the shower. The door was shut, keeping them enclosed in the small space. One face pressed against the side glass in a grotesque distortion of death that brought on the nausea again. But she needed to look. To process. So she could explain what she'd seen should she be so fortunate as to find herself in a position to do so. The face against the glass had a bullet hole just above his right eye. And then she had to look away again.

So, Jeremy had killed them.

Slowly, she got herself together. But the image of their decomposing, green-and-black bodies would haunt her for a long time to come.

Tears leaked and she sniffed. No crying. She had to be able to see. To focus. She kicked away from the horrid scene and finally found herself in the bedroom. With shaking glove-covered hands, she opened the designated cabinet near the bed and found the safe exactly where Todd said it would be.

Her breaths came in hard puffs, and with a glance at her regulator, she realized she was using up way too much air. For a moment, she simply stopped and leaned her head against the wall in an attempt to control her runaway pulse and rapid-fire breathing.

When her heartbeat slowed and she was once again breathing

relatively normally, she used the gripping tool Todd had given her, attached it to the dial on the safe, and ran through the combination. When she was sure she had done it correctly, she let the tool fall from her hand and pulled the handle.

Only it didn't budge.

She had the right combination because the handle turned, but the door wouldn't move.

Of course. Water pressure. That's why she needed the crowbar. *Now would be a really good time to start thinking, Em.*

Maneuvering so she could place her flippered feet against the wall and grab the handle with both hands, she pulled. The door opened a fraction. Just enough for her to grab the crowbar from her belt and jam it into the crack. She pushed to the side and the door opened, allowing another rush of water to flood the inside, equalizing the pressure—and giving her access to the contents. The safe held several plastic bags of cash and a thicker, padded plastic envelope encased in another waterproof bag. She took that and left the cash.

Finally.

With the flash drive secure in the zippered pocket of her dry suit, she turned.

Only to choke on a scream when she spotted the figure floating in the open doorway. The large knife in his hand ruined all of her hard work at breathing normally.

# 26

Todd paced the small area of the boat, wanting to demand what was taking her so long. Unfortunately, while Emily's helmet had the ability to communicate, he didn't have the other equipment necessary to do so. He should have thought of that. With a huff, he slumped into the seat, his eyes on the line. Should he pull her up? Ask her what the problem was and what was taking so long?

His phone rang. "What?"

"You got it yet?"

"No. She's down there working."

A pause. "You're sure she can get it?"

"I'm sure. Just chill, Jeff, okay?" The man was starting to wear on his nerves. He'd been growing more and more tense over the last week or so. "You're going to get your cut. I'm just waiting for her to come up."

"Should have gotten that boyfriend of hers to get it. That was the original plan."

Todd rolled his eyes. "And I told you I wasn't dealing with a cop who'd try to escape or simply refuse to cooperate. This is much better, I promise. Now, just hang tight. I'll let you know when we're on the way. Have the computer ready."

"It's ready."

"Boss?"

Todd gritted his teeth and turned toward Hudson. "What?"

"Got a boat heading our way and that chopper is coming closer. I don't like this."

Todd frowned and the tension across the back of his shoulders doubled. "Talk to you later." He hung up.

Hudson had the binoculars to his eyes.

"What do you see?" Todd demanded.

The man swore. "I see enough to know that we need to get out of here."

"Cops?"

"I think so. In the chopper for sure. Not so sure about the other boat. It seems to have stopped and is just sitting there." He held the binoculars to his eyes a little longer, then lowered them. "I don't know. Something doesn't feel right. We need to go."

"We can't go. Not without that flash drive."

"It's not worth going to prison for."

A gunshot cracked the still air. Red burst from Hudson's chest. He slumped in his seat.

Todd darted to him and pulled the man to the floor, not bothering to check and see if he was still alive. There wasn't anything he could do for him at this point nor did he care to do so. Ducking low, he grabbed the rope that he'd attached to Emily and started reeling her in. Fast.

She'd have the bends, coming up so quickly, but she'd had enough time to get the flash drive and it was time to go. And even if she didn't have it, he had to get rid of her since she knew who he was. He now knew the location of the boat. He could get someone else and come back when things cooled down.

Another shot slammed into the side of the hull and he ducked but didn't stop pulling. Leaving without her wasn't an option.

When the rope stayed slack, his heart skipped into a frantic, desperate rhythm. Had she managed to cut herself loose? When no more shots sounded, he raised his head slightly to see the boat racing for the dock.

What?

Todd gave one more yank on the line and pulled the end into the boat.

Minus Emily.

---

"Who's shooting?" Ryan yelled.

Brady pointed. "That guy in the boat! He's shooting at Emily's boat!"

Only the fact that Emily wasn't actually *on* the boat kept him from diving in and trying to get to her.

Another shot pinged off the craft. Brady kept the binoculars on his eyes. "One guy's down. The other guy dropped low. And he pulled the rope in. Emily's not on the end of that rope!"

Another shot.

The man on the boat returned fire, then ducked low. Nothing happened.

"Can we get close enough to return fire without getting ourselves shot?" Gabe asked.

Anissa shook her head. "We don't have any coverage on this vessel. Look. There he is."

"What's he doing?" Brady muttered. "Stay down, you idiot. Don't give him a target."

The man lifted his head a fraction too far and the next bullet found its mark. A fine red mist sprayed upward. "We've got to stop them or we're next," Brady said. "Can anyone get a bead on him? Ryan?"

"I can't get a visual," Ryan said, his gun aimed in the direction of the craft. He shook his head and lowered the weapon. "I'd need a rifle to hit him at this range."

"I think someone else is down there with her," Brady said,

lowering the binoculars. "Get the chopper to make a pass over the shooter, will you?"

Gabe spoke into the COMMS, and within seconds, the chopper made a low pass over the boat.

The little speedboat holding the killer sped away. The chopper followed. "They'll stay with the boat and hopefully someone can pick him up," Anissa said. "Our lake unit is on the way and I've already called for a forensics team and the ME for the dead guys in that boat."

"We need to get to Emily," Brady said. "Now." Was she hurt? Was she even alive? His heart thundered in his ears as he tried to keep his cool.

Gabe grabbed his helmet. "Let's go get her."

"I'm ready," Adam said.

"Ryan, you're Adam's tender. I'll be Gabe's," Anissa said.

And Brady chafed because he was stuck on the boat with no dive gear. He'd taken off after Emily without thinking he'd wind up on another lake needing to go in.

Thankfully, he could listen in on the COMMS. Otherwise, he'd be tempted to just go in without a suit. And he would if he didn't trust this team.

"Suit up, St. John," Ryan said.

"What?"

"We're about the same size." Ryan handed him his dry suit. "If that was my lady down there, I wouldn't be up here."

Without questioning the gift, Brady pulled on the suit faster than had ever been done in the history of dives. "Thanks, man," he said before pulling the helmet over his head. "I appreciate it."

"I've got your rope," Ryan said. "We'll find another way to let Adam be useful."

"Have him update Linc."

"I can do that," Adam said.

"Can you get us in closer to the boat, Anissa?" Gabe said.

Once they were right over the spot where Emily went down if the boat was any indication, he and Gabe went to the dive platform and slid into the water feet first.

———

The man with the knife had moved closer and Emily had grabbed the rope to give it two yanks. Only to find he'd cut her loose. For several minutes, they'd done a crazy kind of water dance. He'd move closer, she'd dart away, her goal to get to the door. And then he'd move back to block her. The water continued to grow murkier as they stirred things up. What did he *want*?

Panic quickened her breathing, and while she desperately wanted to look at her air gauge, she didn't dare take her eyes off the blurry man in front of her.

He lunged at her. She kicked hard and shot past him, swinging out with the crowbar she still clutched in her right hand.

Her shot in the dark connected with his arm, and the knife sank to the bottom of the vessel. His dark eyes flashed at her from behind the mask, and she kicked backward toward the doorway.

And stared in horror as his hand snaked out to grab at the trailing rope. He missed. Emily continued her exit even as she snagged the rope to reel it in. She had to get out of the boat before she had a full-blown panic attack. Her feet kicked in frantic swipes, propelling her toward the galley. She expected to feel the edge of the blade sink into her back at any moment.

She spun to see him gaining on her, reaching for the still-trailing end of the rope with one hand and gripping the knife in the other. The fact that he'd stopped to retrieve it had gained her a few precious seconds, but not many.

She continued to kick even as she yanked the rope away from his grip. If he managed to grab it, she was done. She darted out of the side door and into the open expanse of the lake.

With frantic kicks, she headed for the surface.

The next raging question was, how was she going to slow down to avoid decompression sickness? No more than thirty feet per second, right? Was it better to risk that or would it be better to let him catch up with her and try to escape later?

Or would he just stab her when he caught her?

*God, please!*

She glanced at her gauge and gasped. Fifteen minutes remained and then she'd be in serious trouble. Her rapid, panicked breathing had used the air faster than was good. Not only that, but she was quickly reaching her no decompression limit.

She inflated the BCD and slowed her ascent. She needed to stop for at least three to five minutes and that just wasn't going to be possible.

The man behind her did the same. Emily continued to gather rope only to have him make a whip-fast lunge and snag the end of it.

A strangled shriek escaped her and she kicked out.

He yanked her back . . .

. . . and slowly reeled her in.

## 27

**B**rady and Gabe kicked their way deeper. "See anything?" Gabe asked.

"No."

"What was she doing down here anyway?"

"I don't know," Brady said. "Everyone's been chasing the location of the *Lady Marie*, which supposedly sank in this area. Whatever was on it when it sank is apparently worth killing and kidnapping over—and they believed Emily could lead them to it due to some pictures that were texted to her by her friend." The conversation was good. It kept his fear for Emily from completely overwhelming him. He could talk and scan the water, mostly because he couldn't see much. It was churned up and visibility was poor. "She could be two feet in front of me and I wouldn't know it," he muttered.

"All right, let's do another sweep. Swim in a grid just like in training. If we don't see the boat, we're going to have to bring in the ROV. Even though we're right under the dinghy, they didn't anchor it and it could have drifted."

"Yeah." Nothing he hadn't already thought about.

"You got that, Anissa? Ryan?"

"Got it."

For the next few minutes, they swept the area, communicating with Anissa and Ryan above, who guided them in the search, making sure they were staying on course and not simply covering the same area over and over.

"There." Brady pointed. "I thought I saw something. Ryan, I need more rope." He swam toward whatever it was his light had snagged. As he got closer, he could see a solid object that grew bigger and finally morphed into the bow of the sunken vessel. "This is it. We found it."

"See if you can see the name on the side," Gabe said.

Brady swung around to the side and used his light to illuminate the port side near the front. "The *Lady Marie*," he said. On the one hand, knowing Emily might be in there, it was all he could do to keep from dashing into the boat. On the other . . .

"All right, let's get in there and see what we can find."

Brady's gut twisted. "I hate penetration diving."

"Right there with you," Gabe said. "Going into those unstable environments is enough to give me nightmares."

"Gabe? Brady?" Anissa said. "Adam said the team just arrived to process the boat with the two dead guys. And the chopper just communicated that they caught the guy who shot them."

"Excellent. Find out who he is if you can."

"Adam's on it."

Brady came to the entrance of the craft and stopped at the sliding glass doors. Was Emily in there? Was she alive? Hurt? He swallowed and pushed on through. He hated penetration diving. There were so many ugly ways to die, so he avoided it at all costs. Only for Emily—or one of his teammates—would he do this. He went inside and Gabe went around him. "Man, bet this was a pretty sweet lady when she was on the other side of the water."

"Yeah." Brady followed. "Watch that drawer full of knives down there."

Gabe gave him a thumbs-up and headed for the short hallway. Brady trailed behind, keeping an eye on the lines. Through the control room, the galley, down the hall . . .

. . . and slammed into Gabe's back.

The man placed a hand on the wall to steady himself and turned. "Dead bodies."

In the span of half a second his heart stopped, then galloped out of control. "Emily?"

"Oh no, man, sorry. Two guys. I think. One's definitely shot in the head. It's not pretty, but it's not Emily."

The thundering in his chest slowed. He slid around so he could see and shuddered at the sight. Horror-movie worthy. He'd dealt with his share of recovery calls, but he never got used to it.

"Dead bodies?" Anissa said. "Plural?"

"Affirmative, but we're not exactly following recovery protocol at the moment," Gabe said.

"We'll sort it out later. Keep looking for Emily."

Brady scanned the lines as Gabe made his way into the bedroom. So far, so good. No snags, catches, or other trouble. Other than the fact that he hadn't found Emily yet. *Please, God, let her be okay . . .*

"The safe's open," Gabe said. He swam over to it. Brady stayed with him, adjusting his BCD pressure slightly. "Lots of money in here. She didn't bother with that. Interesting."

Brady turned and headed for the exit. "Okay, I think it's safe to say Emily's not here. Let's get out of here."

But if she wasn't in the wreckage and her line had been cut, what had she done and where had she gone? More important, who had she gone with?

---

Emily had stopped struggling when she realized that she couldn't escape. Fighting used up her air, and she had a feeling she'd better conserve as much as possible. Her captor didn't seem compelled to try to explain what he had planned, he simply swam next to her, the knife in his hand a constant threat.

The knife she'd pilfered from the galley was still tucked in her belt and she didn't think he'd seen it or he would have taken it. Not sure how he could have missed it, she decided to be grateful and let him lead, since it appeared he was headed to the surface. When he stopped for a moment, she stayed at the end of the line as far from him as she could.

Then he was moving again, pulling her along.

After one more stop, they surfaced. He pointed to the dock. It was similar to the one she'd started out on with Todd and Snake Man, but was farther away and located in a cove lined with large houses. Out of sight of most of the open water area, Emily had no idea where she was. She just knew she needed to get out of the water and away from this man.

He gave her a yank and she swam for the dock. She scrambled up the ladder and sat for a moment, making sure her left arm covered the knife at her side. She was surprised at how tired she was. Exhausted, actually. According to the small computer on her arm, she'd been down there close to forty-five minutes. It had felt like forty-five years. She pulled off the helmet and set it aside. The cold wind lashed at her face and she left the dry suit hood covering her head.

He stood over her and pulled his mask off. "Give me the flash drive. And before you argue about it, I won't kill you, but I will hurt you to get it. Am I clear?"

And he'd find the knife. "Crystal," she said. She pulled the flash drive out of the little pocket on her suit and handed it to him.

"Keep that nice, cooperative attitude and he might be merciful and kill you quickly. Otherwise, you'll hurt for a very long time." As she was processing that, he nodded to her feet. "Get the flippers off and let's go."

She debated arguing with him and decided against it for now.

Keeping her left side away from his line of sight, she wordlessly slid the flippers off, grateful for the neoprene that protected her feet from the chill.

She stood. "Now what?"

"Walk."

Emily walked, keeping her left elbow down and her face tilted away from the wind. "Where are we going?"

"There's a van parked up that hill and around the curve. Fortunately, I work for a man who plans for every contingency. He's had his eyes on Cavendish for a while now, watching him, following him." He scowled. "Following you. He wasn't happy with your bodyguards."

"Sorry to inconvenience him." She shuddered and wrapped her arms around her middle. The fingers of her right hand touched the knife.

"We're going to get in that van and I'm going to take you to someone who's very anxious to meet you."

That didn't sound promising. "Where's Todd and Snake Man?"

He raised a brow. "Snake Man?"

"The guy who was with Todd. Had the big snake tattoo on his neck that ran down to his hand. Grant."

"Oh. Grant Hudson."

"Right."

"He's dead. So is Todd."

She swallowed a gasp. "Okay. But I thought . . ." She stopped. "You work for Paul Bailey, don't you?"

A hard smile curved his lips. "He said you were smart."

"Todd said he and his brother hated each other."

"That's an understatement. Now go."

Emily trudged to the van, wondering if she was making a mistake in cooperating. But that knife hadn't left his hand and she wasn't sure she wanted to risk him using it. Not to kill her, as it was obvious he was keeping her alive for something, but she was quite sure he wasn't lying about hurting her. She shivered and spotted the van. *God, I'm going to have to put this in your hands. You know how I want this to end. I'm scared. Really, seriously scared, and I need you more than ever right now.*

She continued her prayer as she climbed into the passenger seat and buckled her seat belt. While he rounded the van, she slid the knife from the left side of the belt to the right.

*God? Please help me.*

———

Brady pulled his helmet off. "I can't believe this." Would he never catch up with her? "Where'd you see her?"

Anissa lowered the binoculars. "She and another person exited the water using that dock. There was a van parked at the top of the hill. They got in it and drove away. I couldn't get the plate, but I've already called it in and the chopper is looking for it right now."

"Can we head in? I need to be helping search for her."

"Absolutely." Anissa aimed the boat toward the other side of the lake where they'd originally started. Brady skimmed out of the borrowed dry suit, then called Linc. He paced and they schemed while the boat skipped effortlessly over the waves, headed to shore. "Did the chopper get a visual on the vehicle?" he asked his brother.

"Not yet."

"We've got to find her, Linc. I know she's scared out of her mind."

"Hopefully not. She's going to have to keep it together."

Brady sighed. "Yeah."

Finally, the shore came into sight and he saw Linc waiting, leaning against his vehicle. Hopefully, the truck that would take him to Emily.

He turned to Gabe, Ryan, and the others. "Thank you all for your help."

"Anytime," Gabe said.

The others echoed the sentiment and Brady jogged to join Linc. Once he settled in the passenger seat, Linc handed him a COMMS piece and Brady shoved it into his left ear.

"What's the update?" he asked Linc.

"Still no sign of the vehicle description or plate."

Brady closed his eyes and sent up a silent prayer. One thing about this situation, it had him speaking to God again. Begging. Pleading.

Just like Emily had done with Heather.

The thought chilled him and he pressed his palms against his eyes. How had he fallen so hard so fast for this woman? It terrified him. And thrilled him at the same time. As long as he could get her back.

Linc's phone rang. "It's the sheriff of Carrington. They gave him my contact info when they figured out who the two men on the boat were." He hit the Bluetooth button that would allow Brady to listen in as well. "Yeah, Sheriff, what do you have?"

"We've identified the two men. An ex-con named Grant Hudson and a man by the name of Todd Cavendish. Both thirty-four years of age."

"I recognize the name Hudson, but not Cavendish."

"I did a little research. He's had an interesting business career with a lot of ups and downs. As a teen, he was involved in a boating accident that left a bad scar on his face. He recovered and graduated from high school and legally changed his name after his parents got divorced."

"What was his name before he changed it?"

"Todd Garrett Bailey."

## 28

Emily gasped as her captor turned into the driveway of a gated estate, and she leaned forward, taking in as much of it as she could. Not because she appreciated the beauty, but because she needed an escape route.

Unfortunately, all she saw were rolling hills surrounded by a wrought-iron fence with a pointy spike at the tip of each piece.

The vehicle pulled around back and her driver killed the engine. "Try to run and I'll shoot you in the back."

"Kind of defeats the purpose of not killing me in the water when you had the chance, doesn't it?"

He scowled. "Get out."

Emily did so, refusing to acknowledge her pounding heart and wobbly knees. She needed to get a message to Brady or 911 or someone, but how to do that wasn't clear. She had no phone again and the man who'd taken her from the lake didn't appear inclined to share his.

She let him guide her toward the back entrance. He kept a hand on her upper arm, but his grip didn't hurt. Fear wanted to send her running, the knowledge that it wouldn't do a bit of good propelled her forward.

Just inside the back door off the garage, a set of steps led down. "Go down," he said.

Stomach churning, she started down, only the knife at her side gave her the courage to continue. At the bottom of the steps, she stopped. A large wooden door at the bottom stood cracked open. "Inside," he said and pushed it open over her shoulder.

Emily grappled for control of her terror while ordering her heart to slow its frantic pace. She stepped over the threshold and gasped, barely managing to contain the shriek clawing to escape.

The man tied to the chair rolled his head at the sound, but his eyes remained closed. "No more," he said. "Please, no more."

She looked at the contents on the plastic that covered the floor, then looked away before she threw up. The poor man's face ran red as did his exposed chest. But wait . . . she steeled herself and took another look at the battered face. "Jeremy?"

His lids fluttered and he squinted, as though having a hard time focusing. "Emily?"

"Oh my . . . Jeremy . . ." What could she say? Or do? For so long she'd hated him, but now . . . pity filled her. And maybe even compassion.

A man stepped out of the shadows, the knife in his right hand clearly used recently. "Paul Bailey," she whispered his name. "You killed Todd and Snake Man . . . uh . . . Grant Hudson."

"Well, not me personally, but I have very efficient hired assassins. Take Jake over there. Former special forces, sniper, diver, and bomb expert all rolled into one—and worth every penny."

"You killed Heather." Fury rose, almost obliterating the fear racing in her veins.

"Actually, I didn't. You can thank Jeremy for that one. He went out on his own and hired Burnett. I only found out about it later."

"Because Heather had seen him at the lake. How'd she know he was there?"

"Apparently, she'd been following him. The Tuesday before she was killed, we talked a good bit. She was very angry with that man in the chair because of some past misdeed he'd committed against a friend of hers and had taken it upon herself to follow him. When she came upon him, he'd stolen the boat and taken it out to Carrington."

Heather had been following Jeremy because of Emily. The knowledge was like a kick in the stomach.

"How did you discover all this?" If she kept him talking, maybe she could think of a way out. Although, with only one small window in the corner, she wasn't sure what that would be.

"Heather had her laptop in the car and had a document open where she was writing her story and making notes. It was very informative."

A throat cleared from behind him and Emily's eyes probed the shadows of the room. "I think that's enough talking," Paul said. "You can die now."

What? "No, wait a minute, something's not adding up. Please? A few more questions?"

"I don't think so."

"Oh, answer her questions, Paul," the man in the shadows said. "Then you can kill her, get your pictures, and we can be done with all of this. You brought her here to brag about how you bested Todd, so get on with it."

Paul scowled. "Fine. What questions?"

"You hired Martin Burnett and Owen Parker to kidnap me, right?"

"No. That was Jeremy's doing. I didn't want you or Heather dead at first. Unfortunately, Jeremy was quick to act and had Heather killed before I could get to her."

"Because he didn't want you to know the location of the boat."

"Yes."

"Burnett told him about the pictures on Heather's phone that she texted to me."

"Apparently."

Emily rubbed a hand across her head and realized she still had on the hood. She shoved it back. "So, Todd wanted me alive to get the location and later the flash drive from the boat and you wanted me dead in order to prevent that."

"Yes."

"Then why bring me here?"

His eyes flickered. "Because you have been a major thorn in my side. And I wanted you to see who the better brother was."

"What?"

"And now that you know, I think I'm going to allow my friend to get rid of you. You caused him quite a bit of stress too." He turned to the man he'd called friend. "Would you like the honors?"

The man in the corner stepped out of the shadows.

She gaped. "Who are you?"

He gave a slight bow. "Nicholas Jeffrey Raimes at your service. Childhood friend to Paul and Todd Bailey. Also known affectionately as Jeff by those who love him."

His hand lifted, the gun aimed at her, then he shifted it slightly and pulled the trigger. She ducked and covered her ears just as the second shot sounded, then the third.

When she stood, Jake lay on the floor behind her, Paul in front of her, and Jeremy stared with blank eyes at the ceiling.

In horror, Emily turned to the man now aiming at her once more.

---

Linc pulled to a stop at the gated entrance while a helicopter hovered overhead, the blades pounding in time with the beat of Brady's runaway heart. If they had guessed wrong, Emily could die. There'd been no time to do a reconnaissance of the place to confirm she was here.

But it was the only thing that made sense. "So, Annie sent me some interesting information. Paul and Todd's maternal grandparents were millionaires," Linc said above the sound of the rotor. "They moved here in the midsixties and built this mansion. They cut off their daughter when she refused to marry the man they'd picked out for her but reconciled when the twins were born. Then the parents split and Paul stayed with his father while Todd stayed with his mother. Todd and his mother moved in here but were soon kicked out because of Todd's wild ways. Paul came knocking after his father died, and everyone says Paul and his grandparents were very close and he inherited this place when his grandmother passed. His grandfather is now in a nursing facility suffering from dementia. He's had no visitors in the ten years he's been there."

Disgust twisted Brady's gut. Paul Bailey had made millions in the human trafficking industry, working with Jeremy Hightower, Martin Burnett, and Owen Parker. Phone records indicated that Burnett and Jeremy Hightower were in constant communication with one another.

"I pray we're right about this," Brady said.

"You're praying again?"

"I am."

"Emily's influence?"

"Yes."

"I like her."

"So do I."

Linc lifted his phone to his ear. "Annie? Yeah. We're here. Do your stuff."

The gates began their slow open. Linc shot through and the mixture of law enforcement behind them stayed close. "Annie? Are the cameras out?"

"They are. For a short time anyway."

They followed the curving drive, stopping short of the house. SWAT spilled from their van to fan out around the property.

"Blueprints?" Linc asked.

"On your phone," Annie said.

"Thanks."

"I've tapped into the security cameras inside the house. I'm not seeing any movement on the first or second floors, but there are three cars in the garage as well as a motorcycle. A THU is on the way with FLIR. As soon as it gets there, we'll know exactly how many warm bodies we're dealing with and where they are."

The FBI's Tactical Helicopter Unit with FLIR. Forward Looking InfraRed. Only the best for the bureau in heat-seeking technology.

"Got a vehicle at the back. Running the plates," a voice said through the COMMS.

"Looks like the house is empty, according to the cameras," Annie said. "But hold tight. Let me keep looking."

The chopper announced its approach, the blades whomp-whomping far above them. But he knew they already had their heat-seeking FLIR trained on the home. Soon, they should know something specific. Brady's heart thundered. What if they were wrong? Would Emily die because they couldn't find her fast enough? No. No she wouldn't. *Please, God, protect her.*

---

Hands held in front of her, Emily obeyed the command to sit at the computer. She kept her right side away from him, waiting for her opportunity to use the knife. If she could. She thought if he was going to kill her—and she had no doubt that was how it was all supposed to end—she could do what she had to do to protect herself. The irony hadn't escaped her. In the past, she'd used knives, razors, or even a sharp fingernail to cut herself. And now the knife might be the very thing that allowed her to live.

He handed her the flash drive and she inserted it in the USB port before the order left his mouth. She clicked on the icon and a document full of numbers displayed on the screen.

Wait a minute, she knew that routing number.

"These are account numbers."

"They are."

"With a *lot* of money in them." She cut her eyes to him. "Compliments of the human trafficking business?"

"Clever girl."

She stared up at him. "You pitted them against each other, didn't you?"

"It wasn't hard. I had their complete trust. A word here, a word there. Since neither knew that I was 'working' for the other, they were so easy to manipulate. The only real scare was when Jeremy went off on his own and sank the boat. Then killed the one person besides himself who knew where it was."

"He also killed two of the three men who helped him." That black-and-green face pressed up against the shower door flashed, and she shuddered, swallowing the instant sensation of nausea.

"Oh yeah, he was trying to blackmail Paul into paying him more."

"I'm guessing Paul had no interest in that?"

"No." He nodded to the computer. "Those are Paul's account numbers. All told, he has over sixty-two million dollars in liquid cash. I believe I could live very well on that."

"Gabe got you these numbers, didn't he?"

"Yes. Mr. Kingman was the beginning. You see, Paul was a very arrogant man. A psychopath, no doubt. He took joy in killing. I also knew he had pictures of some of his crimes on his laptop. Killings he'd done right here in this room. I simply found someone who needed a lot of money and had the skills to hack into Paul's computer and download the pictures. Reuben Kingman fit that description perfectly. I paid him handsomely to deliver them to Todd Bailey, along with a print of one of the pictures to Paul to let him know someone had breached his security. Unfortunately, one of Paul's men witnessed the exchange and took photos of the transaction between Todd and Kingman. Needless to say, Paul was enraged."

"And killed Gabe."

"Indeed."

"You set him up, didn't you?"

He shrugged. "It wasn't hard. He was greedy and hated his life. He thought the money would buy him some happiness."

Tears clouded her vision and she blinked them away. She could cry later. "So you knew what each brother was up to and finagled things to work against them and in your favor."

"That's a pretty simple summary, but I have to say, it's very accurate."

"Todd knew about the account numbers, didn't he?"

"Of course. He was beyond excited to steal all of that money from his brother. You see, Paul, at my urging, had stolen most everything Todd had ever worked for. So Todd was most happy to go along with my plans. Until he learned about the pictures that could put Paul away for life. Those consumed him to the point that he didn't even care about the account numbers or the money anymore. Of course, once Paul was in prison, Todd would have taken the money and gloated the rest of his life."

"Only you neglected to tell him how the plan was really going to play out. With him dead."

"Yes. I might have left that little detail out."

"And now, you want me to transfer the money to your accounts, then you kill me and live happily ever after."

"Again, a simple summary, but yes."

"Well, if I'm going to die anyway, why should I do it?"

"Because while you're going to die, you get to choose whether it's quick and easy . . ." He placed the gun against her temple. "Or slow and painful." He moved the barrel to her elbow.

She swallowed. *Come on, Brady, I know you're looking for me. Please, God, let him find me in time.*

"So, use your remote login and do your thing." He glanced at a screen over the door and tensed. "Now."

She flicked a glance at the screen and didn't see anything. Her mind raced. How was she going to do this? The transfers would take a few minutes, but she needed to get a message to Brady. But with Raimes looking over her shoulder, she wouldn't be able to do anything.

But she still had the knife.

She logged her way in to the bank software, deliberately messing up her password the first time.

"You better be able to get in."

"Sorry." She shot him a baleful look. "My fingers are a little shaky."

With the next attempt, she was in.

A shadow at the small window to her left caught her attention and she ignored it. However, it gave her hope and sent her prayers into overdrive. "Okay, I need the account number you want to transfer the funds to."

He put it on the table in front of her. "How long will it take?"

"There are a lot of accounts here and I have to enter everything manually. Probably fifteen or twenty minutes."

"Get to it."

Emily did, going slower than her normal rate, praying she was buying herself some time. The man next to her finally started pacing.

But he never had his back to her for very long. However, on his next trek to the far wall, she pulled up the bank's message system and typed in Brady's number. The fact that she actually remembered it astounded her. On his way back, she shut the box and moved to the next account number.

Raimes stopped to look over her shoulder and her heart thundered a frantic beat—until he moved away to pace again. She immediately pulled the box up and typed, "In the basement, back door, steps lead down, door is open. Raimes is behind it all."

She shut the box and returned to the accounts.

"How much longer!"

Emily flinched. "Just a few more minutes."

As she watched the money go into the accounts, she silently prayed. Time was running out. That meant it was time to make a decision.

On Raimes's next nervous stride to the wall, she let her hand go to the knife at her side. Nerves quivered inside her.

And the door flew open.

"Police! Hands up, hands up!"

A hard hand grabbed her by the hair, halting her mid-flight. Her neck snapped back and pain arced through her. But the hard barrel of the gun against her temple froze her.

And she was so over it.

She twisted her right hand and jabbed back. A harsh cry escaped him and he stumbled back. Emily went to the floor. A loud crack had her ears ringing, and she rolled, covered her head, and three more pops filled the air.

For a split second, everything was silent. Then hands were on her biceps pulling her away from the man writhing on the floor. Blood gushed from the wound in his thigh.

He gasped, fear written across his face, and she locked eyes with him. She was watching a man die right in front of her. Soon, he'd breathe his last and step into eternity. A surge of compassion flooded her, and she pulled away from the hands and dropped to her knees beside him.

"Repent, Jeff," she whispered. "Don't die with this on your soul."

"H-how?" He coughed and blood spilled from his lips.

"Call out to Jesus," she said. "Tell him you're sorry and ask him to forgive you . . ." His eyes had glazed over. But another breath rattled into his lungs. "Do you hear me? Did you pray it?"

She thought he gave a short nod before his eyes went blank.

And Emily burst into tears. This time she let the hands lead her away, up the stairs, and out into the sunset.

Brady sank to the ground with his arms around her and simply held her.

# 29

Emily and Brady sat on the end of the dock while the other St. John siblings played a rousing game of Phase 10 on the glassed-in porch.

"You want to dive?" he asked.

"We can, but I'm content just to sit here and talk to you. The dry suit is keeping me warm."

He slid an arm around her. "I hope being next to me has something to do with keeping you warm."

She laughed. Over the past six weeks, they'd spent every spare minute together, working around their work schedules to get to know one another, dive, and repair their battle-weary souls. "I feel so awful Claire Beaumont was a victim of Paul's. His evil touched—and hurt—so many people." The woman had been found dead, wrapped in plastic and stuffed into the extra freezer she'd had in her balcony storage area. "I can't help but think about her every so often."

"Yeah. I know."

They fell silent and Emily leaned into Brady's embrace.

Snuggled against this man's side had become her very favorite place in the world—even if she kept waiting for the other shoe to drop. And hated that she kept waiting.

"Can I ask you a question?" Brady asked. "It's been bugging me for a while."

"Of course."

He drew in a breath and let it out slowly. "How could you do it? I mean it was amazing and exactly what you should have done, and I'm just having a hard time with it."

She drew back and frowned at him. "Do what?"

"Basically lead that killer into heaven. He's in heaven now, thanks to you."

She shrugged. "I don't know, Brady. This world is so messed up. Sometimes, I wonder if there's any good left. And then God places people in my life that say there is. People matter. Even the ones who hurt others. I don't deserve heaven and Nicholas Raimes certainly doesn't, but I don't wish him an eternity in hell, either." She relaxed and rested her head back against him. "All I could see was the thief on the cross and Jesus forgiving him." She sighed. "So many people died over the course of all of that craziness. People who I believe will spend eternity separated from God. I just didn't want the devil to win another one."

"And that's why I'm falling in love with you, Emily Chastain," he said softly. "If you can't think back over what you just said and understand that, then you are way more hardheaded than I thought."

She went still. "You asked me that question on purpose, didn't you?"

"Yep."

"Because you already knew why I did it."

"Yep. It's a clear example of who you are. One of many examples of your true character. And I don't have any trouble at all seeing them."

"But you knew I needed to say it out loud and hear it for myself?"

"Uh-huh. Something like that."

"Okay."

"Okay what?"

"I think I have an inkling of what you're getting at." She smiled. "All my life I've let my weight define me. Well, up until about nine or ten years ago, but it's a constant battle not to let it batter my self-esteem. And while I'll probably never be happy with the number on the scale, it doesn't mean I can't find peace and happiness in other things."

"Like what?"

"Like confirmation that God really does have a plan for me— mostly because I'm not dead and probably should be."

"Well, you were pretty instrumental in bringing down that human trafficking ring. Thirty-seven people in all. And over a hundred rescued victims? That's phenomenal."

"Yeah. I do feel good about that."

"So does Heather's boss. He was really happy when you showed up to talk to him."

"I did it for Heather. She deserved the credit for that story. I'm glad he gave it to her."

"Amen." He paused. "What else can you have peace and happiness about?"

She looked at him from the corner of her eye. "I'm beginning to understand and really believe that I can trust you unconditionally. I don't think I've ever truly had that with anyone but Heather."

"Thank you," he said. "I've wanted to hear that for a while." He cleared his throat. "And the Gilstraps? They're okay?"

"They will be. Mrs. Gilstrap apologized for blaming me. She said she was really just mad at Heather and was projecting that on to me. She asked if she could still be a part of my life. Of course I said yes."

"And your mother and sis—dau—sis—?"

"Sister. She's my sister. And she's happy. I want to get to know her, though, and once I reassured Mom that I had no intention of trying to take Sophia away from her, she was like another person.

And," she said, "she finally said she was sorry for blaming me for my father's death. Apparently, my father was very jealous of me, and in order to keep him from beating her to death, she kept me at arm's length." Which explained why her mom felt free to express love to Sophia. Emily swiped a hand across her cheek and realized she was crying. Again. At least these were good tears. "We won't have a relationship overnight, but I think it's possible that, in the near future, we can at least be in the same room with each other without one of us doing or saying something to make the other one mad."

"That's progress."

"For real."

"So, when are you going on a date with me?"

All of the times they'd been together, he'd never classified them as an actual date. They'd hung out, eaten mostly healthy since they both leaned in that direction. She'd enjoyed the splurge of home-made pizza and a movie. But they'd never called any of it dating.

She laughed. "You've asked me out several times."

"And you've said no every single time."

"I've had some things to work through."

"I know, and I can wait as long as you need." He took her arm, pushed the sleeve up, and traced the white scars.

"What are you doing?" But she didn't jerk away.

"I want to tell you what I see when I look at you. What I think these scars now represent."

"O-okay."

"I see the evidence of how strong you are. The proof that you don't quit. I see a woman whose scars and other past baggage won't define her because she refuses to let it." He locked eyes with her. "I see someone who invests in others' lives so they can see they have a hope and a future."

"Yeah," she whispered. "I think she sees that."

"I'm sure she does. I see someone who doesn't understand how

God could let her best friend die, but still believes he's a good God and his plan is the best one."

"Yeah," she whispered past the growing lump in her throat. "That one's hard, I won't deny it."

"But you believe it."

"I really do. I don't like that bad things happen. I won't deny that I sometimes want to question God's wisdom, but in the end, I know it's far greater than my shortsightedness. I know that God doesn't like the bad stuff either, but we're not robots or puppets and he doesn't pull the strings. We have free will. We all make our own choices. The bad stuff?" She sighed. "It's this fallen world we live in. But God's plan will redeem it all in the end and that's what I have to hang on to."

"You know what else I see?"

"What?"

"I see a woman who makes me want to be a better person. Someone who's changed my life and my faith and made me realize that what I went through with Krystal was bad, but I don't have to blame myself for being unable to help her. I tried. She made her choices. And while I wish things would have ended differently for her sake, the fact that it didn't doesn't have to dictate my future."

Tears spilled over her lashes and he thumbed them away.

"You trust me not to turn to the painkillers?" she asked. "Like Krystal did?"

"Have you touched one since you quit?"

"No. Not one."

"Then if you didn't turn to painkillers when someone was trying to *kill* you, and your stress level was through the roof, I'd say you've got it beat."

"Yeah." She fell silent. Sighed. "I won't say I don't ever think about it."

"I know. I get it. And I'll help you."

"And I'll let you," she said. He was right and she was letting time tick by when she could be doing life with this amazing man. "Ask again."

He blinked. "What?"

"Ask me out. Again."

His eyes brightened. "Emily, will you let me take you out to a fancy schmancy dinner and treat you like you deserve?"

She blinked back tears. "Yes."

"Do you believe I can—and will—do that?"

"I do."

"Good answer. Say it again."

"What? I do?"

"Yes. Again."

"Brady . . ."

"We're practicing. Now again."

"Practicing for—" She gasped. And knew her face went bright red if the temperature of her neck and cheeks was any indication. "Brady St. John!"

"What?"

She grabbed his face in her hands and pulled him down to kiss him. "I love that you make me laugh. I love . . . *you*." There. She said it. And she didn't die. Or have a panic attack. She simply felt . . . happy.

If the look on Brady's face was any indication, his feelings were in agreement with hers.

Emily turned at a particularly loud shout from the porch. Linc had Ruthie in a bear hug while Derek tickled her ribs.

"Uh-oh," Brady said.

"What?"

"Ruthie must have been caught cheating."

"At Phase 10?" she asked.

"Oh yeah. We're a very competitive group, in case you haven't noticed."

"I've noticed."

"They don't scare you?"

Ruthie's shrieks had diminished to giggles while her husband, Isaac, watched and grinned.

"They don't scare me," she said softly. "They're confirmation that God sometimes really does answer prayers just the way you want him to."

He swept a strand of hair behind her ear. "Yeah. He sure does." And he kissed her again. And again. And again.

Until Derek dumped the playing cards on top of their heads.

READ ON FOR
AN EXCERPT FROM THE NEXT
**BLUE JUSTICE** ADVENTURE

# 1

FBI Special Agent Allison Radcliffe fingered the key in her apron pocket and debated about breaking into Vladislav Nevsky's office. "Are you there?" she asked, her voice so low only the person on the other end of the COMMS could hear it.

"Always."

Linc St. John, her partner—and the man she was falling in love with against her better judgment—answered immediately. She smiled, secure in the knowledge that he had her back. Just like she'd have his should their roles be flipped.

*Focus.* She walked past the office and into the kitchen. *Follow the routine.*

"I think this is my chance," she said.

"You're sure?"

"Somewhat."

"That's not good enough. We've waited this long, we can wait a little longer."

"I don't think so. He was livid when his keys went missing then mysteriously turned up under his favorite recliner in the den. Even though I was subtle about it and made sure I was careful, I still think he knows it was me and is just trying to figure out what to do about it." She rubbed her palms together. "My Spidey senses are tingling and telling me time is running out." Unfortunately, she still hadn't located the person she'd hoped most to find and her main reason for pushing for the undercover assignment.

"Then forget it and get out."

"No way. My whole life has been leading up to this. I'm not leaving without getting in that office. Soon."

"Your whole life?"

She bit her lip. "In a manner of speaking."

*Shut up and do your job.*

One year ago, Russian Mafia head Vladislav Nevsky, also known as the *Pakhan*, had moved part of his New York–based organization to South Carolina and the outfit had proceeded to grow like a cancer. Ending part of it was better than none of it, but they'd all agreed taking out Nevsky was the only way to start the process of eradicating the worst of the disease.

They just needed evidence to do so. Solid, undeniable evidence. They'd finally found a way to infiltrate his home.

"He likes to eat," Allie had said, slapping the conference table covered in surveillance photos.

Linc had blinked. "Huh?"

"Look at these pictures. What do you see?" She jabbed a finger at the nearest one. Then another and another. "Nevsky is eating in just about every picture. Well, guess what? I like to cook. Not only that, I'm good at it. Very good, thanks to a college roommate who studied to be a professional chef. I'm going undercover as Nevsky's personal cook. Let's make that happen."

Her supervisor, SSA Henry Ogden, and Linc had exchanged glances, shrugs, and finally nods. Only they hadn't known who else she'd seen in one of those pictures.

Gregori Radchenko.

So, here she was. Looking for a way to take down Nevsky and settle an old score with Radchenko.

Only time was running out and Radchenko was nowhere to be found. It was better to get what she could and get out—and live to fight another day. "No guards in the hallways," Allie whispered. "None in the kitchen either."

The study, accessed from the hallway or directly from the master suite, had been her goal since entering the home. Unfortunately, finding a way into that room had proved impossible thus far, since Nevsky had almost as many surveillance cameras inside his home as he did outside. With no way to disable them without setting off alarms, she'd have to get in the office, get what she needed, and get out. Then pray he didn't have any reason to look at the footage before she could slip out of the house once and for all.

While her mind grappled with when to act, she grabbed the flour from the pantry along with a bag of apples, cinnamon, and everything else she needed to make a mouth-watering apple pie. Nevsky's favorite dessert next to baklava.

"What are you making today?"

Allie swallowed a startled screech and popped out of the pantry to find Nevsky's seventeen-year-old daughter, Daria, perched on one of the stools at the kitchen island. "You scared ten years off of me," Allie said, pressing a hand to her beating heart.

"You're young, you can spare them."

"Ha. No one can spare ten years. Are you looking for another cooking lesson?"

"Nope."

Allie lifted a brow. "Okay." Usually Daria showed up about this time every day after school and the two spent the afternoon preparing dinner. As long as her father wasn't home. If Nevsky was home, Daria sketched or painted. But today was supposed to be different. "What are you doing here? I thought you had that field trip to the museum downtown." She glanced behind her. "And where's Gerard?" Daria's bodyguard was usually ten paces behind her.

"He'll be along soon enough. I gave him the slip." She rolled her eyes. "And I did."

"Did what?"

"Have a field trip. I cancelled it—or at least my participation in it."

"Because?"

"Because life is short and it's time to live, take the bull by the horns, and chart my own course," the girl said. "Or something along those lines."

"I'm sorry, what?" The teen was forever speaking in riddles—or saying one thing and meaning another. Usually, Allie could follow along, but today, she'd been caught off guard by Daria's appearance.

Daria grinned, twin dimples peeking at Allie as she swept her long blonde hair up into a ponytail, then hopped down to turn on the sink. She stuck her hands under the water. "I'm going to do the whole thing by myself." She paused mid-lather to frown. "Unless you don't think I can?"

"I totally think you can. It's just . . ."

"What?"

"Well, it's my job. It's what your dad pays me for, remember?" Allie let out a little laugh. She grabbed a few ice cubes from the freezer, dropped them in the blender, and flipped it on. She leaned in close to Daria's ear. "You and I both know he wouldn't approve, and if he finds out— which he will if he looks at the security footage he has going 24/7—then he'd probably fire me."

"And I don't really care—about the approval and finding out part, not the firing part." Daria's eyes darkened for a fraction of a second. She lowered her voice. "He does plenty of things *I* don't approve of."

"Oh?" Allie said, keeping her own voice casual and soft while she pulled measuring spoons from the drawer to her right. "Like what?" she whispered. She cut the blender off and dumped the ice into a glass.

Daria shrugged. "Doesn't matter."

"Of course it matters."

She gave a small, curiously unreadable smile. "Let's just say"—she motioned to the blender again and Allie refilled it with ice and turned it on—"he's not as smart as he thinks he is."

"How so?"

Daria pursed her lips and her eyes flashed. "He thinks everyone and everything can be bought," she said, her voice so low Allie had to move even closer to hear her. "More than that, he thinks I'm stupid and therefore I'm invisible to him. If I was a boy, I'd be his favorite person. Like my brother."

Allie blinked. "You don't have a brother."

"Actually, I do. He's older and he doesn't live here, though. I never see him. I think I've been in the same room with him maybe four times that I can remember. Truthfully, I'm not even sure he knows I exist. Which is fine because he's just as evil as my father."

A brother? There'd been nothing about Nevsky having a son in their copious amounts of research.

"But I'm just a girl," Daria said. "A stupid, worthless, invisible girl." She doodled on the napkin in front of her. A unicorn emerged beneath her skilled strokes. "But I did something he'll notice. Something he definitely won't approve of." A giggle slipped from her.

"Daria?" Allie wanted to shake her. "What'd you do?"

"It's funny how such a smart man can be so very foolish." At Allie's blank stare, she sighed. "You know what they say about the foolish man who builds his house upon the sand."

"No, what do they say?"

"When the rains come down and the floodwaters rise, the house built on the sand will meet its demise."

"You're talking in riddles again."

Her smile flipped. "It's the only way I can talk around here so I don't get into trouble," she whispered.

Allie bit her lip and avoided glancing at the camera in the far corner of the room. "What are you really trying to tell me here?"

The teen laughed and waved a hand in dismissal. "Nothing. I want to make a pie. You've got the roast in the slow cooker. I can handle the other veggies just like you've taught me. I've got this, so you can take the afternoon off. And that's no riddle."

"But—" Allie turned the blender off. She'd already left it on long enough for Nevsky to be suspicious should he decide to watch or listen in on the footage. "Seriously, Daria—"

"No, no, no. No buts allowed. Literally. So remove yours from the premises and go read a book or something. But first, pass me the apron and then I don't want to see you until six."

Allie's adrenaline flowed a bit faster. "You're sure? I really don't want to get you in trouble," she said, handing over the apron after slipping the key from the pocket.

"One hundred percent." The girl's face softened. "You've taught me so much. I love to cook, and since Papa's not going to be here for dinner, this is the perfect time for me to put my new skills to the test." She bit her lip, then gave Allie a quick hug. Then looked at the blender. "Then maybe I can surprise him one day with something he loves and he'll be glad I took the time to learn." She sighed. "Then again, probably not."

"All right, then. Holler if you need me."

"Will do."

Allie slipped from the kitchen and hurried down the hallway toward the study located past the circular stairwell and the massive living room. The house spanned twelve thousand feet, and at first, it had taken her a good two days to find enough time to sneak away from her duties in the kitchen and learn her way around. And the only thing she liked about the place was Daria's artwork subtly displayed in various rooms. The teen was hands-down talented when it came to creating unique pieces using any medium she chose. Although she did seem to favor using everyday items from Chapstick tubes to measuring spoons in her creations.

After spending a little over four weeks undercover and sleeping in the guest room on the second floor across from Daria, she now knew the place as well as her own twelve-*hundred*-square-foot apartment.

"Allie? You there?"

Linc's voice came through the earpiece. "I'm here," she said softly. Low enough that any mics wouldn't pick up her words. "Did you get all of that?"

"Most of it. There were some spotty places because you were whispering, but I got the gist of it. I'd give my right arm to know what Daria doesn't approve of."

"Same here. I'd also like to know who this brother is that she's talking about."

"Ask her."

"I will when I get the chance."

"You've gained her trust."

"I know." A flash of guilt hit her. From the beginning, she'd played on Daria's desire for a mother figure and had Daria's adoration within days. At least she thought she did. Unless the girl was playing her as well as she played everyone else in her life.

Allie slid the key into the lock and gave a quick sigh of relief when it turned. She slipped inside the office and shut the door behind her. "I'm in."

Without wasting any time admiring the luxurious decor since she knew the money used to outfit it had been gained via the deaths of good people—some of whom had been law enforcement officers whose families still waited for justice—she strode to the desk, inhaling at the sight of the laptop sitting right where she'd last seen it. Next to it were two new EpiPens. The man was terrified of bees, even though he had no allergy that they were aware of. "Is Annie ready to do her thing?"

"She is."

Allie inserted the flash drive that would allow Annie, their IT genius at Quantico, to take over the laptop and crack the password. Once she was in, she'd copy as much of the hard drive as she could. Depending on how much was on the laptop, even with Annie's high-dollar technology, Allie wasn't sure she'd be able to get it all before she had to pull the device.

While the machine worked, Allie opened drawers and riffled through the contents. In the third drawer, she found a stack of file folders.

"Annie's in," Linc said. "That was almost too easy."

"He's not worried about someone breaking in here. He keeps it locked up 24/7 and he's got guards all over the place outside. As far as he's concerned, no one's getting in."

"As long as you can get out."

Allie set the folders on the desk and opened the first one. It looked like legitimate business information, but she took pictures of it anyway and sent those while she went to the next folder. More pictures. Not what she was looking for, but one never knew what would come in handy.

"Hurry up, Allie, you're taking too long."

"I'm fine. Nevsky's not due back for a while." Finally, at the last folder, she opened it and gasped.

"What is it?" Linc asked. "Are you okay?"

"Yes, but you're not."

"What do you mean?"

"They're watching you." Quickly, she worked her phone's camera. "And sending pictures to Nevsky."

"Me? Why would they be watching me?"

"I don't know." She paused and bit her lip. "Unless my cover is blown and they're trying to figure out who I'm communicating with."

The next picture sent her reeling. "He's got a picture of us together, but you can't see my face. The date stamp is from a week ago. It's when we met with Henry at the hotel in Irmo."

"You need to get out of there."

Allie's stomach twisted. "He's got pictures of your family too," she whispered.

"What?"

"You and Brady and Chloe playing basketball in your parents' drive. The dates on the pictures are from last Sunday afternoon." Terrifying, but still not what she was searching for.

And another picture of her and Linc sitting on his parents' back porch swing. Stomach in knots, she shoved everything back where she found it and went to the next drawer. Locked.

"He probably thinks we're a couple, Linc. And he most likely knows who I am." Or at least that she was there under false pretenses. So why was she still in his home and still alive? Something was off.

"Allie—"

She pulled the specialized knife from her front pocket and opened the tool that would give her access to the lock. Within seconds, it popped and she pulled the drawer open. More files. She opened the one on top. "Oh my," she whispered.

"Allie," Henry's voice came through her earpiece this time. "Put everything back now and leave."

"He's got a whole list of military equipment for sale," Allie said. "Where would he be getting that stuff?" She snapped pictures, then shoved everything back where she found it. She stood there for a moment while she sent the pictures to Henry.

"Get. Out. Of. There. Now," Linc said. "Walk out of the house and head to the van."

"Working on it."

The door to the office opened.

Allie jerked her head up. "Uh-oh."

# ACKNOWLEDGMENTS

A huge thanks to the whole team at Revell for all their hard work. I sure couldn't do this without you!

Thank you, as always, to Dru Wells and Wayne Smith for your amazing feedback on all of the law enforcement details. I always do my best to make sure things are accurate. Any law enforcement errors are completely on the author's shoulders. :)

Thank you to my family who always supports me—even when I'm pulling out my hair because time is going too fast!

Thank you to all of my lovely and talented critique buddies and prayer partners: Lynn H. Blackburn, Emme Gannon, Linda Gilden, Edie Melson, Alycia Morales, and Erynn Newman. Y'all are simply the best. Thank you for letting me do life with you.

A special thank-you to Jason Fort for answering tons of Police Procedural questions with accuracy, honesty, and lots of humor! I appreciate you!

I have to give a shout-out to my brainstorming buddy, DiAnn Mills. You have a wonderfully wicked mind. I love it and you, sister!

Another ginormous thanks goes to Carrie Stuart Parks. You simply have THE best ideas and I love picking your fascinating brain. Thanks for letting me!! I love you, my friend—even if you are a <gasp> plotter! :)

And last, but not least, thank you, Jesus, for allowing me to do what I do. I couldn't do it without your blessing and you keeping your hands upon mine as I work each day. Thank you for the stories, thank you for the words, thank you for the lives you allow the books to touch.

**Lynette Eason** is the bestselling author of the Women of Justice series, the Deadly Reunions series, and the Hidden Identity series, as well as *Always Watching*, *Without Warning*, *Moving Target*, and *Chasing Secrets* in the Elite Guardians series. She is the winner of two ACFW Carol Awards, the Selah Award, and the Inspirational Readers' Choice Award. She has a master's degree in education from Converse College and lives in South Carolina. Learn more at www.lynetteeason.com.

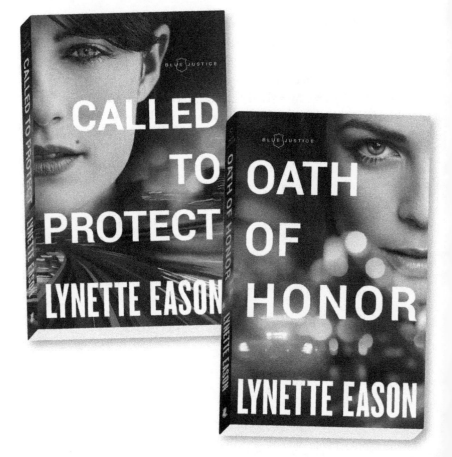

# Want to know more about the
# *Carrington Dive Team?*

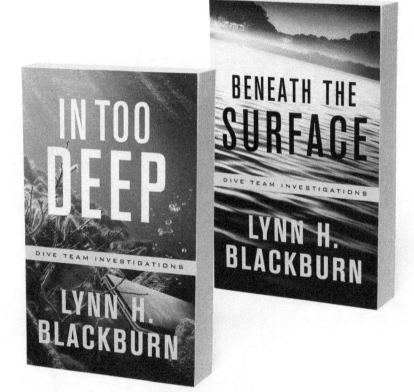

# Catch their other adventures here!

# SECRETS AND LIES.
## DANGER THAT WILL NEVER GO AWAY.

Join three beloved masters of romantic suspense for novellas
of deadly betrayal where the past will not stay buried.

# INTENSITY. SKILL. TENACITY.

The bodyguards of
Elite Guardians Agency have it all.

Connect with
**LYNETTE**

Sign up for Lynette Eason's newsletter to stay in touch on new books, giveaways, and writing conferences.

# LYNETTEEASON.COM

Lynette Eason | @LynetteEason

CPSIA information can be obtained
at www.ICGtesting.com
Printed in the USA
LVHW091436030119
602629LV00006B/49/P

9 780800 735586